i copy 6/07
CRLORPLY
5 8 NOV 2007

8 4 FEB 2010
2 9 DEC 2010
1 2 JAN 2011

− 0 MAR 2008

Don O
2 3 AUG 2008
1 6 JAN 2009
7 6 MAY 2009

6 1 SEP 2009

Please return/renew this item
by the last date shown.
Books may also be renewed by
phone and Internet

Trail of the Silver Saddle

Trail of the Silver Saddle

A Western Trio

LES SAVAGE, JR.

SAGEBRUSH
Large Print Westerns

First published in Great Britain by ISIS Publishing Ltd
First published in the United States by Five Star

Published in Large Print 2007 by ISIS Publishing Ltd.,
7 Centremead, Osney Mead, Oxford OX2 0ES
United Kingdom
by arrangement with
Golden West Literary Agency

British Library Cataloguing in Publication Data
Savage, Les
    Trail of the silver saddle: a western trio. –
    Large print ed. –
    (Sagebrush western series)
    1. Western stories
    2. Large type books
    I. Title
    813.5'4 [F]

ISBN 978–0–7531–7762–4 (hb)

Printed and bound in Great Britain by
T. J. International Ltd., Padstow, Cornwall

Table of Contents

Whip Master

"Whip Master" was Les Savage, Jr.'s original title for this short novel. It was submitted to Malcolm Reis, the general manager at Fiction House, and bought at once. The author was paid $700 for the story in March, 1948. The title was changed upon publication to "Whip-Woman of the Santa Fé" when it appeared in *Frontier Stories* (Winter, 49). For its inclusion here, the author's title and original text have been restored.

CHAPTER
ONE

On that date — April 4, 1861 — the Rocky Mountain House was probably the wildest and most dangerous place in St. Louis, and the wildest and most dangerous man to enter the Rocky Mountain House was Blackie Barr. He shuffled in about seven that evening, making sure there were no troopers in the single, smoky taproom, before heading toward the bar. Here he proceeded to buy a bottle of Monongahela. With the bottle of whiskey in one hand he sought the nearest game of old sledge, finding it in the corner with a group sitting on the floor around a blanket upon which lay the cards and money. He set down the Monongahela, opened his possibles sack, and poured silver into his cap of skunk fur till it was brimming. Then he kicked a pair of the men apart to make a place for himself, and squatted down. A French *voyageur* was dealing out the dirty horsehide cards from a position directly across from Barr.

"I ain't seen you thees far south in many a year, Blackie," he said. "Aren't you taking a chance?"

Barr took a deep drag at the whiskey, rubbed a hairy hand across his wet mouth. "I get tired of playing sledge with the Indians. The Army's got a lot better

3

things to do than looking for me, with this war coming up. Deal me a hand, Frenchie. I'm going to clean you out."

He made an evil picture, sitting cross-legged as an Indian there on the floor, with that chalk-white knife scar drawing its telltale stripe down the oblique plane of his sardonic cheek to disappear in the black brier of his matted beard. His leggings were elk hide, shrunk by so many rains they clung to his legs like a second skin. His shirt was a red Chimayo blanket worn like a poncho, with a hole in the center for his head and the four corners drawn through his belt to hang out beneath that in triangular tails. Behind the belt of Mandan wampum he wore were thrust a naked Green River skinning knife and an immense Henry T. Cooper pistol.

He had gotten halfway through the evening, and more than halfway through the bottle, heaping the silver money up before him till only two men remained in the game, when Smoky Cameron appeared at the door of the den. He stood there a moment, ancient and hoary as the buffalo coat he wore, with a face as ruddy and seamed and furrowed as an old squaw's. When his glance found Blackie Barr, he came over his way, stopping, spread-legged, above the men seated about the floor.

"You better skeedaddle, Blackie boy," he said in his dry, toothless way. "Taos Sheridan is looking for you."

"She won't come here," muttered Barr, intent on his cards.

"You're drunk," offered Cameron. "She'll go any place a man will, and a lot of places a man wouldn't. You'd better get out. She's coming and she's got her whip."

"Whip?" Barr's dark, bearded face lifted for a moment, and a strange look passed through his eyes — something reflective rising furtively from the past to darken them in that instant. Then he cursed at Cameron and put his cards down.

The French *voyageur* in the white blanket coat opposite to Barr allowed a look of pain to fill his face. "I'm pick clean as the bone," he said. "It is sinful to win the way you do, Blackie. It . . ." His head lifted, and he stared ahead of him, as if becoming aware of the sudden silence. Then he twisted around to stare at the door. Blackie Barr had already seen it, as had the others who were faced toward the door.

Taos Sheridan stood there. Her hair was the color of rich taffy, blown into wild, untrammeled curls by the wind to form a frame for her face. It was a face of strong, haunting beauty, with sharp, high cheek bones that left a hint of shadowed hollow beneath them to accentuate the succulent ripeness of her lips. She was a tall girl, with no slenderness to her. She was all woman — a mature curve to the hip that pushed insistently into the tight rawhide leggings she wore, a deep thrust to the breast that lifted proudly against her man's broadcloth shirt. Her eyes — a vivid, startling blue — moved unhurriedly around the room till they found Blackie Barr.

"I told you," whispered Smoky Cameron.

"Barr," said Taos, "I understand you signed on with my train."

Barr's eyes, filmed and bloodshot, had trouble focusing on the woman. "That I did," he told her.

5

"With orders to be at the campfire by eight tonight." Her voice filled the room as clearly as if it had been empty.

"I'll be there in time to string out with you," growled Barr. "You ain't leaving till tomorrow morning."

"But you were to be there this evening," she said. "I'll thank you to come with me now."

"Leave a winning streak like this?" said Barr, waving a hairy hand at his money-filled cap. "No soap."

"You can have your choice," she said. "Walk out or be carried."

Barr's whole broad frame seemed to settle sullenly into itself. "I ain't walkin'," he said. "You hadn't better try nothin'."

"Rubie," said Taos quietly.

Jack Rubie moved out from behind her. The scrape of his muddy boots in the dank sawdust of the floor broke sibilantly against the silence. He was an incredibly beefy man, without carrying any fat, with a neck so big he had to leave the top three buttons of his shirt open. He had been a Mississippi roustabout before turning muleskinner and the muscles of that trade still bulged on him, constantly bursting the seams of whatever clothes he wore.

"Hannibal," Taos said.

Churl Hannibal came out from behind her, following Jack Rubie. He was more typical of a muleskinner with all the lanky, deceptive indolence of a Missouri mule in his tall, gaunt body, so loose-coupled it looked fit to fall apart in sections with every step he took. The flesh of his jaw shimmered like polished leather across the bulge the inevitable chew made in one cheek. Men began to

6

spread away from their advance in a muttering expectation. The men around Barr scrambled to their feet and fanned away into the room, till only Smoky Cameron stood by him. The old mountain man started backing away, too, speaking as he did in his sly, smiling voice.

"You better find your feet, Blackie boy. It looks like they're goin' to do that nothin'."

Barr continued to stare at his cards, sitting cross-legged there beside the blanket. But his face was darkening slowly with diffused blood, turning that white scar red, and the tightening grip of his fingers was slowly bending those horsehide cards double.

"Don't put your hands on me, Rubie," he said in a low, guttural voice, without looking at anything but his cards.

"Not if you get up and walk out," said Jack Rubie, coming on toward him.

The cards were mashed into Barr's fist now. "I'll cut that churl right out of your mouth, Hannibal."

"Others have tried." The indolent Missourian smiled, shuffling on over.

They were within two paces of him, when Barr gave a wild, incoherent yell, and came to his feet. The horsehide cards were out of his hand and that skinning knife was in it, too fast to follow. He threw himself at Rubie with the Green River held to disembowel him.

But Churl Hannibal was fast, too. As soon as Barr had shouted, the lazy length of Hannibal's body uncoiled, diving for that blanket. It took him out of Barr's way, and looked as if he had dodged aside to leave Rubie facing that knife. But as Hannibal ducked

7

down, he scooped up the blanket, and made a quarter turn with it, all his skill with a whip in the way he lashed it up to ensnare Barr's feet.

Barr tried to kick free, but it caught around one ankle, throwing him off balance. He had to spin around to keep from falling, and it took the knife from between him and Rubie. Rubie jumped in, grabbing the knife arm in both his hands and twisting violently. Barr shouted with the pain. The knife slipped from his helpless fingers.

He whirled back into Rubie, bringing his free fist into the man's guts. Rubie gasped, and doubled over, losing his grip on Barr's other arm. Barr saw Hannibal coming in with the blanket, and jumped back from Rubie, catching the free end of the blanket. He yanked hard before Hannibal could release it. This, added to Hannibal's own impetus, pulled the man into Barr, off balance. Barr was bent over to meet him, catching the man's lunging body across the belly with one shoulder and throwing him on over.

Hannibal struck the floor behind Barr with a *thud* that shook the building, and the watching crowd raised a wild, cheering cry. Rubie had recovered from that blow to the stomach now and was charging in on Barr. Barr wheeled away from him to turn and run toward Hannibal. The Missourian was trying groggily to rise when Barr reached him, jumping high into the air and coming down into Hannibal's face with both boots. They stamped the man's head right down into the floor, and he stayed there. At the same time, Rubie caught Barr from behind, carrying him over Hannibal and across the floor into the bar.

8

Both men struck it with the same impact, and reeled away stunned, pawing for each other. Barr recovered first, shaking his shaggy, black head like a wounded buffalo, and jumping back into Rubie. He slugged the man again in the belly, and, as Rubie doubled over, brought a smashing fist up into his face. Rubie caught that fist before Barr could pull it back from the blow, and pulled the man into him, grappling him. There was another savage yell from the crowd, filling the place with deafening sound, for they knew what Rubie meant to do now. His groping hands found Barr's face, and a huge, scarred thumb hooked into Barr's mouth. That was straight from Rubie's days on the Mississippi where more than one man had gotten his face ripped open by those immense hands.

The men stopped most of their movement. They strained together in a static, ghastly pose. The noise died as the watchers stared in fascinated waiting, till the scraping, gasping breathing of the battlers was the only sound. Barr's head was twisted back from Rubie's chest, turned into a grotesque clown's mask by that thumb stretching out his mouth. He had one hand closed about Rubie's wrist, trying to keep it from moving out farther, but Rubie had the better leverage, and slowly, inexorably his wrist moved outward. He had his other arm about Barr's body in a bear hug, pinning Barr's right arm to his side.

Taos Sheridan watched without expression, still in the doorway, and Churl Hannibal lay sprawled, unconscious, on the floor, threatened by the boots of the heedless, awed crowd. Blood began to dribble from one corner of Barr's mouth into his beard. He made a strangled, rattling sound in his throat. Then, without warning, he released Rubie's wrist with his left hand. There was a sick, sighing sound from the crowd. But before Rubie could rip Barr's mouth out, Barr brought that left hand up in a looping blow to Rubie's temple. It was like felling an ox.

Rubie stiffened above Barr's bent body, a stunned expression fixed onto his face. His thumb was still in Barr's mouth, but he did not use it. Barr shifted his weight and hit the man again, in the same place, a vicious hammer blow that had all the weight of his body behind it. This time Rubie toppled, like a great tree going over to one side, stiff and straight, to strike the floor a shuddering blow.

Wiping his mouth, gasping in a drained exhaustion from the struggle, Barr started to turn toward the woman. Before he could see her, there was a deafening, crackling explosion that seemed to fill the whole taproom. Barr reeled back, blinded by a pain that seemed to have detonated in his very head, lifting his whole body up. He could not identify it yet. He felt himself staggering against bodies, and then released as they stepped aside. There was a loud, shouting, scurrying noise all about him as the crowd scattered. Again that explosion caught him up, leaving a stunning agony that seared his body like a stripe of fire burned into his chest. He was stopped by a hard painful pressure, and realized he was up against the wall. Here, hands groping out before him like a blind man, he sought to find his sight again. Finally vision came dimly. Salty blood filled one eye as he opened it, but with the other he could make out the woman.

The crowd had spread away to the walls and back along the bar, and she was striding across the deserted center of the floor past Hannibal where he lay on his back, past Rubie, lashing the twenty feet of her whip back and forth in front of her like a vicious, restless snake.

"Now," she said, "are you coming, or do I have to take you there in strips?"

"No woman whips me!" he shouted hoarsely, lunging at her.

Her wrist flipped upward. That was the only noticeable motion. The whole length of the snake came up and lashed about his legs, pinning them. He fell helplessly forward on his face. He kicked free, sought to roll over. There was that immense explosion, seeming to be inside him, and he was blinded again. He finally did roll over, only to get knocked back against the wall. Here he crouched, with the strength to rise whipped out of him, unable to see, dripping his sweat and blood into the sawdust beneath him.

"Are you coming?" she said.

He made one more attempt to rise. Couldn't. He heard the hiss of that whip again, gathering.

"I'm comin'," he whispered.

CHAPTER
TWO

Twenty Conestogas left St. Louis the next morning, with spokes of their wheels painted red and their high swagger beds trimmed in blue, with Taos Sheridan riding her vinegar roan up at the head, and Blackie Barr shambling along beside the team of the last wagon. West of the river it was Delaware Springs, Lone Elm, Round Grove, Council Grove, rising up before the train and passing behind the train, a noon halt or a night's camping place. West of the river it rained incessantly, till saddles and harness were sticky as glue, and the double thickness of Osnaberg sheeting covering the wagons would no longer shed water.

After Council Grove it stopped raining, and it was the blowflies. Muleskinners cursed and slapped and scratched all day long and sat with their heads in the smoke of their campfires at night. Then they reached Turkey Creek, the limit of the blowflies' range, and left that behind. Beyond Turkey Creek the country was emerald green, rolling like a sea, the cut banks of its streams black-soiled. Sunflowers shone like gold nuggets above a mantle of grass so tall it brushed a horse's belly.

This was a part of the trip Taos Sheridan loved. She had lost count of how many times she had passed through this country. It had started as a little girl, when she rode with her father back and forth each year from Santa Fé to Missouri with his half-dozen battered Conestogas that constituted the beginnings of the Sheridan Freight Company. Her mother had died when she was three, and her father was killed by Kou-Ailee and his Apaches near Raton when she was seventeen. Taos had taken over the freight company then, building it till, at twenty-four, she had one of the most successful, vigorous shipping concerns on the Santa Fé Trail.

She spent most of her time in the saddle, riding up and down the train or scouting far in its lead with the outriders. She was the first to put her horse in the water when they reached the Narrows. This was a treacherous crossing, where the Kansas and the Osage Rivers flowed so close that only a narrow ridge separated the two rivers, formed of black mud and shifting bogs of quicksand that had claimed more than one hapless wagon.

Each year a new route had to be charted through the ford. The roan looked like a circus horse, dancing this way and that across the mud bank, shifting back abruptly from quicksand and fiddling around to find a new way. There was something Indian in the way Taos rode, gauging her balance delicately, always in perfect accord with the animal's slightest movement when he had to step quickly away from a dangerous bit of ground, till she had finally gained the opposite side of the strip, reaching the comparatively safe waters of the Osage, where the ford was gravelly and firm.

Then the wagons started following her, one by one, sliding down the steep bank of the Kansas with their rough locks on and swaying bed-deep through its turgid waters. Ford Martin was the first to bring his outfit across the Narrows and into the Osage. He was acting wagon boss whenever Taos had to be away, a big, smiling man with curly black hair and fine white teeth that always gave him a way with the ladies when he was in town.

Coming up to Taos, he bent down out of the seat, grinning at her. "Are you still riled about last night?"

"Let's forget it," she said.

"I always heard you took the whip to any man who tried to kiss you," he said. "Can't I take it as a good indication that you didn't whip me?"

"I didn't have my whip with me," she said. "Next time I will."

He leaned closer, his engaging grin broadening. "There'll be a full moon tonight, Taos."

"Ford," she said, "you're a good teamster, and I would have hired you a long time ago if it hadn't been for your reputation with the ladies. I wouldn't have hired you this time if Peddigrew hadn't quit to join the Army and left me short. As much as I need you, if you try anything like last night again, I'll give you the sack."

He sobered abruptly, studying her in a gravity foreign to him. "It's strange that a woman so wild can be so cold," he said.

She tossed her head irritably, staring down the line of laboring wagons. "I asked you to forget it, Ford. Is that Barr having trouble on the Kansas bank?"

14

He turned to look. "Looks like it. He'll get her down. It isn't his muleskinning you'll be bothered with, Taos."

"Meaning what?"

"Don't you know who he is?"

"There are a lot of men in this train with a past, Ford. I've heard some shady references to Barr. I've never gotten all the details. I couldn't be too picky who I hired this time. This war talk is making for a bad shortage of drivers."

"I thought surely you'd know about Barr," said Ford. "It happened at Taos."

"My father named me after the town because I was born there on the way to Santa Fé," she said. "I never actually lived there, and all I know about Barr is that it had something to do with the Taos rebellion. That was the Indian uprising after the Americans took over Santa Fé during the Mexican War, wasn't it?"

"It was thought to be a purely native rebellion at first," he told her. "But the American traders had profited immensely under the graft and lax rule of the Mexican government. They stood to lose a lot of that in the rigid restrictions General Kearney imposed when the Americans captured Santa Fé. They saw in a native uprising a chance to return to the old ways, and more than one white trader had a hand in it."

"Barr was running a string of wagons between Saint Louis and Santa Fé at that time, wasn't he?" she asked.

"And making money off it," Ford told her. "The Indians had formed a secret society called the Brothers of the Skull. On the day of the uprising, they were to mark themselves by a turquoise ring in the shape of a

15

skull. Just one day before the Taos massacre, Blackie Barr was found in a back room at La Fonda, dead drunk, wearing one of the turquoise rings. General Kearney tried to make Barr tell when they planned to strike, but Barr wouldn't. Two days later it happened. The American governor was killed in the massacre at Taos, along with others. Two of the ringleaders were hung by the Army. Barr was slated for the same fate, but he escaped."

Taos felt the shock fill her face. That changed to a savage anger. She wheeled her roan sharply in the shallow water, putting it into a gallop. She heard Ford call to her, but would not answer. She knew there were hunted men in her crew, possibly even murderers, but a traitor, a man who would betray his own people in a thing like that . . .

She passed the wagons that had already come down off the Narrows into the ford of the Osage, and drove her roan up the slippery bank on one side of the dug way. Churl Hannibal's wagon was in the dug way, the rough locks on his wheels preventing their turning as he skidded down the steep, muddy channel into shallow water. Behind him came Jack Rubie, standing up on his seat with the jerkline in one hand and his mule whip in the other.

The ridge of mud separating the Osage from the Kansas was several hundred yards broad, but only Smoky Cameron's wagon was on top here, the tongue of his outfit lashing back and forth with the lunge of mules against their collars in the unremitting struggle to pull through this mire. Beside Cameron, up on the high seat, sat his squaw, with the single dot of vermilion on her cheek proclaiming her Cheyenne blood. She was a mysterious, burnished statue, in her gaudy dress of yellow buckskin, trimmed front and rear with rows of elk's teeth.

"Giddap, you calico va'mints!" Smoky shouted at his mules. "Giddap!"

Intent on Barr's wagon, Taos hardly took notice of what Smoky was doing. Barr had finally fought his team down off the Kansas bank and was rattling through the shallows toward this mud ridge. He was up on the seat before the arch of canvas, the scar making its chalky, diabolic slash into the matted beard. Taos was at the rear of Smoky Cameron's outfit now, and she pulled her vinegar roan up to wait for Barr. As she did, Smoky's high, cracked voice filled the air again, screaming at his mules. The broken urgency of it made her wheel to stare at him, realizing for the first time how far he was off the trail she had chosen.

"Smoky!" she called. "You're not following Rubie! Gee them, or you'll slide off this ridge into that quicksand! Gee them . . ."

"Gee, there, you outsize burros, gee there!" shouted Smoky, tugging wildly at his jerkline. He did not give enough time between the jerks for the mules to get his signals, and the confused animals began fighting each other. Taos wheeled her horse around and slopped back through the mud to the leaders, trying to grab their bits and lead them back onto solid ground. She almost got her hand bitten off. Then she tried for the jerkline, but Smoky was yanking on it wildly, and it whipped out of her hand.

They were too far down off the ridge of solid ground for her to reach them now. She saw how they would be lost completely in another moment unless they could be headed into a right turn. She rode around their heads and plunged down off the firm strip into sticky, warm mud. Farther out, she could see the rusty hoops of a wagon thrusting a foot or so above the surface, pushed down by the quicksand in some former year.

She drew her horse in against the mules' left flank, and uncoiled her twenty-foot whip, laying it on as she shouted at them with all the vitupertive familiarity of a muleskinner: "Gee, you canaries, before I lop your ears off and stuff them down your throats! Smoky, quit jerking on that line, you've got them so mixed up they don't know which is off . . . quit pulling that line or I'll lay this whip on you . . . gee, there, gee, you mules . . ."

Her cracking whip turned the plunging, frightened leaders back up toward solid ground. But when the front wheels started turning, that brought the stern sliding down off the high ground it had held till now. The unexpected shift of weight behind them panicked the wheelers, and they began lunging wildly off to the left.

"They're pulling us right out into that bog!" screamed the squawman, whipping at the beasts like a man gone mad. "There's quicksand out there, Taos, look at that wagon, they're pulling us right out in it . . ."

Taos could hear him no more. The din of braying mules and the frenzied squeals of her own roan drowned out the farther sounds. The mules had turned back into the horse, driving it farther into the ooze.

Taos felt the animal clutched in the abrupt grasp of quicksand, and tried to spin it around and spur it into a last desperate run all at once. She only got it headed far enough around to run down the line of mules, smashing in against their tossing heads and lathered rumps, till she came up against the wheelers. Their wild lunging knocked the roan backward. Again there was the fearsome clutch of quicksand.

The roan struggled crazily, trying to buck. It felt like the animal's hoofs were tied. The roan let out a shrill, pitiable whinny, the muscles of its body rippling and bulging like snakes in pain. But the beast's legs would not move. Looking down, Taos saw they were up to the knees in the mud and sinking deeper fast. The wagon was creaking and swaying past her now, hauled a few feet onward by the last efforts of those frenzied mules. In a moment, the tailgate would be beyond her reach, and she would be left on the sinking horse alone. She took the one chance left, jumping for the wagon bed.

She caught the tailgate, was almost torn off, and hung there a moment, toes trailing the ugly ooze. It cost her great effort to crawl in over the gate. Buffeted back and forth by loose cargo, she made her way to the front. The seat was empty. She saw that Smoky and his squaw had jumped, minutes ago, and had failed to make firm ground. They were waist-deep in the black mud. Taos blocked her impulse to jump after them. The wagon was much farther out, and, if they could not make it from where they had jumped, she had utterly no chance from here.

Lunging, braying, trying to pull their hind legs out of the mud to kick at each other, the frenzied mules fought on forward, pulling the wagon farther and farther out. They were up to their rumps in the mud now. Taos could not understand why the quicksand did not stall them. The ooze was lapping at the stakes and bolsters of the wagon itself, curling myriad black tongues at the gay blue trim of the sides. The desperation filling Taos was as black and viscid as that mud. Desperately she tried to focus her whirling thoughts, to think of a way out. She had dropped her whip when she had jumped for the wagon. She tried pulling on the jerkline, to turn the mules, but they only fought it. Jumping was out of the question now.

The teamsters had run from the other wagons to line up along the edge of that high, firm strip of ground. They had already tossed ropes out to Smoky and his squaw, and were hauling them in. Someone made a throw for the wagon, but the rope fell short. Ford Martin appeared in the crowd with another coil of hemp, and began to feel his way out.

"Don't come any farther!" Taos shouted at him. "It'll pull you down!"

"But you must be on a firm strip of ground!" Ford yelled back. "The mules couldn't pull you that far out otherwise!"

"If we are, the mules have chewed it up as we went!" she cried. "They've been kicking and fighting all the way out, Ford! There won't be any good ground left behind us . . ."

As if in answer, his arms went up over his head as he dropped suddenly into a pocket, up to his waist. He made a desperate cast of the rope from there. It dropped short of the wagon. She saw his face twist, and he started struggling empty-handed out toward her. But he kept sinking deeper and deeper, and finally he stopped helplessly. Taos had been right. The mules had cut away their own bridge behind them, chewing up so much of the good top ground with their sharp, churning hoofs that it only left ooze, quickly mingling with the quicksand underneath.

The men on high ground got a rope out to Ford, and pulled him back. They had Smoky and his Cheyenne woman in now, too. They tied two ropes together, and made a toss with this longer length, one end weighted with a rock. But it still dropped short.

Something cold and heavy sank to the very bottom of Taos. For the first time, the true helplessness of her position reached her. She found herself looking again at the rusty hoops of the other wagon out there. It was not the only outfit that had been claimed by this bog, she knew. Where were the others, then? Underneath? How long would it take?

There was a wild, ear-splitting bray from the lead mules, freighted with such awful terror it stiffened Taos on the seat. She turned to see that they had stopped at last. The mules were threshing around wildly. It looked as if their legs were tied. Only their gaunt bodies moved, twisting and writhing. She realized they had reached the end at last, and had stepped off into the true quicksand.

Then she saw the turbulent group of helpless men on good ground part in the middle. Quietly, without a word, Blackie Barr appeared among them, a little shorter than most, but half again as broad as the biggest, with mud blackening his leggings to the knees. He was leading a whole team of mules unhitched from their wagon, and he brought them right up to the brink. His voice rolled out like the guttural snarl of some beast.

"Shut your damn' traps and give me a hand with these mules! You're just makin' them nervous with all that yammer!"

The men's surprise stopped them for a moment, and then there were a dozen voices telling him why he couldn't take the team out there, with Ford Martin's voice finally becoming clear above the rest. "If a man can't get to the wagon, a whole team of jacks certainly can't, Barr. Smoky's team walked out on a ridge, but they cut it away beneath them as they went."

"Then there must be other ridges of good ground," said Barr. He pointed his whip stock at the hoops of the wagon beyond Taos. "How could that outfit have got that far unless the animals followed a ridge?"

"This bog changes every year," said Martin disgustedly. "That might have been solid ground last year."

"There must be other paths of firm ground through it," repeated Barr stubbornly. "I can find it with a team where a man trying alone wouldn't have a chance. Get out of my way . . ."

"Barr, don't be crazy . . ."

22

"Just hobble your jaw and get me another team of mules!" shouted Barr.

"Another team?"

"You don't think one team is going to be long enough to stretch from this dry ground out to that wagon, do you? Now quit bellyaching and get me some more jacks!"

It was the same voice he used on his mules, and it had the same effect. Taos saw Martin wince as if it hurt his eardrums. He stared at Barr, then looked out toward Taos. At last he turned and walked down to Rubie's outfit, where he began unhitching traces from the doubletree. Meanwhile, Barr had begun backing his team off the bank into the mud.

Taos had never heard such profane eloquence. The mules seemed to have an even more acute appreciation of it than she. Barr could bring a look of unholy fear to their eyes with a single epithet, could let out a string of expletives that sent them laboring like equine demons to carry out his commands. She saw now how he meant to find a path through the bog. Half a dozen times he backed those wheelers off into the mud. They balked and fought, kicked and brayed, but he kept driving them down into the bog. Each time, when the quicksand clutched at them, and they started to sink, he still had three or four pairs of mules on dry ground, enough to haul the trapped ones out. She had lost count of how many times he had driven those balky, frightened animals off into the bat-black ooze, when the wheelers finally found firm ground. It was far to the west of the stranded wagon in which Taos crouched. A great cheer went up from the men as Barr backed the wheelers on and they did not sink. The pointers followed, and then the swingers. When Barr saw that they still did not sink, he caught the headbands of the leaders, yet on high ground, and swung himself between them. They began kicking and rearing, but a single roaring word from him turned them to statues.

He put a foot on the whiffletree and from here stepped onto their backs. Then he walked down the team, using whiffletrees and traces, rumps and withers for his stepping stones. Whenever they became fractious, he laid their ears back with his roaring voice, or stilled their lunging rumps with a crack of his whip a foot above their hides. Finally he reached the wheelers and sat down on the off-mule's rump. The beast started writhing and pitching, trying to lift his hind hoofs from the mud for a kick. He merely raised his coiled whip over its stern. The jack's ears laid back and it ceased all movement. The whole team stood quiescent before the threat of him seated like a muddy, bearded idol on the rump of that off wheeler.

"Now, Martin!" he shouted. "Hitch your wheelers to my leaders!"

"Barr, are you crazy . . . ?"

"Damn you, Martin, if you don't hitch up, I'm coming back there and put you in the harness, too. I'm going to back on out, but I want to keep enough mules on dry land to pull me out. Now, hitch up!"

The last was a savage roar that set Martin to backing his wheel animals into the leaders of Barr's team, which were still on high ground. When the two teams were together, Barr started backing the animals upon which he sat farther out into the bog. Like a ringmaster in the circus, he drove them delicately, daintily, directing each hoof as it was put down, picking a way out of that thin band of firm earth as if the whole team were walking on eggshells. More than once they lost their way and mired down in the treacherous quicksand. Then Barr left his perch to run up the team, driving them back toward good ground till they had pulled the trapped animals free. And all the time, the wagon was settling beneath Taos. The chuckling, popping mud was lapping higher and higher up the sides of the bed, oozing through the cracks, licking at the soles of her boots.

She watched Barr in a terrible fascination till he had finally reached a point with his wheelers opposite to her leaders. He was still off to the west, however, with a gap of quicksand between his last animals and the leaders of Smoky's team. Every hitch of his two teams was down into the mud now, and he turned to call for Martin to hitch on another team. This time there was no protest. They already had Churl Hannibal's dozen mules waiting.

Taos realized this was the final test. It seemed impossible that he could force the last three or four hitches of his own team across that gap of quicksand without miring them down. She understood now why he had not actually touched a single mule with his whip till this point. He had saved it for this final effort. He sat there on the gaunt, hairy rump of his off wheeler, staring darkly at that black stretch of treacherous bog that lay between him and Smoky's leaders. Then he raised his whip.

The mules had been fidgeting around, snapping at each other, twitching their ears nervously. It all stopped, as if they sensed what was coming. The silence after all the noise pressed in against Taos with physical weight.

"All right," shouted Barr, "gee-up!"

His words ended with a stunning detonation of his mule whip in mid-air. The wheelers jumped beneath him, lunging off toward the right. Their first plunging rush carried them a few feet before the quicksand caught at their hind legs. Barr stepped on a whiffletree, caught a hame, pulled himself down to the pointers. He cracked his whip over their heads again, letting out a string of vituperation that had their ears smoking. The pointers lunged off dry ground, forcing the stalled wheelers ahead a couple more feet. Then the pointers were mired.

Barr worked his way back to the swing animals, driving them after the pointers and wheelers. The constant pressure of pair after pair lunging off dry ground pushed the mules already stuck on forward a little, till only a few feet separated the rumps of Barr's wheelers from Smoky's leaders. He dared not stop now. Sweating, panting, black with mud, he moved back and forth via whiffletree and rump, exhorting them to one last immense effort. Still he had not laid on that whip. The wheelers lunged once more, moved a foot, stalled. At last, with a wild, feral scream, he let that lash fall on their rumps.

"Gee-up, you damn' fuzzy excuses for a sop-and-taters hawss! I'll cut so much blood out of you it'll bleach you white!"

A great spasm of pain and fear gripped the animals. In a final, incredible burst of energy, the wheelers and pointers surged up out of the mud, the swingers pressed in from behind, mud flying beneath churning hoofs, rumps driving in wild unison. Then the whip stopped, and the voice, and the whole line of them pressed to sag back into the mud, tongues lolling, eyes bloodshot. Taos saw that the rumps of those exhausted wheelers were within reach of her sinking leaders. She started climbing down off the seat, meaning to make her way forward and hitch up for Barr.

"You stay there!" he roared. "I ain't having no hinny mess up the works at this time!"

"You can't talk to me like a mule . . ."

"I'll stop talkin' and start whackin' unless you climb back there and behave!" he shouted.

She looked at the implacable darkness of his face, utterly without humor in this moment, and knew he meant it. She climbed back aboard the wagon. Then he came back along his team. The clutch of quicksand was filling his animals with panic now, tired as they were, and he had to stop half a dozen times to quiet them. He finally reached the wheelers, hitching their traces to the tree of Smoky's leaders.

After this, he turned and made his way once more back up through his teams, stepping on trees, catching at hames, walking on rumps and withers, till he had reached the leaders of the first team. He jumped from them to solid ground. She could see him standing there, chest heaving. There were four teams hitched together now. Forty-eight mules, strung out through the bog and up onto high ground in a great snake of tall ears and sharp withers and muddy rumps, more animals than Taos had ever seen in one hitch before. A tingling thrill went through her as she waited for Barr to start them. A cottony silence had settled over the whole scene. His yell smashed it, making whatever he had shouted before sound like a whisper: "*G-i-i-i-d-a-a-p!*"

There was a wild, erupting surge along the whole line. Four dozen mules hit their collars with a slap of leather that rattled the Osnaberg sheeting on the wagon. Mud churned up over straining shoulders and swelling ribs and driving rumps. Great gouts of it filled the air from the pumping legs. The sounds lost identity in the one great din of shouting and braying and whipping and cursing.

The first team began moving forward on high ground. The second team began climbing from the bog onto the firm land. The third team seemed to lift out of the bog. Taos watched fixedly for the first movement from Smoky's leaders. For a long time, they remained there, braying pitifully, ears laid back. She did not think the traces and chains could stand the strain. Then slowly, painfully, Smoky's lead animals began to rise a little from the mud.

A small sobbing sound filled Taos's throat. Her eyes flashed to that black-bearded demon on high ground. He was laying his lash on with awesome skill now, picking out the laggers, nicking their ears, flaying their backs. When Barr saw Smoky's leaders move, he jumped up between the hitches and started making his way down the struggling line into the bog, shouting something to each mule as he passed.

Finally he got to the spot where he could reach Smoky's leaders with that whip. "What now, you broken down flea grubs!" he bellowed. "Am I going to strip you nekkid, or would you rather work with your fur on?"

The pitiful braying ceased. The mules took heart, began writhing and twisting in the suction of the mud. Barr turned back toward higher ground.

"Hitch up some more teams," he said. "We've got 'em goin'. Get me some more jacks."

They brought another team, hitching it up. The line of them stretched out of Taos's sight now, straining, heaving, braying, fighting to pull their brothers out of the bog. Slowly, maddeningly Smoky's team lifted. Their bellies were visible now, dripping viscid mud, and then the wagon.

The first little chuckle of thimbles in the axle was like a cry of joy to Taos. Then dogs began popping. Bolsters creaked and stakes rattled. The cargo shifted sullenly.

"Blackie," Taos heard herself whisper. "Blackie . . ."

The wheels began to roll. She could not hear dogs or thimbles or stakes or cargo now. The din was too great. She could not even hear Barr shouting any more. His mouth was open up there, as he plunged back and forth along the line. His yells seemed to mingle with the mules' brays, their brays seemed to become the squeal of tortured leather, the grating of grinding iron, the sucking ululation of a thousand hoofs churning at all the bogs on earth.

Taos shut her eyes against the mud flying into her face, gripping the seat in both hands, squinting her whole face against the raucous, deafening thunder of it all. She seemed spinning in a sea of sound. It lost reality to her. It lost time. It lost everything but that one little flame of hope away down inside of her, and that picture of a man that she could not shut out even with closed eyes — a savage, bearded, diabolical man with a scar on his face and a whip in his hand, like no one she had ever seen before in her whole life.

Thus the peak of sound subsided, and she seemed to be swaying back and forth. She opened her eyes to see that the wagon was on dry ground, surrounded by the men. She fell off the seat into their arms.

When the scene gained coherence again for her, she was sitting against one of the muddy wheels, and Ford was offering her a drink from his flask. Then Barr's sweating, mud-blackened face appeared before her.

"What were you coming back to the rear of the caravan for in the first place?" he said.

Her laugh held a little hysteria. "To fire you."

"To what?"

"Yes." Her laugh faded into a puzzled frown. "But I guess I can't do that to a man who has just saved my life, can I?"

CHAPTER
THREE

It was April 11, 1861 when Blackie Barr pulled Taos Sheridan from the quicksand at the Narrows, sixty-five miles west of Independence. On high noon of the same day, at Big John Springs, 140 miles west of Independence, a war party of thirty Apaches stopped to water their horses. One of them was Aztec Miller.

There were many stories concerning this man along the Santa Fé Trail. Some glorified him, some condemned, many would not be told in the presence of a woman. Few, however, were based on facts. Aztec's father had been Corcoran Miller, one of the early Yankee traders in Santa Fé, who had taken a Pueblo Indian for his wife in 1839. Whenever Corcoran went to St. Louis with his wagons, he left his squaw with her own people at the pueblo of Pecos, near Santa Fé. In 1850, ten years after the birth of their only son, Corcoran was killed by Comanches on the trail. His mother took their son to her people, to raise him as an Indian, but, before the year was up, Apaches raided Pecos, killing his mother and taking him away with them. The Pueblo Indians, especially the people of Pecos, had a legend that the Aztec Emperor Montezuma had originated among them, and that they were of Aztec descent. The Apaches scorned this tradition, so it must have been sheer mockery that caused them to name the boy captive Aztec. But somehow it clung, and, as he grew to manhood among the Apaches of the Mimbres drainage, it became as respected as the name of the most valiant warrior, for Aztec had developed into that kind of a man. Thus, at twenty-one, he was one of the Indians standing knee-deep in the white primrose that filled the hollow of Big John Spring.

He was taller than most of them, and the sun had burned his flesh to the color of ruddy bronze. His white heritage gave him a heavier quilting of muscle over chest and shoulders than an Indian, and showed itself again in the way his hair curled whenever it was dampened with sweat — although it was black enough to be Apache, worn in a long braid over his left shoulder. He wore a remarkable jaguar vest made from a pelt of the beast he had killed while on a raid into the mountains of northern Mexico, and his leggings were of yellow-dyed doeskin, soft and malleable as silk, yet tough as iron.

The Indians were silent for the most part, watching their steaming horses soak up the spring water, weary and jaded from the many days they had been on the trail. Up on the higher ground, Aztec could see Hachito, riding restlessly up and down in search of fresh sign. Unable to find it, he finally turned his pied pony down off the bank and walked it through the sand to the water. He slid off the animal, making a disgusted, spitting sound.

"*Ako alin day hahdah!*" Hachito said in the guttural, swallowed language of the Apaches. "Where are they now? I see no sign. No tracks of the wagon or the shod hoof."

"You expect too much," Aztec told him, speaking the same harsh, brutal tongue. "If they left the River of the Big Mud during the quarter moon, they would not be here yet. At best they could only have reached the place where the Kansas and the Osage flow together."

The other man turned restlessly, sourly to watch his horse drink. Aztec still studied him, acutely aware of the antipathy between them. Although the Apaches had fought Spanish and Mexican rule through four centuries, and had never been subdued, this unremitting contact had left its insidious imprint. One of the marks was the way many Apaches had come to use the Spanish forms of their names. Such as Hachito. Little Hatchet — after the bright-bladed weapon thrust into his belt with which he had gained such bloody infamy these last years. A weather-scored, rawhide whip of a man with a hungry, rapacious face, so fleshless the cheek bones shone yellow through the saddle-colored skin, and the eyes were sunken and feverish in their sockets. He got down to drink himself, and then rose again, spitting out the last mouthful.

"It seems a long ride for a few guns," he said.

"More than a few guns," Aztec told him. "The Cheyennes said there would be enough to arm our whole tribe."

"*Zeetzaian,*" swore Hachito. "The whole thing smacks of a bow string so weak it will snap when

33

drawn. Did it not seem strange to you that a Southern Cheyenne would appear alone so far away from the hunting grounds of his people? Would you go alone into a Cheyenne camp? They would have your scalp in an instant."

"This man was a traveler," said Aztec. "He knew much of our language. I don't think his people would have slain me had I appeared among them with such a story as he brought. The Cheyennes need guns as badly as we. He said the wagon train would leave the River of the Big Mud during the quarter moon of this month. There is a man with the train who will contact us. That is the best part. There will be no fight. We will not have to give any payment for the guns. They will be ours for simply contacting this man."

"A thin story to make a ride of three hundred miles for," said Hachito.

"Then why did you come, Little Hatchet?" Aztec asked. "Were you afraid Kou-Ailee would look elsewhere for a chief to replace him if he thought you were shirking danger?"

This had long been a tension between these two, for a great part of Hachito's restlessness was his insatiable ambition. The hollows under his cheek bones seemed to grow darker, and his eyes burned with a more febrile light.

"You speak dangerous words," he said. "Kou-Ailee is not that old. He has many more years on the warpath. A man could become suspicious of your own intention, hearing you talk like that."

"Which is better, to say what you think, or to hide the words in your head and think it anyway?" asked Aztec.

Hachito released the woven bridle of his horse and moved toward Aztec. The sand crushed sibilantly beneath the turned-up toes of his knee-high war moccasins. When he was within a pace of Aztec, he stopped, placing a hand upon the handle of the hatchet in his belt.

"I have never hidden my ambition to become chief of the Mimbrenos, Aztec. I hope that when Kou-Ailee retires in the ordinary course of things and it comes time to choose another, I will have proven myself worthy for the honor. On the other hand, it is you who have kept your words in your head. Why are you so intent upon getting these guns? If you were chief of the Mimbrenos, what would you do?" A sly look curled Hachito's lips. "Take us down to Mexico City, perhaps, and get back the gold shoes the Spaniards took from Montezuma?"

Aztec's chest began stirring more perceptibly. "You make a joke of it."

Hachito smiled thinly. "I actually think you believe in the superstition. Where is the fire kept burning constantly till Montezuma returns to Pecos? I have been all through the mountains around the Pueblos and never found it."

Aztec let the bridle of his own horse slip from his hand. "If you want to fight, Hachito, why don't you say so, instead of poking your head up like a prairie dog from its hole and insulting the beliefs of my mother?"

The other man made a small rattling sound in his throat and started to jerk the hatchet from his belt. Before he completed the movement, a loud, commanding voice stopped him, and Kou-Ailee came from among the other Indians. He was an imposing figure of a man, this war chief of the Mimbrenos, with his tall, military carriage, the tails of a red Chimayo blanket flapping at his burnished calves. He moved with as much savage, restless vigor as the youngest warrior in the party, despite his mane of pure white hair and his face scored and lined with the wisdom and weather and pain of fifty years.

"Are my young fighting cocks at it again?" he said in a half-angry, half-indulgent way. "If you do not stop this, I will leave you both here to fast. Save your fighting for the white man. There will be plenty of it."

With the reluctant surliness of a child, Hachito turned to him. "Then we do attack the caravan?"

"Not unless we have to," Kou-Ailee told Hachito darkly. "The Cheyenne who brought us words of these guns was very definite that we did not have to fight for them. Don't spoil things with your eagerness, Hachito, till we learn if what he said was true. Let us mount and ride."

The chief turned to walk toward his horse. Hachito picked up his bridle. Before mounting, he turned to Aztec, those eyes burning like banked coals in his head.

"You and I will finish this, *Pecoseno* . . . sooner than you think."

Aztec said nothing, holding Hachito's eyes till the man turned to swing aboard his horse. Then Aztec picked up his own bridle, and the lead ropes of his three spare horses, and mounted himself. As he did so, another Apache rode up. He was Hachito's blood brother, Little Sun, a vain, gaudy boy of no more than eighteen winters. He was mounted upon an Appaloosa horse he had gotten from a northern raid, and a bright yellow scalp gleamed like gold from among the string of scalps tied to his buffalo-hide shield.

"Why do you never fight Hachito?" he asked, smiling slyly. "Always it is talk, and the big words, but never a fight."

"Sometimes there are things more important than the petty feuds of a single man," said Aztec. "I wouldn't expect you to understand that."

Little Sun's hand closed tightly around the handle of his lance, tipped with the blade of a butcher knife, but before he could answer, Aztec turned his back and kicked his pony up out of the hollow.

This was buffalo country, with deep buffalo trails crisscrossing the short, matted grass that stretched beyond the eye's reach, their wallow filling the air with the reek of stagnant water and petrifying mud, their bleaching bones and hoary flaking horns strewn everywhere from the countless centuries of their life and death in this land. Noon. Afternoon. Night. Brief halts in gullies to rest the horses. An evening meal of jerked beef and dried corn. Then the huddled, blanketed figures gathering closely around the fire in age-old fears of the spirits pervading the darkness. Dawn came with a burst of song from the snipe and killdeer haunting the wallows, and after a meager, fireless breakfast, into the saddle again.

Then, on noon of that day, their scouts returned with word of riders ahead. Four whites, they said, well-armed, looking like the scouts for a wagon train. Kou-Ailee pulled the whole band of them into the bottoms of the Neosho River, awaiting sight of the whites. Each man had three or four horses to hold, and they began to fiddle as soon as the alien horses were near enough to scent. Then the riders came into sight. Aztec could make out a tall, black-haired man in jeans and a sack coat. Beside him was an older, shriveled scout in buckskin. The third was heavily bearded, riding a paint animal.

"The black-haired one is Ford Martin," said Aztec. "He has been in Santa Fé many times. He must have left his wagon to his swamper so he could come with these outriders. The man in buckskins is Kantrace. He has been scouting for trains since Becknell first came through. I cannot recognize the one on the pinto."

"And the fourth . . . with the blonde hair?" asked the chief.

Aztec squinted his eyes against the sun. "It is strange that she does not ride her vinegar roan, but it looks like the woman . . . Taos Sheridan."

The whites passed the spot where the Indians were hidden, heading straight for a copse of hackberry trees that stood at a bend in the river, the only decent timber within miles. They had almost reached it when a sharp whinny came from one of the fiddling, nervous Indian ponies. Aztec whirled to see a fight among Hachito's spare beasts. A buckskin had turned to nip at a fuzzy little mare, and the mare reared up, breaking her halter. Realizing that she was free, the half-wild broomtail wheeled and scrambled up through the rushes of the bank.

"Hachito!" cried Kou-Ailee. "Stop that animal!"

Hachito dropped the lead rope of his other spare animals, leaped aboard his mount, and kicked it up after the mare. But the prairie was already thumping like a tom-tom beneath the beat of the mare's hoofs. The whites had wheeled their animals to stare as Hachito burst from the bulrushes after his mare.

"We are revealed now!" shouted Kou-Ailee. "We must prevent them from returning to their wagon train with the word! Fifteen of you men ride across their path and make a show that will drive them into that timber for cover! The youngest three here for horse holders! The rest of you with me!"

Aztec quickly passed his bridle and lead rope into the hand of one of the youngest men, following Kou-Ailee down the river bottoms. Already the other Indians were streaming up onto the prairie, yelling and pirouetting. At sight of this band, cutting off flight back to the wagon train, the four whites wheeled their animals into the hackberries, dismounted, and opened fire. The mounted Indians kept cavorting around out of range, while Kou-Ailee and his men ran toward the trees in the cover of the willows and bulrushes filling the river bottoms.

When they neared the timber, the Indians spread out, till Aztec was crawling through the undergrowth with no more sight of the others than if he had been alone. Desultory firing clapped like muffled applause in the stifling heat of early afternoon. Finally Aztec caught sight of shadowy movement within the hackberries, the flash of a gun. On his belly, he squirmed through the swamp grass, short bow in one hand, arrows in the other. A voice rose from ahead, so near it stiffened him in startled surprise.

"It's too late to get out the back way, Taos. I can see horses being held downstream. There's a bunch of them coming up through the bottoms on foot."

"Then stay right where you are, Ford. If we can hold them off till the train gets here, we're safe."

Kou-Ailee snaked through the grass to Aztec's side, whispering in his ear: "Call to them. Tell them to put down their arms and they will be safe."

"White men," said Aztec in English. "Put down your arms and you will not be killed. We do not —"

A shot smashed his words, and lead whistled through the berry bushes a foot to his right. "There's your answer to that!" shouted Ford Martin. "I'd rather get my throat slit with a gun in my hand than see it done otherwise!"

The other Apaches could not understand him, but the shot set them off. With wild, piercing yells, they popped up out of the grass on every side. Aztec himself came to his feet, notching an arrow. Over the bushes, he saw Ford Martin, twenty feet ahead, feverishly reloading his Sharps. He got the rifle ball dumped and wheeled toward Aztec, bringing the gun up. Aztec had his bowstring against his ear, but before he could let it go, Hachito plunged from the bushes behind Martin, hatchet raised. The rattle of brush whirled Martin toward him. Unable to bring the gun into position to fire, Martin swung it upward, knocking Hachito's weapon aside. At the same moment, Little Sun came charging in on Martin's other flank, lance leveled. Martin tried to head away from this, but it caught him through the shoulder carrying him over backward.

Up near the front of the grove, the woman and the other two men whirled from where they had been watching the Indians out on the open prairie. Aztec had a momentary, flashing impression of Taos Sheridan, the beauty of her striking him with poignant shock. The hair, rippling like a golden pennant in the wind. The gleam of grease-slick leggings across the deep curve of her hip. The hot flash of anger on her face.

Then the buckskinned scout beside her was leveling his Sharps at Kou-Ailee. This time Aztec did let his arrow go. The short bows had incredible force at this close range. The shaft caught the scout in the chest before he could fire, carrying him backward and downward till he was standing on his feet, and then dropped him like a sack of meal. The woman stood with her legs apart, eyes blazing, emptying her revolver into the rush of Indians. Aztec saw two of them go down, tumbling and rolling to a stop. At the same moment, the white man on her other side dropped his gun and fell back, pin-cushioned by arrows. Seeing that her three companions were done, the woman threw her gun at the Apaches, in a last wild defiance, and whirled to grab at one of the excited horses.

41

The gun struck Kou-Ailee in the face, as he ran toward her. He veered off to the side, going to his knees in a stunned way. The four animals of the whites had been tugging frantically at their reins, tied to the branches of trees, and one of them broke free. Taos grabbed the reins and threw them over its tossing head, leaping for the saddle. An arrow drove deeply into its hip, and the beast screamed and reared. But she put her spurs to it, beating at the arched neck with her fist. The horse came back down, bolting.

Aztec was on the side of the grove to which she wheeled the animal. She drove spurs to its flank and the beast leaped into a gallop. But Aztec was already quartering in. As the animal raced by him, he caught her leg. It almost jerked his arm from the socket. It took her off balance, and she tumbled from the horse onto him. They rolled over and over across the ground. He had a dazed expression of dusty, resilient flesh forced against him, of the heat of breath bursting against his face, of blue eyes flashing rage and pain.

They came to a stop against a tree. She still had a fight in her. The pain of clawing fingers raked his face. She tried to tear free. He braced a knee, threw himself against her. For a moment, he had her pinned up against the tree. It was like trying to hold an enraged cat. She got an arm free and struck at him, hand fisted, like a man. It had more force than he had anticipated, knocking him partly off her. She writhed free, jumping to her feet, taffy hair whipping around her twisted face, red lips parted. Before she could wheel and run, someone stepped from the trees behind her. Getting to his feet, Aztec caught sight of a rifle butt swinging down. It caught her at the base of the neck. She slumped to the ground, and Hachito stood above her. He stared down at the body, something more than triumph in those feverishly burning eyes.

"We will keep her for a hostage," he said.

"I told you we didn't need to do anything like that for the guns," panted Aztec. "It is for Kou-Ailee to decide."

"He will make no more decisions," said Hachito.

Slowly Aztec turned till he could see through the trees to where most of the warriors had gathered around a fallen body. Forgetting the woman and Hachito in that moment, Aztec walked over to where Kou-Ailee lay. He stared down at the chieftain for a long time, knowing as much grief as was possible in a man reared to the stoicism of these people, for he had had much reverence for Kou-Ailee.

"Surely the gun the girl threw at him didn't do it," he said.

"There is a bullet hole," answered one of the warriors. "One of her shots must have told."

He squatted down to examine the wound. As he saw where it had entered, and where it came out, a curious, fixed blankness entered his face. With this expression, he rose and walked back to where Hachito was tying the woman's hands with the gut from the bow of a dead Apache.

"The bullet enters Kou-Ailee's left hip and travels upward to come out at the upper right side of the chest," said Aztec in Apache. "It could not have come from the woman's gun."

"The scout, then," said Hachito, rising.

"My arrow struck Kantrace before he could shoot," said Aztec.

Hachito turned to face him, the blood filling his face till it had a dark, tainted hue. "What are you thinking, then, *Pecoseno?*" he asked, putting all his sly contempt into the last word.

Aztec lowered his eyes to the Sharps in Hachito's hand. "Ford Martin's gun."

"If you are speaking of the one with the black hair, yes," said Hachito. "He is not dead. The lance went through his shoulder."

"And he was behind Kou-Ailee and myself, and to our left, as we ran in," said Aztec. "That means you would be in the same position when you got the gun, about the time Kou-Ailee was struck by the girl's revolver."

"It would be dangerous to go any further with your suppositions," said Hachito softly. "All the others are sure it was one of the white men's bullets that killed Kou-Ailee. They want vengeance for that. They wish to attack the wagon train."

"We will not do that," said Aztec.

The other warriors had drifted around these two by now, except for one left to watch the body of their chief. Hachito turned to them with an expressionless face.

"There is need of a new war chief now," he said. "Who shall lead you?"

The Indians looked narrowly from Hachito to Aztec, and then one of them, the gleaming sweat of his body blotted out here and there with dirt, stepped forward.

"He shall lead us who follows the will of the majority."

The trace of a smile twitched at Hachito's lips. "And what is your will?"

It arose from them in a guttural chorus. "Attack the wagon train."

CHAPTER
FOUR

Twelve o'clock. April 11, 1861. Have reached spot six miles east of the Neosho River. Am giving Sergeant Coffin and the men twenty minutes for noon halt and lunch. Still no sign of Taos Sheridan's caravan. I still cannot believe she would smuggle guns.

Lieutenant Wade Kenmore stopped writing in his diary, sitting there in the dubious shade of a scrawny cottonwood, six miles east of the Neosho, and swabbed absently at his sweating face. It was a long, angular face, brick-hued with the sunburn of a blond that would never turn tan, a face reflecting the surprising contradictions of the man himself, as if all the dogma and precision of a rule book had been mixed in with the reckless defiance of a wild horse. That precision was in the square, carefully molded lines of his mouth and jaw, but whenever the sun caught them right, the chilly night was blotted from his gray eyes by a startlingly wild-looking flash.

He could see the men of his half troop sprawled in the meager shade of more cottonwoods at the base of this rise. There was something nervously resentful to their positions, as weary as they were. He could not blame them. He himself had resented being sent West on this mission when every soldier worth his salt had been dreaming of an assignment to some Eastern theater, with this war so imminent . . .

He shook his head doggedly, closing the diary and rising to walk down the hill. The vague path took him from sight of the troops behind an outthrust of earth, and, when he came from behind this, they were gathered around Sergeant Coffin, so intent upon what he was saying that they did not see Kenmore's approach. There was a drawling indolence to Coffin's voice that had always galled Kenmore.

"Have they got any right to send us West, that's what I want to know? I'll allow Anderson's surrendered Sumter already. Why, do you know Major Buell has orders to pull every regular out of the Department of New Mexico as soon as war's declared? And where will they send them? East. Why would they turn around and send us West?"

"A little disaffection, Sergeant?" asked Kenmore.

Coffin could not hide his surprise as he wheeled to find the lieutenant standing there. Then he rose to his feet, that insolent defiance stamped into his face. He was a long, loose-jointed man, the cavalry stripe running down the seam of his blue trousers faded till it looked almost white. A network of weather wrinkles spread from the corners of his eyes into his cheeks, roughening them to the texture of old leather. It was the eyes that had always intrigued Kenmore, reminding him of holes burst through a blanket, so contrary to the man's loose-jointed indolence in their black intensity.

"Ain't disaffection to wonder where you're going, Lieutenant," he said.

"Seems to me you wonder a lot," said Kenmore. "I'm used to troops griping, Coffin, and I'm used to my non-com griping. But I've never seen them do it together."

"Maybe you've never had a sergeant with the interests of his men really at heart, Lieutenant."

"Is it really the interests of the men, Coffin?"

The man's face stiffened, his voice softened. "Just what do you mean by that?"

The words were in Kenmore's mind, ready to say: *I mean to reprimand you, Sergeant. If you keep it up, you can expect a summary court when we get back.* But he became aware of how intently the troops were watching, and for the first time realized how far his own frayed nerves had driven him. He knew he would lose their respect by criticizing Coffin before them, no matter what the non-com had done. He forced himself to smile.

"I mean that we'd all better take it a little easy, Sergeant," he said. "We've been pushing hard, and I don't blame you for being jumpy. In fact, you do have a right to know what we're doing out here. The colonel ordered me to keep it to myself till we neared our destination. Did you ever hear of Beecher's Bibles?"

A puzzled look mingled with the hostility in Coffin's face. "No."

"Guess you wouldn't, not being a Kansas man," said Kenmore. "When the state entered the Union, it was touch and go whether it would be slave or free. The feeling rose pretty high around here. Henry Ward Beecher had raised a lot of money by his preaching against slavery, and a lot of it went to buy Sharps rifles for his Abolitionists. That's how the guns got called Beecher's Bibles. Last month, a big consignment of those Sharps fell into the hands of Confederate sympathizers. We thought they'd try to run them south to the Confederate Army, but they had different plans."

"The West?" asked Coffin.

Kenmore nodded. "Tucson and Santa Fé are going to be hot points in the contest for control of the Territories. Our forces will be pretty thin around there when the Department of New Mexico packs up its gear. You know what a host of Indians there is in that country. If enough of them were armed, they could be a deciding factor in who gained control. And it's obvious they would favor the side that supplied them with guns and ammunition."

"And that's where these Beecher's Bibles are going?" said Coffin.

"The last caravan to leave Independence was Taos Sheridan's. The Army has strong reason to believe the guns are in her wagons. This is more than the mere fact of these specific rifles. If the Confederates get these guns through, it will set a precedent that will snowball. The Indians will know they can get guns through these channels and will fall in with the Confederate plans completely. On the other hand, if we block this first

49

shipment, the Indians will lose faith in the South's ability to supply them. They didn't send us West for a joke, Sergeant. It's a big responsibility. Now, will you mount them up?"

Coffin's burning black eyes held his for another moment. There was no relenting to them. Then he turned and sourly ordered the men into their saddles.

The dusty file of them rode out of the meagerly timbered hollow at the trot. For a long, sweltering space, Kenmore did not speak to Coffin, riding beside him. Thought of Taos Sheridan kept darkening his mind. How could he have been such a fool? There was an insidious shame needling him at having to see her again in this capacity, so soon after that night at Fort Leavenworth. How young he must have seemed to her, how naïve. But she had been through Leavenworth three times this year, with her wagons, and each time he had been her escort to the officer's ball at the fort. Barrack rooms talk had convinced him she had never shown another man so much favor. And he had fallen under her spell. He had the picture of himself once more, out there in the moonlight, by the battery, proposing to her in that stumbling, passionate burst.

It had been surprise widening her eyes. But there had been amazement, too, starting up, then blotted out deliberately for his sake. How grave and studied her reply had been, so careful not to hurt his feelings. It was so unlike the stories he had heard of her, whipping any man who tried to kiss her. Slowly, into his thoughts, crept the awareness of Coffin's attention on him. Kenmore turned to see those black eyes studying his face.

"If you want to give me a little talking to now, Lieutenant, the troops can't hear."

There was something mocking in the man's voice that brought Kenmore's teeth together. "Never mind, Coffin. I've just always thought that one of the most valuable functions of a non-com is to act as sort of a buffer between the officers and men. A lot of unnecessary tensions can be eased off passing through him."

"Maybe I learned in a different army."

"Maybe you did. I understand you were with Taylor when he stormed Monterey during the Mexican War, Coffin. What day was that? The twentieth?"

Coffin stared at him sharply. "How can a man remember dates in a thing like that?"

"I can remember the date of my first action very well," said Kenmore. "I've always heard it was an old Yankee custom to answer one question with another question, Sergeant. Was it born in you, or did you pick it up somewhere?"

Coffin lifted a little in his saddle. "What are you getting at, Lieutenant?"

"If you've been in the Army since the Mexican War, you must have been away from your home state a long time, Coffin. Just what was that state?"

A furtive, shuttling look sharpened Coffin's face, but before he could answer, one of the scouts appeared on a rise ahead, coming down through the spring grass at a gallop. Sweat made dark channels in the alkali caking his horse as he pulled it to a halt before Kenmore.

"I think we've found the wagon train, Lieutenant. They're about three miles ahead, corralled, fighting off a bunch of Indians. Looks like Apaches."

There was a ridge of bluffs rising from the river bottoms to flank the alkali flats upon which the wagon train had corralled. Reaching these, Kenmore dismounted his men at their base and climbed to the top for a look at the scene. He counted twenty wagons, pulled into a rough circle with the spare animals in the middle. As near as he could make out, there were between twenty and thirty Indians in the hurrying, plunging, cavorting line of horsemen riding around and around the wagons. The scout told him they had spotted three more Apaches in the river bottoms, holding the spare horses of the war party. Kenmore sent two of his men down the river to get these horse holders, and then mounted up his troops.

The trail through these bluffs had been cut for thirty-five years by the wheels of Conestogas, a deep, hard-packed way, laced with ruts, echoing mutedly to the trotting gait of the men filing to the top. Here Kenmore halted them.

"I'll take five men in the first wave. Coffin, you take the rest. Swing out to my flank and spread as thin as you can. It will look like more that way, and present a poorer target than if we bunch. Don't fire till I give the order, and make that first shot count. We'll be right on their necks. Ready?" He felt the faint thread of trembling nausea that always drew itself through his belly just before an action. His big red bay fiddled nervously beneath him, sensing the charge. Kenmore raised his saber. "Left front into line, gallop . . ."

They poured out of the defile and covered the downslope in a thin, spreading line. The whole bluff trembled to the drum of their collected gallop. That sound filled Kenmore's ears till he could hear nothing else. The first wave struck the alkali flats, and still he held them in that steady, controlled gallop. 300 yards now? A few of the Apaches had seen them and were turning out of their wild circle around the wagons. 250 yards. Kenmore saw a heavy-shouldered warrior in a jacket made from the spotted hide of some Mexican cat trying to attract the attention of his fellows to the troops. 200 yards.

Kenmore felt himself lifting up in the stirrups. 100 yards to go. An arrow dug into the ground between his horse and the ring of Indians. 50 yards. Most of them had seen the soldiers now and were trying to pull around to meet them, a wild swirl of pinto ponies and twisted, painted faces, and open mouths.

"Charge!" screamed Kenmore, standing up in his stirrups and lifting his saber high. "Charge . . ."

The gallop was collected no longer. The drum of hoofs lost regularity, lost identity, became a vast surf of mottled sound lifting him toward the riders ahead.

"Fire!"

His hoarse shout was drowned in the roaring volley from behind him. He saw a buckskin horse go down. The Indian rolled like a ball and came up to his feet. Kenmore switched his saber to the hand holding his reins and yanked his Navy revolver out. The Indian wheeled, bow in hand, and notched an arrow. Kenmore fired. The

53

man fell backward before he let his taut bowstring go, and the notched arrow flew straight upward into the air.

At the same instant, off to his flank, Kenmore saw one of his men fighting to control a horse crazed by the pain of three arrows buried deeply in its rump. The man did not see the Indian who burst from the cloud of dust and swirling horses, long lance leveled, a string of scalps streaming from his buffalo-hide shield.

"Duneen!" shouted Kenmore. "Off to your side, off to your side!"

The man did not hear him. Kenmore spun his horse, firing at the Indian lancer. But the range was too great for his revolver. The butcher knife tipping the lance went into Duneen just above his hips, coming out his belly on the other side. It carried him off over one shoulder of his horse, to fall flat on the ground, lance sticking perpendicular as a flagpole from his spread-eagled body. The Indian had to release the lance as he thundered on by, to keep from being pulled out of the saddle. But he reined his gaudy Appaloosa horse around viciously, and came back to pull the lance from the body. For a moment he kept the excited, prancing horse there, looking down at Duneen. Knowing the Indian was thinking about that scalp, Kenmore spurred his bay toward the man, bringing his gun up to fire again.

As he did, a dun-colored mustang raced across his front. The Apache was hanging off on the opposite side, by a leg, and firing under the neck of the horse. The arrow whizzed from the animal's tangled mane. There was a thick, thumping sound beneath Kenmore. His bay screamed, shuddered. Kenmore kicked free as it went down.

The jarring impact of ground stunned him. He rolled over, mouth full of dust. He saw the Indian on the dun-colored animal wheeling around, coming up straight on its back to fit another arrow to his bow. It was the one in the spotted vest. Kenmore's gun was gone, but he still held his saber. He rose to one knee in a desperate, final defiance, raising the sword. The man had the string drawn back to his ear again. The horse looked big as a house, bearing directly down on Kenmore. Off to one side, the lieutenant saw a trooper wheeling to fire, but he knew the man would be too late. He found a curiously detached thought floating into the chaos of his mind: *I'll never get those Beecher's Bibles.*

Then something happened Kenmore could not believe. Another Apache came charging out of the dust and smoke to crash broadside against the one in the spotted vest. The blow of it knocked his bow aside, and the arrow dug half its length into the earth, ten feet to Kenmore's right. For that instant, the two Apaches were up against each other — the heavy-chested one with the spotted vest, and the taller one in knee-high war moccasins with a gaunt, feverish face and burning eyes. He held a heavy Sharps rifle out to one side, but it was smoking and must have been empty. His other hand rose into the air, and Kenmore saw the bright flash of a hatchet blade.

The one in the spotted vest dropped his bow, trying to block the hatchet. His elbow struck the other man's wrist, deflecting the blow so that the hatchet buried itself in his back instead of his neck. Face twisted with the pain of it, he slid off to the side, blood already covering the spotted vest. With a fiendish shout of triumph, the other Apache wheeled, still holding his hatchet in one hand, the Sharps in his other, and booted his horse away after the other Indians.

Kenmore rose to his feet. The dust was settling over the scene like a chalky pall. The Indians had scattered, to leave their dead, a streak of copper here and there against the pale alkali, a wounded horse kicking its last over by the wagons. Sergeant Coffin came over at the trot. The Indian in the vest stirred, moaning. The sergeant's horse squealed and tossed its head with the viciousness of Coffin's reining, as he drew it up to step off beside the Indian. He bent over the man, face compressed with intent study. Then he turned to pull his carbine from its boot.

"Coffin," Kenmore asked, "what are you doing?"

"This one's still alive," said Coffin, opening the breech on his gun.

"Sergeant," Kenmore told him, "I forbid you."

"What the hell," growled Coffin. "You'd kill a wolf in a trap, wouldn't you?"

Kenmore's lips made a pale line through his dust-stained face, barely moving as he answered. "Put your gun back in the boot, Sergeant, and gather up the men. Put a detail under Corporal Maine and patrol the corralled wagons."

Coffin met his hot young gaze for a moment, then turned and slipped the carbine back in its boot. "Yes, sir," he growled.

Kenmore went over to hunker down beside the Indian. He saw that the blade had sliced deeply into the man's back, high up. It was an ugly wound, and he doubted if the Indian would last long. He took off his bandanna and set about stopping the blood and trying to make a bandage. The wagon crew was emerging now, a motley stream of bearded teamsters, led by a tattered old whang-hide with a great flowing mane of white hair.

Irritably Kenmore recognized Smoky Cameron. He was too well acquainted with the man's vile temper and unreliable disposition, having ridden tour with him more than once when Smoky was acting as guide and interpreter for the 3rd during the Comanche troubles of 1857. The whiteheaded plainsman stopped above Kenmore, leering down at him.

"Our regards for breaking up the fandango, Lootenant. Looks like you bagged a prize. That's Aztec Miller."

Kenmore started to raise his head sharply, then looked back down again at the wounded man. The face, dark as it was, had a finely chiseled aquilinity to its high brow. The hair was black, but sweat had put a definite curl to it. Kenmore waited for some emotion to come, after the surprise. He felt little. After all the legends he had heard of this man, there was nothing particularly notable or imposing about the long, rather gaunt body, with its ribs thrusting against the coppery flesh like a washboard along suds row, lying there in the alkali, blotted with chalky dust and muddy blood.

"Are you sure?" asked Kenmore.

"Couldn't be anybody else, with that spotted vest. Hachito was with the band, too. He was the one that chopped Aztec up."

Kenmore rose, ordering a couple of the teamsters to make a litter and get Aztec to the wagon. "And now, Smoky," he said, "where is Taos Sheridan?"

Cameron tilted his greasy old hat forward to scratch the back of his head. "Well, now, I couldn't rightly say . . ."

"Smoky, I'm not going to stand for any of your vagaries. Where is she?"

"All right, Lootenant," grumbled the teamster. "She was scouting ahead with Ford Martin and Kantrace and Bulloman. She hasn't shown up yet. We are all just hoping and praying the Indians come in from the north or south and didn't see her."

Kenmore felt the blood leave his face at the implications of that. He saw a quizzical, studying glow fill Smoky's eyes, and turned aside, trying to hide his own sick look. He was glad Coffin came up at that moment. It gave him a chance to recover, while listening.

Coffin made his report without dismounting. Two wounded, one dead. Kenmore had expected more casualties, but it had been a quicker fight than he had looked for. That was the Indian way, to touch and run, and wait for another day. He ordered Coffin to detail a man for the wounded, to bring him the dead man's horse, if they had it, and to start to search the wagons.

"Search the wagons?" echoed Smoky Cameron. "You didn't bring a whole half troop out here jist to git Blackie Barr, did you?"

Kenmore whirled on him. "Barr?"

Smoky cackled. "No, I can see you didn't. You won't git him anyway. He's probably hightailed it by now."

"*He* was with the train?" asked Kenmore softly.

"If you'd brought him and Aztec Miller both back, they probably would have made you a brigadier." Smoky laughed.

Kenmore's eyes went blank. He allowed himself a moment of regret that Barr had escaped. Any man in the Army would give a year's pay to bring that traitor to justice. Then, squaring his shoulders, Kenmore made a parade quarter turn and walked toward the wagons. Coffin had already dismounted his men and was going through the second Murphy by the time Kenmore and the teamsters reached the corral. A big kettle-bellied man was shouting at the sergeant from a hind wheel and brandishing his whip.

"You don't tear my load apart like that. It'll take three or four hours to get it balanced up again. What in God's little wagon are you damn' blue-coats doing here?"

"I'll have your name, if you don't mind," said Kenmore.

"I'm Jack Rubie!" roared the man. "And this is my outfit. And if you don't tell your non-com . . ."

"I've already told him what to do," said Kenmore. "We are searching for an illegal shipment of guns, Mister Rubie, sent by Southern sympathizers to arm the very Indians that almost had your scalp."

Jack Rubie's Adam's apple made a greasy bob in his muscular, unshaven neck, and he dropped his coiled whip to his side. The other teamsters had heard him, and they gathered around Kenmore in a muttering, eddying tide. He paid no attention to them, climbing into the wagon himself. Coffin and a private were climbing over the crates of cargo, poking about with the barrels of their muskets, moving a box here and there.

"What kind of search do you call this?" said Kenmore in a voice rent with anger. "Open those boxes, Sergeant. Take those bolts of cloth out and unroll them on the ground. Empty this wagon down to the bottom of its bed. Then tear out a plank to make sure it isn't a false bottom. Take that Osnaberg sheeting off the hoops and separate it. The stuff comes in two layers, you know. Come on, now, on the double!"

Coffin turned his narrow face toward Kenmore. Those eyes glittered in the dusky light. Then he turned back, ordering the private to take the other end of a long crate. Kenmore backed out through the pucker, dropping over the tailgate, and ordered the teamsters to get to work unloading their wagons. He saw the angry refusal rise up in their faces and spoke before they could answer.

"You might as well. If you don't, I'll have my troops do it, and that will take five times as long. You'll be here three or four days unless you help me."

60

That had more effect than any direct exercise of his authority. The heaps of cargo grew all about the wagons. Cotton goods, coarse and fine, cambrics and calicoes, stemloom shirtings. Kenmore pried open half a dozen long crates that took four men to unload, found their load to be butcher knives with leather-wrapped hilts. He personally unrolled countless bolts of calico, long enough to hold a rifle, and found them empty.

He was standing amidst a pile of these when one of the men he had detailed to take care of the Apache horse holders came riding in. With him, on an Indian pony, was Taos Sheridan.

"Private Bidwell is still riding herd on as many of the Indian horses as didn't get away, sir," reported the trooper. "We killed one of the Apaches . . . the other two escaped. They were holding this woman and another man prisoner. The man got a lance through his shoulder. Says his name is Ford Martin."

Kenmore hardly heard the man. He was staring at the woman. She sat for a moment on the bareback Indian horse, as easily, as casually as if she had been born there, staring about her at the carnage. The haunting, oblique planes of her face darkened with a flush of growing anger, and the afternoon light caught a bright-bladed flash in her eyes when she finally looked at Kenmore.

"Is this some sort of revenge, Wade?" she asked. Her voice trembled a little.

He tried to keep the humiliation from his eyes, inclining his head to one side in an apologetic gesture.

"Believe me, Taos, it isn't any of my choosing. I was ordered after you, to seize a shipment of smuggled Rebel guns."

"Guns? Do you think I'm crazy, Wade? I wouldn't let a Secessionist ride with my train, much less ship a cargo of their guns."

"Nonetheless, I was sent out here to get a shipment of Sharps rifles from this wagon train."

Taos slid off the horse, her glance sweeping to Coffin, who had ripped the top from a flour-barrel and was thrusting a stick to the bottom of its contents. "Why don't you just dump the flour out on the ground," she said acidly. "You've torn apart just about everything else. Where else could the guns be?"

"Perhaps you could tell me," said Kenmore.

Taos swung to him with her eyes blazing, but, before she could speak, Corporal Maine and a private came riding through the wagons with a surly, black-bearded man stumbling along between their horses.

"We saw this one riding away from the wagon train right after Coffin put us to patrolling it, sir," said the corporal. "We gave chase and finally had to shoot his horse to stop him."

Kenmore stared at the man's filthy, scarred face, half hidden by the curly, matted beard that grew heavily up the angle of the jaw to meet the shaggy hair growling down from the temples. The eyes were sullen and bloodshot, half concealed by dissolute blue lids, and the black brows had a peak of the devil in them.

"Blackie Barr," said Kenmore finally. The man met his glance balefully, not answering. "I find your sentiments about Secession hard to believe, Miss Sheridan," said Kenmore, still studying Barr, "when you harbor traitors of this stripe in your train."

"I didn't know his whole story when I signed him on," she said. For the first time, there was a hesitance in her voice. "I . . . I guess I won't try and prevent your taking him back, if you're a mind."

"In good time," said Kenmore. "I'll have the guns first."

She waved her hand impatiently at the piles of goods. "But you can see there aren't any."

Kenmore gazed at her in troubled silence, seeking some softening of the thought in his mind. But there was none, and he had to put it in words. "I hate to say this, Taos, but if they aren't here now, there's a possibility you will pick them up later. I've got to take that possibility into consideration. I won't hold you up. But I'm going to be with you . . . till I find those guns."

CHAPTER
FIVE

Beyond the Neosho the spring days beckoned them ever onward, past the big bend of the Arkansas, down that river to Cimarrón Crossing, taking the north fork of the trail here that would lead them into the mountains. Beyond Cimarrón Crossing, the land became a desert. Alkali flats and sand hills filled the horizon. Mirages turned a knoll to a lake, a cut bank to a mountain. The night was filled with the eerie chorus of wolves down from the far mountains to prowl. Dust storms swept out of nowhere, choking animals to death in a few minutes and often halting the train for hours while the beasts and men huddled behind the high wagon boxes beneath a sun that had turned to a pale silver disk in the sky.

This was the land Aztec Miller rode through, in the shadowy depths of a jolting, rocking wagon. All they had for his wound was a poultice of lard and gunpowder. It would either kill him or cure him, the way it began to draw. He had a high fever and spent most of those first days in delirium. The fever, the heat of the land, the constant pain — all melted the weight off him till he looked like a starved ghoul. In this inferno of pain and fabulous visions, he could not tell whether he was having a feverish delusion, or whether it actually happened, when, on one of those nights, he was awakened by someone shaking him. He could see nobody in the darkness. Could only hear the voices.

"You were a damn' fool to attack the train. You could have had the guns by merely contacting me. I thought the Cheyenne was to make that clear."

"He did," groaned Aztec. "But our war chief was killed, and Hachito argued the rest into attacking."

"Little Hatchet? He's still out there?"

"He'll be back," Aztec moaned. "He'll get more warriors and be back, sooner or later."

"Then you've got to get word to him somehow to stop him."

"Nothing could do that. He will want vengeance."

The voice swore softly, then said: "At least, if he does attack, we've got to stop him from burning the wagons."

"For what reason? The guns aren't here. I heard the talk."

"They _are_ here! That's the whole point. Hachito may be coming back for vengeance, but the biggest reason is still those guns. Now, if you want them, you've got to do it my way."

"I am too weak to reach him."

"Tell me where he'll be and I'll send a man."

"I don't know where Hachito will be," Aztec said. "He is like the smoke."

"Damn you . . ."

The man started shaking him, but there was a muffled rattling noise near the end of the wagon. The bed shifted, there was a soft whispering sound, the *creak* of strained wood, the faint *thud* of feet striking earth — and Aztec knew that the man had left him. Then someone was climbing in over the front, fumbling through the cargo. He finally heard a rattle and knew whoever it was had found the shielded lantern and was lighting it. The dim glow blossomed over the crates and bolts of calico, picking up the shadowed obliquity of a woman's face. It was Taos Sheridan. She had found out already his fluency with English, and spoke in that language.

"Heard you stirring around. Thought you might be in pain."

He watched her suspiciously. "I must have had bad dreams."

She smiled. "You even think like an Indian, don't you? Dreams have such a different meaning to them than to a white man."

"Why shouldn't I think like an Indian?" he said. "I've lived with them most of my life."

She shrugged, moved over in a swift, impulsive way, reaching out for his waist. He pulled back sharply, wincing with the pain it caused him. She stopped, the smile fading. "Look," she said, "if I'd wanted to hurt you, I could have done it before this. I was only going to roll you a cigarette."

He tried to relax. Strange thoughts struggled in his mind. He had never before thought of himself as wild or jumpy or suspicious. In a life where a man died if he was not always on watch, his reactions had seemed normal. Now, every time Taos came to him, they seemed cast into an unnatural light, as if he were a wolf among sheep. Was it only the contrast she provided, with her utter lack of any suspicion, in relation to him, her apparent desire to help him as much as possible, her softness?

As she reached for his tobacco pouch, her hip brushed him. It had a hot, resilient feel. He began to breathe more heavily.

Another thing she had early discovered about him was his taste for the corn-shuck cigarettes that so many of the Apaches had adopted through their contact with the Mexicans. She found the little tube within the pouch, made from a length of hollow reed, and uncorked this, pouring a small mound of tobacco into her hand. She put this back and fished out one of the brown corn shucks he used for papers. The ring tumbled out of the pouch with this.

"I've wondered about that," she said. "Good medicine?"

His attention was focused so intently upon her face that he did not give much thought to his words. "No. I lost my medicine bag in the fight. The ring belonged to my mother."

"The Pueblo woman," murmured Taos, rolling the cigarette. "I thought it was the Navajos who worked with turquoise."

"My mother did not make it. It belonged to my uncle. My father had one, too."

She handed him the cigarette. "What happened to it?"

"I don't know. My mother said it disappeared when I was about te —" He caught himself abruptly, a strange, taut expression filling his face, as he realized how unguarded his tongue had been.

Drawing a spark from his flint and steel, she lit the punk and held it to his cigarette. "You were going to say the ring disappeared when you were ten," she said casually.

He did not answer, a sullen, retiring look blanketing his face. She handed him the cigarette, the sad expression in her blue eyes disturbing him.

"Here we go again," she said. "For a minute, I thought I'd broken through that wall. Why do you have to get this way again? Why should you mistrust us just because we're whites? You have as much white blood as Indian, whether you like it or not."

"The blood is not all that matters. My life has been Indian. I have come in contact with many whites. What I saw never made me want to be one of them."

"You haven't much cause to be so high and mighty," she said impatiently. "What about a people who would attack a party without any warning, burn all their earthly belongings, kill them, and torture to death the ones who didn't die in the fight?"

"What about a people who would make seventeen treaties in a period of twenty-five years, and break every one of them within six months after they were agreed upon?" he said.

She shook her head angrily. "All right, all right. I guess you're right. All we can see is the worst side of your people, and all you can see is the worst side of us."

Her face hardened a little. "I should hate you, you know. Two of my scouts were killed by your attack there in the grove. I saw you put an arrow through Kantrace myself. Ford Martin's shoulder is still swelled up like a poisoned pup." She paused, studying him in the dim light. "But, somehow, I can't hate you. You aren't to blame for the things that have made you this way."

"Because I have lived with the Indians all my life, I think of them as my people," he said. "And your people and mine have been at war from the beginning. We were enemies long before we met in that grove."

His fatalistic mood must have touched her, for her face darkened. "I suppose you're right. I'm sorry for it."

She snuffed out the lantern and turned to climb out. The only light, after that, was the round glow his cigarette made in the darkness. He could not help remembering the feel of her hip against him, the smell of her hair. He stirred impatiently in his blankets, trying to blot the thoughts from his mind. They were soft thoughts. She was his enemy. When Hachito got more warriors and came back after those guns, she would be killed. He knew Hachito would try to kill him again, if he were still alive, but Hachito was only one man among his people. The man's enmity did not change Aztec's wish to see the Apaches get the guns. *And kill Taos?* He stirred again, cursing his own softness in Apache. Why could he not forget her?

CHAPTER
SIX

Taos Sheridan went to her blankets beneath a wagon, after leaving Aztec, but she felt too restless to sleep. They had reached Red Shin's Standing Ground, near the upper end of Big Timbers. The huge round rock, named after some Indian battle, overlooked the Arkansas River, streaked yellow and chocolate with spring tides. The wild tang of poplars filling the air only accented Taos's nervousness. That ring was in her mind. It coupled her thought to that of Blackie Barr.

Kenmore had wanted to put Barr in chains, within a wagon, but two of the teamsters had been wounded in the fight with the Indians, and it would have left Taos shorthanded. Kenmore had finally compromised by putting a guard on Barr all the time. She saw the trooper now, leaning against the front wheel of Barr's outfit. Barr himself was sitting, leaning moodily against the rear wheel. What men had not already turned in were over by a lone fire near Ford Martin's wagon, playing cards. It was silent near Barr's wagon. The trooper turned in a startled way as Taos reached him, then lowered his gun.

"I'd like to speak with Barr privately, if you don't mind," she said.

The soldier touched his hat. "I'll move off a little, if you like, miss, but he's in an ugly mood tonight. He got hold of a bottle somewhere and he's pretty drunk."

Her eyes dropped to the coiled whip in her hand, a borrowed one, since she had lost her other in the quicksand. "I don't think he'll cause me trouble."

The man nodded and walked toward the next wagon. Barr looked up when Taos approached, leered evilly.

" 'Evenin', Queen."

She stared at the man, trying to define the strange attraction he held for her. At first, she had tried to deny it, had tried to feel the repulsion she should feel for such a filthy, sullen beast. But she had found herself studying him, and had to admit at last the insidious fascination he exerted upon her. She had come to realize that even without the beard, the scar, the surly, defensive hunch of his shoulders, he would not be handsome in the accepted sense. It was something else, then. The pure, animal magnetism of a restless beast. Perhaps that was where the intrigue lay. The fascination a surly, dangerous bear could hold, moving constantly in its cage, glaring balefully at the world with its sullen eyes, evincing its awesome power in every motion.

"I guess you could get hold of a bottle if they shut you up in a church, couldn't you, Barr?" she said without much anger.

He grinned slackly. "I got my connections."

"One of my men?"

"You don't really want me to tell you, now?"

71

"Not particularly," she said. "I guess I'd seek some means of escape myself, if I had a past like yours." He did not answer, and she bent toward him slightly, saying in a quiet voice: "I was with Aztec Miller a few minutes ago. He has a turquoise ring shaped like a skull in his tobacco pouch. Wasn't that the identifying mark of the society who caused the Taos massacre?"

His head jerked up to her, eyes wide. Then he dropped the heavy, bluish lids over them again, veiling his shock, and reached up to grab a cherrywood spoke, pulling himself to his feet.

"You want to ride me," he said. "Why don't you do it with the whip?"

"I'm not riding you," she said.

He had the bottle in one hand, and he turned away from her, taking a long drink. He wiped his hand across wet lips. "Then go away and leave me be," he said thickly.

"I've heard the Taos massacre was instigated by white traders who stood to lose a lot of graft under American rule," she said. "They hoped to throw off the Americans and reinstate the Mexican governor. Aztec's father was Corcoran Miller, wasn't he? I imagine you knew him, Barr. Was he the type who would take illegal profits?"

"He was a . . ." Barr cut himself off, sending her a savage glance. Then he emptied the bottle in another drink, and threw it from him viciously. It broke against some rocks, and Taos saw the trooper stiffen up by the next wagon. Barr's face was flushed a little, and his head wagged from side to side now. "I asked you to leave me be."

"I'd like to know your side of the story," she said.

He turned to her with a loose, drunken leer. "Would you, now? So you can testify in court when Kenmore gets me back? Did he put you up to this?"

"Don't be a fool . . ."

He turned toward her, chuckling deeply in his throat. The guttural, bestial vibrations of it played over her nerves till they tingled, filling her with an excitement she had never felt before. Her lips compressed in an effort to blot it out. How could the sound of a man's laugh do that? Just the sound of his laugh?

"You want me to tell you my story?" he said in drunken humor. "Here it is. You're the most beautiful woman I've ever seen. And ever since you whipped hell out of me at the Rocky Mountain House, I haven't known whether I wanted to pay you back with my own whip, or this . . ."

Before she realized his intent, he had lurched forward, snaking his other arm about her waist. For a moment, the breath was crushed from her by the awesome, demanding strength of him. Before he could lower his face to kiss her, however, she shoved her free arm up between their faces. For a moment, they swayed there. She tried to wedge her elbow deeper and deeper between them, knowing he would release her with one hand or the other to grab at it finally. She felt his weight shift, and knew it was coming.

The pressure of his left arm left her back. It allowed her to twist away. But he still held her right wrist.

Panting, trying to catch her free arm and drag her to him again, his face broke into a drunken leer.

"Thought I'd let go the other arm, didn't you? Thought I'd let you take that whip to me . . . ?"

"Barr," she gasped, pain twisting her face, with that grip of his on her wrist, "let me go. You're drunk."

There was the pound of running feet. She saw the guard coming from the other wagon, and on the other side Kenmore appeared, shirtless, holding his revolver. Barr did not see them. Fearing one of them might shoot, Taos let herself be pulled into Barr suddenly. It took him off balance. She got one foot snaked behind the ankle and shoved. He tried to keep hold of her wrist as he fell backward, but she tore it free. Without thinking, she leaped back to give herself room, shaking out the whip. She stopped herself with the twenty feet of lash stretched out on the ground, staring at Barr with eyes wide as an enraged cat's. Slowly, however, they narrowed, and the heaving of her breast subsided. Kenmore and the private stood on either side of Barr, who had rolled over to one elbow without trying to rise. All three men were staring at her. With a soft, disgusted sound, Taos whirled, pulling in the whip with vicious little flirts, and walked away. She heard Kenmore tell the private to put Barr in irons, and then the soft *thud* of his feet coming after her.

"Taos," he called, "are you all right?"

She slowed down, trying to subdue her anger. She found it strange that it was not an anger directed at Barr, for trying to kiss her, but at herself, and at Kenmore actually and the other soldier, for coming upon her in such a situation. Kenmore came up to her side.

"I thought you were going to take his hide off for a minute," he said.

"He was drunk," she said.

"Does that excuse him?" asked the lieutenant.

She shrugged irritably, unwilling to meet his eyes. "I don't know."

"I've often wondered," said Kenmore. "I've heard so often how you've whipped men who tried to kiss you, Taos."

"It's not just a story, Wade. This trail is almost eight hundred miles long. I've been traveling it since I was a kid. Two, sometimes three times a year. With anywhere from twenty to a hundred men who haven't seen a woman in months. Often, I don't have any better chaperone than someone like Smoky's squaw. Ordinary measures don't suffice in a case like that, Wade."

"I guess you're right," he said. A faint, wry smile touched his lips. "Why did you never take the whip to me, Taos?"

She turned, gravely. "You were always a gentleman, Wade."

"Maybe that's where I made my mistake . . ."

"No, Wade, don't say that," she said.

"Then what was it, Taos? My age? Was I just a foolish kid?"

"You aren't a kid and you aren't foolish," she said. "If I fell in love with anybody, Wade, I'd want it to be you, but . . ."

"Then I have a chance," he said, his face lighting eagerly.

She turned away from him impatiently. "I don't know, Wade, how can I know . . . ?"

The eagerness seeped from his face before a suddenly speculative frown. "Taos," he said, "I've never seen you this way before. What's the matter?"

A lot of things were passing through Blackie Barr's fogged brain as he sat by the wagon wheel, waiting for them to get the irons. The private watching him had called the corporal of the guard, and the corporal had set about looking for something that would suffice. They would have to improvise, Barr knew. The closest thing he could think of was trace chains and the padlock off Ford Martin's tool chest. It would take them a few minutes to find out about that. Meanwhile, the private originally put to guarding him was still here. Barr heard the restless stirring of his booted feet off to the right.

Turquoise ring. That was one of the thoughts in his head. The others were of Taos, confused, shadowy, the rich soft resilience of her in his arms, the scent of her hair, the ripeness of her lips, shining red as new paint in the moonlight. But coming up from beneath was the other thought. *Turquoise ring. Corcoran Miller. January Nineteenth, Eighteen Forty-Seven. Had that been the date of the Taos revolt? Then why does January Seventeenth keep popping into my mind? Had that been the night I was found at La Fonda?* How often had he tried to remember the details of that night? It was lost in such a drunken fog. Time added its haze now. *Turquoise ring. Corcoran Miller. Aztec Miller.*

He realized suddenly that he had to get to the half-breed. It came as impulse more than any thinking decision. It cleared his head a little. It lifted his head sharply, to look at his guard. The man straightened up, bringing his rifle around toward Barr. Drunken cunning veiled Barr's eyes.

"Stand easy, sonny," he leered. "I'm rollin' in."

He crawled under the wagon and started straightening his blankets. The soldier stopped for a moment to watch him, and Barr lowered himself with drunken babblings into the messy bed. The trooper straightened. Barr could see as high as the man's chest now.

Each wagon carried a length of hickory slung beneath its bed, from which could be fashioned a spare tongue, if necessary. Barr reached up and began untying the lashings. Down the line, Ford Martin's voice broke the uneasy silence of the camp.

"What the hell are you prowling around about?"

"We're looking for something we can use to manacle Barr with." That was the corporal of the guard. "He's drunk and raising Cain."

"Best we can do is a padlock off this tool chest and some trace chains," said Martin impatiently. "Let a man sleep after that, will you?"

Barr had the hickory shaft untied now. Holding it up, he rolled over to one side. The sentry's legs stirred uneasily. They were within reach. Barr lowered the shaft, swung it out with all his might. It whacked against the sentry's legs, carrying them from beneath him. As the man fell, grunting heavily, Barr rolled from beneath the wagon, coming to his knees, bringing the hickory shaft up, above the soldier's head, down again viciously. Another sharp whack. The trooper made no sound this time. His body lay limp and motionless as a sack of grain.

Barr stared up toward Martin's wagon. The spare animals were making a lot of clatter, braying and nickering, and Barr hoped it had covered these sounds enough. He got to his feet, keeping in the shadow as he worked around to the wagon in which they had put the half-breed. His head had cleared enough to realize just how drunk he was. The shadows moved, sometimes, and he kept trying to grab things for support that weren't there. It was a weird, maddening state. He reached the wagon he wanted and climbed in over the tailgate. There was a sharp, stirring sound farther up, then silence.

"Aztec?" he said.

"Ah," breathed the voice from farther up. "The man with the guns again."

"Whadda you mean?"

"I recognize the voice. You are the man who came before. What is it this time? Are the guns ready to be passed out?"

"The hell with the guns," said Barr. "Where did you get that skull ring?" There was utter silence. He could not even hear Aztec breathing. Barr spoke again. "I know you have it. Taos saw it. She said you got it from your uncle. She said your father had one, too. Why wouldn't it be him who passed it down to your mother? Why was it your uncle's ring?"

Again that silence. A desperation entered Barr. He forgot that the man was wounded. All the bitterness, the hatred, the ostracism of more than thirteen years of running and hiding and wandering seemed to well up inside him, overflowing in a wild, uncontrollable tide, as he threw himself upon the man. He felt feverish flesh in his hands, a writhing body. He found the throat, sunk thumbs against an Adam's apple.

"Now tell me, damn you," he said hoarsely. "Why does Corcoran Miller keep coming to my mind? That was your father's name, wasn't it? What happened that night? I can't remember. Was your father with me?"

"I don't know," gasped Aztec.

"You do, damn you. Was he in the society? Why didn't your mother get his ring, too . . . ?"

Barr stopped with the sound of running feet outside, the tinkling of chains. That would be the corporal of the guard passing. Aztec was struggling again, tearing one of Barr's hands from his throat, sinking his teeth into it. Barr shouted in rage and pain. It was caught up outside, as the corporal must have discovered the unconscious sentry.

Aztec lunged upward, and Barr was carried back toward the front. There was the final, adrenal strength of despair in the half-breed's violence. The spasm of it carried Barr across the box seat, twisting him beneath Aztec's body. From here he had a glimpse of the aroused camp, shadows flitting back and forth before a freshly lit fire, the sharp explosion of shouts buffeting the night. Barr got his hold on Aztec's neck again, flinging him off so that they lay on their sides across the seat, facing each other.

"Tell me, damn you," snarled Barr again. "What do you know? I swear, I'll throttle it out of you if you don't . . ."

"There he is!" yelled someone. "Up on Garrett's wagon . . ."

A man came running from the next outfit in line, halting when he was close enough to see Barr. It was Smoky Cameron, just dropping a half-ounce ball into the muzzle of his Sharps. A strange, wild expression filled his face.

"What are you doin' to him, Barr?" he cried, lifting the gun. "When did you find out . . . ?"

Even to Barr's befuddled senses the intent of the squawman was plain. With a grunt, Barr heaved Aztec off him and got a knee beneath him, throwing himself from there right down at Smoky's face. His flailing arm struck the gun barrel, knocking it aside as it went off with a deafening explosion. Then he crashed into Smoky and they went to the ground. Smoky clawed at his face, snarling at him in rage.

"What did that half-breed tell you, Barr? You won't stay alive long enough to tell it. Churl, get him. It's Barr. He was with that half-breed, kill him . . ."

Fighting to free himself from the clawing, kicking old squawman, Barr saw Churl Hannibal coming out of the darkness. He tore free of Smoky and wheeled to meet Hannibal. He was still on his knees when the man struck him. He twisted his shoulder into Hannibal's belly and threw the man's oncoming body right over him. Smoky tried to keep him from getting on up. He kicked a wild boot into the man's seamed face, and staggered to his feet, free.

He saw the corporal of the guard and two troopers running headlong from where he had left the unconscious sentry. He wheeled, seeing Hannibal coming to his feet behind him, and dodged between two wagons. Rounding the rear wheel of this outfit, he ran head-on into Sergeant Coffin. The non-com had been running hard, too, and it took them both from their feet to tumble on the ground in a stunned tangle. Barr tried to roll free, shaking his head dazedly. Coffin caught him by the collar, beating him back down. Barr stiffened for the rocking jar of a blow, but it did not come. Coffin was shaking him.

"You were in that half-breed's wagon?" he said. "What did he tell you? Where are the guns, Barr . . . ?"

"Everybody in this wagon train want those guns?" panted Barr.

"Where are they?" snarled Coffin, shaking him again.

Barr heard running feet coming between the wagons and knew this was his last chance. He swept an arm against Coffin's wrist, tearing the man's grip from his collar, and brought his other fist into Coffin's face. It knocked the man aside, and Barr rolled with him, slugging again. This last blow knocked Coffin completely off, to flop over on the ground. Barr rolled over onto his hands and knees. Boots pounded behind him, and he wheeled, not yet risen, to see Churl Hannibal stop above him, a savage leer on his equine

81

face. He had Smoky's Sharps held high up in the air with the butt pointed downward. Barr stared wide-eyed up at the heavy weapon, knowing he could not avoid it, knowing it would smash his head in. Hannibal grunted, and the gun descended.

The rifle butt was six inches from Barr's head when the shot crashed. The butt splintered in a dozen pieces. It must have shivered the barrel in Hannibal's hands, for he cried out sharply, twisting aside and releasing the gun from numbed fingers. It drove into the ground at Barr's side. Both he and Hannibal wheeled to see Lieutenant Kenmore standing, shirtless, between the two wagons, his smoking Navy in one hand.

"I'll thank you not to be so free with my prisoner," he said. "If he gets killed, it will be after a court-martial, not before."

CHAPTER
SEVEN

After Big Timbers was Bent's Fort, Hole-in-the-Rock, Purgatoire Creek. They were deep in the real mountains now, approaching Raton Pass, and tension mounted in the wagon train, for it was believed by all that Hachito would strike again before they reached Santa Fé. Over the protests of Taos, Kenmore put Barr in irons and kept him inside a wagon under constant guard. This forced Taos to put a swamper to driving the last wagon, which had been Barr's, and it slowed them down considerably. The man forgot to dope the wheels and they were held up half a day at Hole-in-the-Rock, afraid to leave him alone, while he repaired the hot boxes that had developed. He didn't lash his rough locks on right at the grade coming down into Purgatoire, and the whole outfit got away and rolled over on its team, drowning three mules. And still, Kenmore would not allow Barr out to drive.

Beyond Purgatoire, the trail wound upward through heavily timbered slopes that broke away here and there to take the breath with views of the country beyond. A rocky defile framed a glimpse of the badlands to the west, a rolling sea of lava, black as sin, that swept up against the base of the Snake Mountains beyond. A saddle fell off to the east, revealing the mesas squatting on the lower land in that direction, channeled and turreted by wind and water till they looked like ancient castles. It was such a lonely, pristine country that Kenmore was surprised to see a Mexican appear on the road ahead with a string of rat mules. He was a small man in dirty cotton clothes. He raised his prod pole to them as they went by, with the inevitable: "*Vaya con Dios, señores.*"

Then, near noon, while Kenmore and Coffin were riding ahead of the wagon train, the rider came. At first it was the faraway drum of hoofs, causing Kenmore to halt his file of riders. He was about to order them off the road into cover when the horseman appeared, rounding a sharp turn. He pulled up when he saw the soldiers, a white man in buckskin and a buffalo coat. He fought his excited horse around in a complete circle, long enough to shout it.

"Takin' the news up to Bent's Fort! Sumter was fired on! The war's started! Virginia seceded the Seventeenth and Arkansas is goin' to foller! What in hell are you bluecoats doin' 'way out here?"

Before he was through shouting, his horse had completed the circle, and he booted it on past the line of cavalrymen. For a moment, the astonished troopers were quiet behind Kenmore. Then they began whooping, tossing their hats in the air, and some actually pulled their carbines to fire them. Kenmore wheeled on them.

"Quiet!" he shouted. "Quiet! Attention!" He was riding down the line, then, straightening them up.

"Dress right. Attention, there, Maine. Do you want to draw every Apache in New Mexico down on us? Dismount and pick up your cap, Corell. I never saw such a bunch of schoolboys."

Smarting under the reprimand, they sat stiffly in their saddles. The wagons were coming into view behind from around a turn. Kenmore found his eyes on Coffin. The lieutenant realized he had not heard Coffin shouting, or reacting in any way to the news.

"Didn't you want the war?" he asked.

"On the contrary," said Coffin grinning. "I'm right glad."

Kenmore gave the forward march order, and settled once more into his saddle. His attention came back to the timber, the ridges, the high slopes on either side of them — for he knew Hachito would attack sooner or later. He had scouts out, and flankers, and there wasn't much more a man could do if he wanted to keep enough troops with the wagon train to give it protection. The tension of waiting had settled into his face, forming ridges of white flesh about his compressed lips, toughening the skin across his cheek bones till it gleamed faintly. But something else was nagging at him besides Hachito now.

Sergeant Coffin, with a hitch going clear back to the Mexican War, was unable to remember the date of his first action. Coffin, so indifferent about his search for those guns. Coffin, right glad for the war, yet not joining in with the others in expressing it. That set him apart from them, and it was the key. With it, Kenmore had the knowledge he had been trying to form ever since they left Leavenworth on this tour.

He pulled in beside Coffin, far enough ahead of the other men so they could not hear, and asked quietly: "Which one was it, Sergeant? Virginia or Arkansas?"

Coffin turned his gaunt head, without surprise. For a moment he hesitated. Then he grinned, and answered: "I'm from Arkansas, Lieutenant. Little Rock."

"You've been waiting for them to secede."

"That's right, Lieutenant. Jest waiting."

"And now that they have seceded?"

"I guess that makes me a Rebel, don't it?"

Kenmore looked him fully in the face. "I think you were a Rebel long before Sumter was fired upon, Coffin."

"Well, now, mebbe I was, at that." Coffin grinned.

"And you were never at Monterey."

"I enlisted in Eighteen Fifty-Six, Lieutenant. A lot of men in the South could see this was coming even then, and they started planning for it. There are quite a few men in the Army, like me, placed in strategic spots. A clerk working with us managed to pretty up my service record so it would look like I was a real old-timer. A man with that kind of record would be more apt to get important assignments like this."

"You mean you're here to see that I don't get those guns."

"I am, Lieutenant," said Coffin mildly. "I will."

For a moment, Kenmore stared at Coffin, amazed at the calm conviction of the assertion. Then he sidled his horse over against Coffin, hand lifted to grab Coffin's wrist and prevent him from reaching for his gun.

"Perhaps you overestimate your powers, Sergeant. Will you tell me who else is in it with you, before I put you under arrest? Is Barr one of them?"

"I don't know, Lieutenant. All I'm supposed to do is keep you from turning back with those guns." He savored the words in his mouth, as if he relished them. "And I will."

Kenmore started to raise his voice, without taking his eyes from Coffin, and call the corporal up from the rear to put the sergeant under arrest. But the direction of Coffin's eyes held him. The man was not actually looking up into timber — his eyes were pointed ahead — but his attention encompassed the slope to their right flank and that sly grin was on his lips. Kenmore understood, then, the man's bland self-assurance.

Coffin saw that Kenmore had become aware of it, now, and spoke again. "Won't do you any good to call the corporal, Kenmore. They've been pulling in over the ridge for some time now. They'll jump any minute."

Kenmore spurred his horse, wheeling it around, and started to shout. "Corporal, left front into line —"

The long, quavering yell cut him off, starting clear at the top of the ridge and rolling down through timber, becoming an eruption of shadowy figures that filled the avenues of pine with a downswinging rush. Kenmore caught Coffin's jerky, twisting motion, from the tail of his eye, and knew what the man intended now. He wheeled his animal toward the sergeant, but Coffin already had his rifle out, swinging it around toward

Kenmore. The lieutenant knew he could not get his own gun out in time. There was only one thing to do. He kicked free of his stirrups and jumped off his horse at the man.

An arrow made its *whooshing* sound past his head as he struck the sergeant's horse, knocking the animal to one side. One of Kenmore's flailing hands caught in Coffin's belt. The man's carbine was too long to bring into position for firing now, and he clubbed wildly at Kenmore with it. But Kenmore's weight pulled him from the saddle, and they tumbled to the ground together.

Kenmore was under, and it stunned him. Lying on his side, gripped by a buzzing paralysis, he was detachedly aware of Coffin's rising to his feet. The man started to lift that carbine, but a howling Apache swept into Kenmore's vision. Coffin wheeled, firing from the hip. The Indian pitched off his horse over the withers. The falling body struck Coffin, knocking him backward. He stumbled into the ditch at the side of the road and rolled to the bottom.

The paralysis was leaving Kenmore. Another Indian raced by him, ignoring his body there, apparently thinking he was dead. Kenmore forced his numb right hand down to his holster, pulling his gun. The battle around him made a deafening, swirling panorama. He could not tell what had happened to his troops. He could see a whirl of pinto ponies and war feathers farther down the road, and a blue coat flashing among them. The air was filled with squealing horses and shouting men and crashing guns. He knew Coffin would be crawling back up out of that ditch to get him. It was needling agony to force his will against that numbness. It was like pulling a wall back, inch by inch. His fingers were on the Navy .36. He twisted his head around, waiting for Coffin to show, waiting for that expressionless, mahogany face with its glittering black eyes. His whole body tingled with needle pricks.

He had the gun free. He only had to bring it up and aim it toward the lip of the ditch. Then, before he had the Navy into position, he saw two more riders bearing down on him. One was a gaunt, ferocious Apache in knee-high war moccasins, his eyes burning holes in a face so dark it looked black. He had a Sharps buffalo gun across his saddlebows. The one on his inside, nearest Kenmore, was armed with a bull-hide shield and a butcher-knife lance. There was a string of scalps on the shield, and one of them shone like yellow gold in the sun. When the two Indians saw Kenmore, they veered out of their path to ride him down. The man with the lance leaned forward with a wild, triumphant cry twisting his face.

At the same moment, Sergeant Coffin appeared above the lip of the ditch, carbine aimed. Kenmore had that last chance, knowing he would die whichever one he took. Calmly, as though on target range, he lifted his Navy on up toward Coffin and turned toward the man, shutting the Indians completely out of his vision. Their guns roared simultaneously.

Aztec Miller was in his fetid, gloomy bed in the fifth wagon when the Indians attacked. For several days now he had been awaiting it, knowing they would choose some spot in these mountains on the approach to Raton Pass. When the first long, quavering yell came down off the ridge, he stiffened in the wagon bed. Then, face set against the pain, he hauled himself to a sitting position.

Through the pucker, he could see the teamster standing in the seat, trying to turn his mules and form a corral along with the other wagons. The clash of forces in Aztec was as painful as his wound in that last space of time. He could not help thinking of the Apaches as his people still — and he could not help wanting his people to get the guns. Too long they had been waging an unequal war against the inroads of the whites, bow against rifle, lance against revolver. The fact that Hachito led them now did not change Aztec's attitude. He knew Hachito would kill him, given another chance. But the other warriors had been good men to ride with, accepting him as one of them.

And then, insidiously, his mind was filled with thought of the girl. The softness of her, the richness, bringing a whole new world of sensation and emotion to him, a world he had not dreamed existed. He knew poignant longing for more of it. Could he not help Hachito conquer these men in the wagons and still save the girl? He shook his head savagely. It was a childish question. Taos would not be saved, even if he could save her. She would die fighting with her wagons. That's the kind of woman she was.

He tried to thrust the softness she brought from his mind. He had to make his choice now. It should be the choice of a man, a warrior. It should honor the memory of Kou-Ailee, his mentor, and the code he lived by most of his life. He looked again at the head of the driver. The wagon was shaking heavily as it turned. The din outside seemed to press in against it, rattling the canvas. An arrow whipped through the Osnaberg sheeting to bury itself in the oak sideboard. Aztec snapped the shaft, and used the broken end to pry up a board in one of the crates at his side.

This box held those butcher knives. He started fishing one out. The leather wrapping on the handle caught on a nail and ripped, unwinding as he pulled the knife on out. In the dim light, the haft had the dull gleam of lead. He stared at it, realizing now why they were so heavy and why Kenmore had not found any ammunition for the guns that were supposed to be with this train. The handles of these knives were made of pure Galena lead. Melted down and molded, they would each supply twenty or thirty rounds of ammunition. There were many crates of these knives. Enough in their handles for thousands of pounds of shot. It sent a thin, tingling sensation through Aztec's loins. He had to get to his people. He had to stop them from burning these wagons.

Painfully he hauled himself forward over the cargo. The muleskinner was swearing and shouting at his animals. They had hauled the wagon into the ditch beside the road, where it was tilted precariously over to one side, threatening to fall off any minute. Aztec pulled himself up behind the seat. The muleskinner heard him, whirled. Aztec rose and drove, hard and deep, with the knife.

It went to the hilt in the man's neck. Aztec was up against him, and, when the man fell, he did not have the strength to keep from going down with him. They plunged off the left side of the high seat, onto the road. As they left the wagon, it tilted on over into the deep ditch, pulling the whole team of kicking, braying mules with it. A vast pain blotted out everything else when Aztec struck. He did not know how long he lay there in the poignant giddiness of it.

Finally, sobbing with agony, he started pawing feebly to pull the knife out of the muleskinner. Then he saw Taos Sheridan, farther down the road. Her horse had been shot out from under her. She was lying flat in the middle of the road, using the carcass for cover. Jack Rubie's wagon was the nearest outfit to her, fifty feet down the road, its lead mules forming dusty, arrow-studded heaps in front of the frenzied, braying other animals. Rubie himself was beneath the wagon, firing through the spokes of a front wheel, and shouting at the woman.

"Come on down here, Taos! You'll be ridden down out there!"

"I can't show myself, Rubie!" she answered. "You unhorsed a couple of Indians with that buffalo gun of yours, and they're over behind those rocks with short bows! I'll be a pincushion the minute I lift my head!"

Rubie turned and started firing at the rocks. A trio of wild, yelling young bucks passed on the other side of his wagon, filling it with arrows. Then the road began to shake beneath Aztec. He looked up the other way and saw a pair of riders coming straight down the middle of it. The first wave of Apaches had already scattered the file of troopers, up ahead. Three of the troopers lay wounded or dead on the road, and the rest had dismounted and sought the cover of timber, where Aztec could see a corporal trying to rally them. Of the teamsters driving those four wagons ahead of the one Aztec had occupied, one still sat up on his high seat, pinned to its back by a pair of arrows, and another was draped over a front wheel of his outfit in limp death. The other two were not in sight. It gave those two Indian riders plunging down upon Aztec a freeway right to Taos Sheridan.

One of them was Little Sun. He had already counted coup, for on the blade of the butcher knife tipping his lance was pinned a dusty blue forage cap. Aztec recognized it as an officer's cap. *Lieutenant Kenmore?* The other rider with Little Sun was Hachito.

Aztec stared up at the oncoming animals, swelling up till they looked all out of proportion, like huge, lathered nightmare horses. He doubted if either Hachito or Little Sun saw him, lying here, they were so intent upon Taos ahead. She had turned to see them now, too. The utter pallor of her face twisted something inside Aztec. There was no fear in it, but the flesh looked like parchment.

Jack Rubie's gun would account for one. That was a possibility. But it was only a single-shot weapon. Even if he made a hit, there would be one left, whether it was Hachito or Little Sun, riding down on her. There was only a woman left. That bloody lance with Kenmore's fringed cap already pinned to it, dipping down, lifting her beautiful body up with the thrust. Or that buffalo gun in Hachito's hands, blasting the life from her.

"No!" cried Aztec, without realizing he said it, and, with the two riders almost on top of him, rolled over to free his knife arm. His whole body heaved up with the throw. Then he dropped back, unable to hold himself up longer.

The earth shuddered beneath him, and they were by. He turned his head feebly to look, amazed that he had not been trampled. They were past him, both men still sitting upright in the saddle. But Hachito looked stiff and awkward. In that last instant he dropped forward onto the withers of his horse and then pitched off, and his turning body revealed the butcher knife buried to the hilt in his chest.

As Hachito fell, Little Sun dipped forward into the thrust of his lance. The woman tried to rise and dodge aside. Little Sun veered his horse so that he would ride her down. The blade of the butcher knife was but a foot from her back when Rubie's gun cracked.

Only that kind of a shot could have stopped the lance from pinning her. It caught Little Sun squarely in the body, lifting him upward and backward with its heavy impact so that the jerk of it lifted the butcher knife, carrying it over Taos's head as he roared by.

Aztec lay feebly there, watching Taos wheel the other way and dart for the wagon, to drop beside Rubie, a stunned blankness to her face. She did not look up this way, and Aztec realized she still did not know who had killed Hachito. Then Rubie and the woman wormed out behind the wagon and started moving toward the rear of the train, gathering the muleskinners up one by one. Soon they were out of sight. Aztec wondered why the bowmen had not shot at Taos when she ran across the open space. Then he saw that the troopers had rallied and were working down this way, forcing the bowmen to turn on them.

There was a rattling fire. One of the bowmen lurched up from behind the rock, clutching at his stomach. The other scuttled to higher timber and disappeared. A line of blue-coated men flooded up out of the ditch, running for the cover of the wagons. The man leading them veered off to drop on his knees beside Aztec.

"Kenmore," gasped Aztec. "I thought Little Sun had killed you. Your hat, on the end of his knife . . ."

"That's all he did get," said Kenmore grimly. "I ducked."

Aztec noticed Kenmore's left arm, dangling helplessly at his side. "Hachito shot you?"

"No," said Kenmore. "That's Coffin's work."

"Sergeant Coffin?"

"Yes," said Kenmore. "He was from Arkansas." A bleak look entered his face. "He'll never get back to Arkansas."

The battle had swept on down the road, and in the lull, their voices sounded strangely clear. Kenmore dropped his eyes to the teamster Aztec had killed, then glanced down the road to where Hachito lay, knife hilt still protruding from his chest. Finally Kenmore looked back at Aztec.

"I saw you do that," he said.

"And can't figure it out?" asked Aztec feebly.

"Hachito was their war chief," Kenmore said. "You know they'll break up without him."

"Yes," murmured Aztec. "I know."

"You could have forgotten your feud with him in order that your people might have the guns."

"I could have."

"Except . . ." — Kenmore glanced down the road to her dead horse — "for Taos."

"Can you understand that?"

Kenmore looked back into Aztec's face. "Yes," he said finally, "I guess I can."

"There is a white man's word that the Apaches have no equivalent for," said Aztec. "As much English as I know, I never learned it."

"Love?"

"Yes," answered Aztec. A strange peace pervaded him, relaxing the tension of pain in his face. "Lean close, now," he whispered. "There is one more thing I have to do. There is something I must tell you . . . before I die."

CHAPTER
EIGHT

Blackie Barr crouched behind a rear wheel of his
wagon, rattling irritably at the makeshift manacles they
had locked on him, and cursing the luck that had left
him without a decent gun. The trooper left to guard
him had been swept away in the tide of battle, and Barr
had gotten out of his wagon to find a dead teamster
lying in the gully beside it, an old Greene breechloader
under his body. The gun was made for paper cartridges
holding sixty-eight grains of powder and a Minié ball,
but there had been only a small handful in the dead
man's pockets, and Barr had quickly shot these up.

The battle had swept from the front of the train to
the rear, and was now raging around this wagon.
Farther up the line, Smoky and his squaw were
huddled behind an overturned wagon. The old
mountain man had a Sharps buffalo gun, but the balls
for that wouldn't fit Barr's breechloader. Beyond
Smoky, a wave of dismounted troopers was working
down through the wagons, driving the Indians before
them. A trio of Apaches swept by on the far side of the
road, hanging on the offside of their ponies.

An arrow made a sharp, knocking sound, burying
itself six inches in the sideboard above Barr's head,

drawing a fresh curse from him. Smoky's Sharps bellowed, but none of the horses went down. Barr had never known the old hawk eye to miss at such close range. Then Barr caught sight of Jack Rubie, jog trotting down the ditch that paralleled the road on this side. "Rubie!" he shouted. "Bring me some cartridges. You've got a Greene, haven't you?"

Rubie scrambled up the ditch and threw himself beneath the wagon with Barr. "I'm out of shot. You seen Taos?"

"No," said Barr.

"She was with me about five minutes ago," said Rubie. "Hachito tried to ride her down and somebody put a knife in him. We never did see who it was."

"If Hachito's gone, they won't stay together much longer," said Barr.

"Taos and I started working down this way. We got separated when another bunch of Apaches cut through the train." Rubie turned his head at a sound from the front of the wagon, and then shouted. "Hey, Churl, you got any Miniés left?"

Barr turned to look. Churl Hannibal was working at the doubletree on Barr's wagon, unbolting it. Apparently he had not heard Rubie. The big teamster beside Barr turned and crawled on his hands and knees to the head of the wagon. Coming out from between the front wheels, he startled Hannibal. The man wheeled, with a guttural sound, a wild look to his face.

"What in hell are you doing?" asked Rubie, started to stand up.

"Leave me be," said Hannibal, turning back to the doubletree.

Rubie grabbed his arm. "I want some Minié . . ."

With an inarticulate snarl, Hannibal whirled on the man, striking at him. Rubie's head rocked to the blow, but he caught at Hannibal before he was knocked away from the man. Barr stared at them, unable to guess what had gotten into Hannibal. They were locked together now, and Hannibal was snarling wildly, kicking and clawing at Rubie. His right hand disappeared for an instant. Then Rubie gasped and stiffened. Churl Hannibal stepped back from him. Rubie sank slowly to his knees, clutching his belly with both hands. There, on his knees, he stared up at Hannibal with an open mouth.

"Churl," he said, as if still unable to comprehend it. "Churl . . ."

Holding the bloody knife in his hands, Hannibal panted, "You shouldn't've tried to stop me, Jack." Then he turned back and grabbed the doubletree. The surprise of it had held Barr till now. He dropped his useless gun and crawled out from under the wagon at the rear, running up toward the front. Before he reached it, Hannibal had wheeled with the doubletree in his hands.

Rubie was still on his knees, and he pawed at the man, getting his arms around Hannibal's knees. Hannibal struck with the knife again, but Rubie blocked it. Then there was a great blasting sound. Rubie was carried away from Hannibal clear back to the wheel, where he hung for a moment, then slumped over on his face. From behind the bed of the overturned wagon, Smoky lowered his Sharps and called to Hannibal.

"All right, Churl. Get going now, and show them."

Barr rounded the corner of his wagon then. Hannibal was already scrambling down into the ditch, carrying the doubletree. Barr ran after him, but Smoky saw him, and crawled out from behind the bed of his wagon, running with the single-shot rifle clubbed to quarter in between Barr and Hannibal. Barr saw that the old scout would reach him at the lip of the ditch. He ran as hard as he could up to the ditch, and then stopped suddenly. Running just as hard to catch him, Smoky could not halt himself as quickly, and ran across in front of Barr, swinging wildly with the clubbed rifle. Barr ducked in under it, tackling Smoky. They rolled off into the ditch together.

At the bottom, Barr came up on top, and slugged at Smoky's face with all his might. Smoky went limp beneath him, and Barr got up to climb out of the ditch and up onto the timbered slope. Ahead, he caught sight of Churl Hannibal dodging through the trees. Then, above Hannibal, he saw a pair of mounted Apaches coming down from the ridge.

Hoping they had not seen him, Barr kept closer to cover, as he moved up through the trees. The Apaches disappeared from his view into the timber. He went more slowly, muffling his sound, heading for the approximate spot Hannibal would meet those Apaches. The pattern of this was beginning to take form in his mind now. At last, he heard a rattling, thumping sound from ahead. He crept through the piñons, straining to see Hannibal. Sight of the man came in a flash, from behind two rocks, sending Barr to his knees behind one of them. One of the two Apaches was holding a drawn bow at Hannibal, while he beat the doubletree against a rock. The other was circling restlessly back and forth, keeping a lookout. Hannibal was talking to them in Apache while he worked, and Barr could not understand him. He stared at the doubletree, trying to imagine what Hannibal was doing. It was a long section of hickory that was made to be attached to the rear of the wagon tongue by a swivel fitting. At each end it normally had a singletree, another, shorter hickory bar on a ring bolt, to which the traces of the animals were attached. Hannibal had taken the singletrees off at the wagon, and was now apparently trying to break one of the iron fittings off the end of the doubletree.

It rubbed off, finally, and Hannibal went to his knees with his bloody knife, feverishly prying at the hickory. It came apart in two longitudinal sections. From this he pulled a rifle barrel. The Indians gave a shout, and rode in close to Hannibal, forgetting caution. Then one of them grabbed the barrel from Hannibal, and the other leaned from his saddle to swoop up the doubletree, and they galloped recklessly off down the hill. Hannibal watched them go, sweat gleaming on his face. Barr stood up and stepped from behind the rock.

"You got to them a little late, Churl," he said. "Kenmore and the teamsters have gotten together down there and have about finished the fight."

Hannibal whirled in startled surprise. His eyes flashed through the timber behind Barr. When he realized Barr was alone, the surprise, the fright left his face.

"You a Secesh?" asked Barr.

"I ain't got no particular sympathies, North or South," said Hannibal.

"I figured you would have," Barr told him. "I figured the feeling must be pretty strong, to make you kill your best friend like that."

Hannibal's face contorted. "Rubie shouldn't have surprised me. I thought he was trying to stop me."

"Maybe money makes the feeling pretty strong anyway," said Barr. "How much were you and Smoky going to get for seeing that the Apaches got these guns?"

"Enough so's I could quit hiding mules forever," said Hannibal. A slow, leering grin broke over his face, as he saw that Barr was empty-handed, and he pulled his knife. "But you won't be able to tell anybody else about that, Blackie. I killed Rubie by mistake. This won't be any mistake. It's been coming to you ever since the Rocky Mountain House. I'm going to cut your guts out."

The battle was dying, now, down at the wagon train. Taos Sheridan could see that from where she stood by Churl Hannibal's wagon, directing the fire of the half dozen teamsters she had collected. She and Rubie had become separated a few minutes before — when the two of them had left Rubie's outfit to come down this way — and she had thought he would be here at Hannibal's outfit, for the two of them always stuck together. Picking up men along the way, she had gained this wagon to find neither Hannibal nor Rubie in sight.

Up at the head of the train, just coming around the turn in the road, she saw Kenmore and his troopers, dodging from wagon to wagon, keeping the bulk of the Apaches down this way. The Indians, with no one to rally or guide them, were rapidly becoming disorganized. As Taos deployed her teamsters to meet the band the troopers were driving toward them, she heard a single, booming shot near the rear of the wagon train, surprising after the lull that had fallen at that end. She turned to see some kind of struggle going on down there, but it was blocked off by the mules and wagons. Calling to Ford Martin to take over here, she wheeled to dodge down through the high-sided Murphies. She had reached the outfit in front of Smoky's when she saw two figures tumble off into the gully from between the next two wagons. A moment later, Blackie Barr scrambled up out of the gully and labored up the slope, disappearing into timber.

She was not surprised at this attempt to escape, but ran on down past Smoky's outfit, with the old man's squaw still cowering under the wagon bed. She rounded the tailgate to see Jack Rubie slumped against the front wheel of the wagon. She ran to him, dropping to her knees. He was dead, his belly soaked in blood. It could only have been a knife wound, the way his shirt was torn. It made her think of Blackie Barr's Green

River blade, and turned her sick with disgust and anger that she had ever felt compassion for the traitor.

She rose to run up to the head of the team, meaning to dodge between the leaders and the tail of Smoky's outfit. She knew the fight with the Indians was about over, and there was no compunction now to stop her from bringing Barr back and handing him over to Kenmore. She felt a great, vengeful need for this, with the sight of Rubie's dead body branded into her mind. As she ducked around the leaders, however, the sight of Smoky's squaw caught her eyes. The woman had crawled to the tailgate of the wagon and was hurriedly brushing something off the ground into her skirts. It halted Taos momentarily. She saw that a vague trickle of black stuff was leaking through the crack where the gate was hinged, to pile up on the ground. It was powder. Black powder. Too much to have leaked out of a powder horn.

Taos moved toward the wagon. The squaw shrieked something in Cheyenne, leaping at Taos. Taos dodged aside, but the squaw caught her wrist, biting it savagely. With a hoarse sound of pain and anger, Taos wheeled on the squaw, catching her across the jaw with the heavy butt of the mule whip. The Indian woman fell back, stunned.

Taos unhooked the tailgate of Smoky's wagon and let it drop. Half the man's cargo was flour. Wild bullets had made holes in the barrels and flour was sifting out to form conical drifts on the planks of the bed. But here and there, where the bullets had struck near the bottom of the barrels, the stuff dribbling out was black. Taos swung in and rolled a barrel off onto the ground. Then she dropped back after it.

"You don't have to look," said someone from behind her. "It's a false bottom, all right. Each barrel has it. Enough to hold about four inches of black powder. But it ain't going to do you no good to know about it."

Taos had already whirled to see Smoky standing there. He must have just scrambled up out of the gully, for he was covered with dirt, his beard matted and muddy. He had his old Sharps muzzleloader leveled at her.

"Smoky," she said in a soft, amazed whisper.

"Why not?" he said. "I'm from the West myself. Why should I care whether the South or North wins? If the South wants to pay me a goodly piece to run a few guns through for them, I'd be a fool to turn it down. Trouble is, I get paid after delivery. You ain't going to keep me from getting paid, Taos."

He cocked the gun. At the same time there was renewed firing from the head of the train, and a man came dodging between the wagons.

"Taos!" he called sharply.

It was Ford Martin's voice. It snapped Smoky's head that way, for just an instant. Taos did not have time to throw her lash back over the shoulder, in the ordinary manner. She pointed her arm down so that the whip uncoiled off it like a snake, and, when the lash lay heaped on the ground, whipped her arm back and forth in a vicious motion. It snapped Smoky's head back. The gun roared. At the same instant, however, the poppers

105

on the end of that lash had struck it, knocking the barrel upward.

With the slug whistling over her head, Taos brought the whip back again. Smoky's face twisted, and he clubbed the rifle, running toward her. The twenty feet of braided rawhide sang, popped, snarled back toward him. It plucked the gun from his fingers so precisely that it looked dainty. But the true force of it jerked at his arms so hard his whole body lifted up. With consummate skill, she slackened the whip in mid-air to drop the rifle, and then brought the lash singing back over her shoulder. Smoky stopped, the fear of that whip in his eyes now.

"No, Taos . . ."

The great roaring *crack* of it drowned his voice. It caught him on the shoulder, spinning him backward into the wagon so hard the whole outfit shuddered. He dropped in a stunned heap to the ground, and, as Ford rounded the tailgate, Taos ran for the gully, tossing her words back over her shoulder.

"Take care of this, Ford. He's one of the men Kenmore wants. I've got something else to do."

It was heavy work running up through the timber. She had to slow down at last, chest heaving with the breath passing through it. She saw a pair of Apaches break into a glade above her, haul up. One of them held a long section of wood, with fittings at each end. It looked like a doubletree. They saw her, but they seemed to be staring past her, at the battle. She flung a look over her shoulder to see that it was over, down there. The remaining Apaches were fleeing into timber on the other side of the road, with the triumphant troopers following them. The two Apaches above Taos finally turned, and disappeared into the trees, heading northward.

She continued on upward, till she heard a shout from above. It was savage and guttural, like a raging animal. She had heard that kind of sound before, from Blackie Barr, in a fight. She started running again, and broke from timber into a small rocky meadow. At the far side, Barr was just rising off Churl Hannibal. He had a rock in his manacled hands, covered with blood. He saw her and wheeled, raising the rock as if to throw it.

Taos let out her whip again in a swift flashing motion, and brought it back over her shoulder. Barr tried to dodge, but she was too quick for him. The lash snarled out once more, catching his manacled wrists and snapping them up. The rock flew from his fingers. She slackened the whip and drew it back.

"I always did think they ought to horsewhip traitors, before they shot them," she said. "I know they won't do it where Kenmore's taking you, so I think I'll oblige, Barr. I saw Jack Rubie back there."

"Taos," he cried, "I didn't do that . . ."

Hardly hearing him, she lashed out. It caught him across the chest, knocking him off his feet with the force of the blow. He rolled over toward Hannibal, coming to his hands and knees.

"All right," he said. "If it's whippin' you want, I guess I owe you one anyway."

Most of the teamsters habitually slung their blacksnakes around their necks when not in use and

Hannibal must have carried his this way when he came up here, for it lay across the ground by him now. Barr's manacled hands snaked out and closed around the handle. Taos lashed at him again, catching that right arm. He screamed with the pain as she jerked it. But he would not let go of Hannibal's whip.

She had to slacken up and withdraw her lash, and he leaped to his feet, face twisted with the pain, laying his lash out along the ground. She threw hers over the shoulder and it sang out to the end of its length and roared like a Sharps. Then she brought it forward with a lashing motion of her arm, hearing the snarl of it past her ear, seeing the braided rawhide unfurl toward his face. At the last instant, he whipped the lash up off the ground and fouled hers in mid-air.

It was an old trick, but whatever she did now would necessarily put her on the defensive. It gave him a chance for an over-the-shoulder movement while she was recovering. Accepting this position, she slacked her whip to let it drop freely, expecting him to leap at the advantage this gave him. He did the utterly unexpected. Instead of allowing her lash to free itself, and throwing his own lash, still in mid-air, back over his shoulder, he ran in toward her, keeping their lines fouled. When he was halfway down her whip, he jumped sharply aside, giving a chopping, downward motion with his own whip stock that sent a series of whorls down his lash.

Desperately she tried to raise her lash, knowing what those flirts would do to the slack she had achieved. But before she could lift it freely, those flirting whorls had caught up her lash. When he jerked his whip back, they caught like half-hitches, holding fast. It shortened both their whips to five feet, giving neither room to slacken, and, when he jerked up with both his manacled arms, leaning back into the pull, the rawhide stretched out straight as a reach pole.

She had seen that coming, and tried to step into the jerk. Even knowing Barr's strength, she had underestimated the force of it. Her right arm was yanked so hard she cried out in pain. If she had hung onto her whip, the arm would have been pulled from its socket. The whip stock flew from her opening fingers, flying high back over Barr's head.

He gave his own whip slack, disengaging it in mid-air, and wheeled to face Taos again. She felt her whole body go rigid, waiting for that first stunning agony of the leather biting into her body. Barr drew his arm back. The popper crashed behind him. Taos knew how futile it would be to try and escape that whip, yet her every impulse was to turn and run. She refused to do this, facing him defiantly. The lash snarled out. Her lips parted, but she blocked the cry in her throat. The lash hissed around her waist, winding around and around till the poppers struck. She twitched in expectancy of pain. There was only the dull whack of those poppers striking leather, the layer upon layer of lash twisted around her waist cushioning the biting blow till there was no pain. Then, with a growl, Barr pulled her violently forward. It took her off balance, and she stumbled toward Barr, pulled by that whip, till she came up against him.

"Now," he said, "I'm going to do something I been wanting to do for a long time."

She was too surprised to fight it at first. His arms went about her and he lowered his face to hers. When she finally realized he was kissing her, she started writhing. But there was appalling strength to his arms. When she realized she could not fight him, and the first flash of rage left her, she began to feel other things. The matted beard did not feel as repulsive as it had looked. In fact, she could hardly feel it. All she felt was the insistent, demanding pressure of his lips, forcing her head backward. Her whole consciousness seemed slowly enveloped by a sardonic, mysterious animal magnetism. And she found herself meeting it. Her arms stole up around his shoulders and she was returning the kiss. When he finally released her, she stared at him with parted lips.

"Barr," she said huskily.

"I thought so," he said. "If you hadn't taken the whip to every man that tried to kiss you, mebbe you'd've found out a long time ago what you were missing."

At this moment, Ford Martin and Lieutenant Kenmore broke from the trees, followed by a trio of troopers. A hunted look flashed through Barr's eyes, and he started a wheeling motion away from Taos.

"Hold it, Barr!" called Kenmore. "It's too late."

Barr halted, looking at the revolver in Kenmore's hand, and stood there sullenly, awaiting them. Kenmore trotted up, breathing heavily from the uphill run. His eyes found Taos first. There was a strange

110

expression to them. Then his gaze dropped to Churl Hannibal.

"Dead?" he asked.

"No," muttered Barr. "He'll just have a sore head."

"What happened?"

"You wouldn't believe me if I told you," said Barr.

"Maybe I would," Kenmore told him.

Barr frowned at him, spat disgustedly. "All right. Churl got a doubletree off my wagon. When Rubie tried to stop him, Churl knifed him and run up here. I followed Churl. He broke the doubletree apart. There was a rifle barrel in it."

Kenmore looked startled. "In a doubletree?"

"It ain't so impossible," said Barr. "They probably even have them in the axles, and any other fitting on the wagons long enough to hold a barrel."

"How could an axle hold up, weakened like that?"

"Wouldn't need to be weakened. Just split it and groove the middle for the barrel, the way that doubletree was fixed. Put it together with extra fittings in the middle and it's as strong as ever. A good blacksmith could do it, even a carpenter. Smoky was in on the deal. He had access to the wagons while Taos had them in Independence. They had time to put a thousand rifles in those wagons."

"How about the rifle butts?" asked Kenmore dubiously.

"There are a dozen half-breed carpenters in Santa Fé who'd fit those guns up with rifle butts for the Indians," said Taos. "It was a pretty clever scheme, Wade. They had the powder in false bottoms of the flour barrels."

111

"And the lead molded into the handles of those butcher knives," said Kenmore. He turned with effort to Barr. "I have something to tell you, Barr. Aztec Miller told me just before he died. His father and his uncle belonged to the secret society that instigated the Taos rebellion. They were both inveterate gamblers and heavy drinkers. They were both wearing the skull ring of the society the night they went into Santa Fé. When they came back, near morning, they were blind drunk, and broke, and Aztec's father didn't have his ring. When he sobered up, he told Aztec's mother he had gambled with you at La Fonda, and had thrown his ring into the last pot, which you had won."

Barr stared at him a long time. As the full significance of it reached Taos, she saw the sullen, hunted look slip away from the bearded man. He seemed to grow taller, as that hunched, defensive position of his shoulders squared out. The eyes ceased to dart balefully from side to side, like a trapped animal, and met Kenmore's gaze squarely. Even the guttural, bestial tone of his voice was gone as he spoke.

"You aren't taking me in, then?"

"I think Aztec's testimony clears you," said Kenmore. "You're a free man." He turned to Taos. "That pleases you."

She faced him, not trying to hide her joy. "I'm sorry, Wade," she said softly.

He gazed at her a moment longer. Then, with an obvious effort, he drew himself up and his voice had fallen into the clipped, parade-ground tone.

"We'll go back to the wagons. There's a lot of work to be done."

He wheeled and marched back down the slope. Ford Martin grinned at Barr, in naked envy, and then followed Kenmore.

"I guess a lot of men have fallen in love with you," said Barr.

She turned to find a grave, watchful repose in his face. "I've never loved any of them," she said.

"Do you now?" he said.

"I don't know." She stared at him. "It's so new to me, Barr. I want to talk about it. I want to see it completely."

He came to her, and, knowing he meant to kiss her again, she did not fight it this time, she met it eagerly.

"We'll have a long time to talk about it," he said. "A whole lifetime."

Secret of the Santiago

Les Savage, Jr., narrated the adventures of Elgera Douglas, better known as *Señorita* Scorpion, in a series of seven short novels that originally appeared in *Action Stories*, published by Fiction House. She was, by far, the most popular literary series character to appear in this magazine in the nearly thirty years of its publication history. The fifth short novel in this series, "The Brand of Penasco", is included in *The Shadow in Renegade Basin: A Western Trio* (Five Star Westerns, 2000). The seventh, and last, story in the series, "The Sting of *Señorita* Scorpion", is collected in the eponymous *The Sting of Señorita Scorpion: A Western Trio* (Five Star Westerns, 2000). The short novel that began the series, "*Señorita* Scorpion", can be found in *The Devil's Corral: A Western Trio* (Five Star Westerns, 2003). That story so pleased Malcolm Reiss, the general manager at Fiction House, that he wanted another story about her for the very next issue. The sequel, titled "The Brand of *Señorita* Scorpion", is collected in *The Beast in Cañada Diablo* (Five Star Westerns, 2004). "Secret of the Santiago" first appeared as "Secret of Santiago" in *Action Stories* (Winter, 44). It was bought by Fiction House on March 5, 1944 and the author was paid $330.

CHAPTER
ONE

The angry flush in *Señorita* Scorpion's golden-tan face turned her cheek to a darkly etched line, startling against the gleaming darkness of her long hair. She stood looking out of the window of the big room, slim hands clenched tightly against the soft buckskin of her Cheyenne skirt. Basket-stamped Hyer boots covered her bare legs halfway up to the knee, spiked heels accentuating the long slim line of her rigid body. The exasperated rise and fall of her bosom was apparent beneath her white camisa; sun streaming in from the outside caught the dangerous flash in her wide blue eyes as she turned sharply to the man sitting by the fireplace.

"I never heard anything so fantastic," she snapped. "How can you possibly be any relation to me, how can you have any claim on the Santiago Mine? The Douglases have been in this valley . . ."

The man held up a thin, imperious hand. "Spare me the details, please, Miss Douglas. I know the story well enough . . . how *Don* Simeón Santiago and George Douglas discovered this valley and the Santiago Mine in Sixteen Eighty-One. How, a year after they began working the mine, the Comanches raided the valley and

117

cut off its only access to the outer world, trapping Douglas inside. It only seems rather far-fetched to me that Douglas and his descendants would be able to live here for two hundred years without finding their way out again."

Elgera drew a sharp breath, fists clenching. "That mine shaft through the mountains is the only way in or out of the Santiago Valley . . . the shaft the Comanches caved in behind them on their way out after the raid. And you saw the mountains beyond that, you know you'd never have gotten through them alive to the shaft itself if my brother hadn't brought you. That's why we were never able to get out . . . The Dead Horses. They're all around us, and the Douglases who tried to go over them never reached the outside . . . and never came back. It was only fifteen years ago that my own father succeeded in digging the shaft through again, and got on through the Dead Horses alive. Fifteen years. And yet you sit there and claim to be a Douglas!"

The man who had given his name as Harold Bruce-Douglas leaned back in the ponderous hand-carved armchair, stretching patent leather boots languidly toward the cracking flames in the stone fireplace. He turned his narrow head toward Elgera slightly, and again she was struck by the supercilious curl of his thin lips, the inbred arrogance in his aquiline beak of a nose. He threw aside the heavy lapel of a blue greatcoat, reached a slender hand beneath it, drawing forth a small gilt box. Elgera had never seen a man take snuff before. Bruce-Douglas pinched it testily between a pale thumb and forefinger, tilted his close-cropped head back slightly. He snapped the box shut and thrust it beneath his coat again, then he took out an embroidered silk handkerchief, voice condescending.

"My dear girl, your vaunted ancestor, George Douglas, was over thirty years old when he was captured by the Spaniards in the Caribbean and subsequently ended up in this valley in Sixteen Eighty-One, as *Don* Simeón Santiago's slave. Thirty years old, I say, and he left a goodly family in England when he decided to go free-booting . . ." — the man dabbed at his nose with the kerchief — "yes, a goodly family. A wife and two sons, as I recall. Sons who had sons, and who handed the name down unto me. Now, the very fact that George Douglas's first wife was living undivorced in England while he was begetting children by another woman in this valley renders invalid whatever claim you, as a descendant of that second union, have on the estate, namely the Santiago Valley and the Santiago Mine."

The girl stepped toward him jerkily. "You . . ."

"Elgera, Elgera," said Avarillo, catching her arm. "Let us hear the *hombre* out." He turned to Bruce-Douglas. "You must handle our *chiquita* gently, *señor*. She is not the demure type, if you understand what I mean. No? *Sí*."

He chuckled till his gross belly quivered against the broad red sash bound around it. He was the mining engineer Elgera had brought down from Alpine to work her Santiago, Ignacio Avarillo, a pudgy barrel of a Mexican with big, sad, bloodshot eyes that always reminded her of a hound dog's. His fat hams took all the slack in his gray whipcord jodhpurs, and his postoak calves strained a pair of English riding boots till their seams looked ready to burst. Elgera shook off his heavy hand.

"I hope you don't think you can just come in here and take the valley," she told the other man. "In the first place, proof . . ."

"What I prove to you, or what I don't," said Bruce-Douglas indifferently, "has no significance. My lawyer is already entering my claim to the Santiago in the Texas courts, and it will be established soon enough. However, I have brought with me a small portion of the total evidence that validates said claim. I see you have the old pistol case on the mantel. It has one weapon in it."

The flush left *Señorita* Scorpion's face suddenly; her eyes shifted to the leather box on the hand-hewn mantelpiece. How could he know there was only one gun? Only members of her immediate family even knew what the case contained. Bruce-Douglas caught her eye, inclined his thin head imperiously toward the mantel. Frowning, Elgera moved around him. The skin of her slim hand made a golden-tan glow against the battered black leather as she opened the lid of the case. A single dueling pistol lay against the purple satin inside, a large "GD" inscribed on the golden plate over the gun's old-fashioned firing pin. There was a place for the second gun below it, empty.

"You know where it came from, of course," said Bruce-Douglas.

120

"George Douglas brought it back with him when he came here in Sixteen Eighty-One," said the girl, watching the Englishman narrowly.

The skin was drawn across his bony forehead like transparent parchment with a tiny network of blue veins visible beneath. His eyes were the gray-blue of shadowed ice, and for a moment the girl saw something almost feral in their depths. She drew away slightly.

"Have you ever wondered what happened to the other gun?"

"This is the only one we've ever had," she said.

"It is an Adams dueling piece, my dear, made by that famous gunsmith in London about Sixteen Seventy," said Bruce-Douglas, reaching beneath his greatcoat again. "George Douglas valued the guns highly. He left one of them with his first wife in England, took one to the New World with him."

Elgera's glance was drawn to the hand he took from beneath his coat. It held a dueling piece with "GD" inscribed on the golden plate above its old-fashioned firing pin. Avarillo's riding boots made a swift scuffle on the earthen floor.

"*Con su permiso*," he said, reaching for the gun.

Bruce-Douglas handed it to him disdainfully. The fat Mexican examined the weapon, muttering to himself.

"Adams, you say, Sixteen Seventy? The same firm that made the self-cocker in Eighteen Fifty-Two?" asked Avarillo.

Douglas shrugged, watching the fire. "Perhaps."

121

Elgera shook her blonde head angrily. "Do you think I'd hand over the Santiago just because you have a gun like the one I have?"

Bruce-Douglas leaned back, thin lips curling superciliously. "Hardly, hardly. As I said before, my lawyer is handling everything, and actually I am under no compulsion to prove anything. However . . . how about the secret of the Santiago?"

The dull, metallic *thud* turned Elgera sharply toward Avarillo. The fat Mexican stood there with pudgy hands empty, the gun he had dropped lying at his feet. He had turned pale beneath the natural coffee color of his moon face; his inevitable black *cigarro* dangled slackly from one side of his mouth. Finally he tore his wide eyes from Bruce-Douglas, clamped his lips shut on the *cigarro*, bent to pick up the gun. He handed it back to the Englishman, muttering a garbled apology.

"What is it?" demanded Elgera. "The secret of the Santiago?"

Avarillo made a helpless gesture with his plump hands. "*Dios*, Elgera. I didn't think, that is, I didn't know . . ."

Bruce-Douglas's thin laugh was unbelieving. "Miss Douglas, are you trying to tell me you don't know the secret? Are you trying to tell me you don't know what my knowledge of it signifies?"

Avarillo took a vicious puff on his *cigarro*. "How . . . ?"

"How did I know?" supplied the Englishman. "Isn't it logical that the true heir to the lost Santiago should know the secret?"

"What are you talking about?" cried the girl. "Avarillo, what is it?"

Avarillo's eyes dropped before hers and he made that helpless gesture with his hand. "I don't know, Elgera. I didn't think anybody else in the world knew about the secret. I don't know . . ."

She would have said something else, but someone came across the porch outside in a hard-heeled walk, shoving open the big front door. Natividad Douglas stood there a moment, lighted by the Texas sun slanting in through the jagged red peaks of the Dead Horses. He was Elgera's older brother, tall and lanky in reddish *charro* leggings; he came on in, removing a black soft brim from his dark hair.

"We've got the mules all packed for Alpine," he said, glancing at the Englishman, "but the men . . ."

Elgera turned to him, frowning. "Why do we have so much trouble with them? Avarillo, you said you picked good men."

Avarillo was still watching Bruce-Douglas. "Better not go up there, Elgera. They aren't in any mood . . ."

"It's my mine," she snapped, glancing pointedly at Bruce-Douglas, "and I'm settling this once and for all."

Behind the hall door was her big Army Model Colt hanging on a peg. She slipped it around her slim waist, notched the cartridge belt up to its last hole, jammed the heavy gun down till it hung snugly against the curve of her thigh. Natividad held out his hand protestingly.

"Elgera . . ."

"You stay here and see that Mister Bruce-Douglas has whatever he needs," said Elgera to her brother. "That train's going to Alpine if I have to ride it myself!"

The Dead Horses rose, barren and forbidding, on every side of the Santiago Valley, waterless slopes shadowed by gaunt skeleton trees, dry river courses marked by the bones of men who had died trying to penetrate the unknown mountains. The Santiago was the only spot in the whole range with water enough to support animals and people. The sprawling adobe ranch house had been built by *Don* Simeón when he first arrived in 1681, the wings of its U stretching back on either side of a flagstoned *placita* where a pair of greening willows dropped their shade over a red-roofed well. The scrub oak grew upslope behind the house to the mouth of the shaft that led through the heart of the mountain for many miles, dug there by the Indians many centuries before.

"What is this secret?" Elgera asked Avarillo as they climbed the hill. "I've never seen you so shocked before. What is the significance of his knowing it? Does it mean he *is* the heir of George Douglas?"

Avarillo shrugged, puffing like a windsucker from the climb. "It might. I didn't think there were three men in the world who knew about the secret of the Santiago. You know there are a thousand and one legends about your fabulous mine, Elgera. As a mining engineer, I thought I had heard of them all. But three years ago, a blind priest down at Monclava let slip something about the secret. He didn't want to talk, and I didn't question him directly. All I found out was that there is a secret."

"Then you don't know what it is?" she said.

He shook his head. "Only of its existence. *Dios*, it isn't enough we have this trouble with the diggings. Now somebody has to show up claiming them."

"What trouble?" *Señorita* Scorpion said. "What's got into the men?"

"Have you ever noticed how each level of the mine only goes back into the earth, so far, then stops dead? It looked as if Santiago sunk them that far, then quit and punched the vertical shaft another few feet, and started digging back on another level. He did that with each level. We are on the seventh level now, and we have dug back about as far as Santiago's first six went."

"But the ore you took up assayed true." She frowned.

They skirted the split-rail corral and went on up through a clearing of curly grama. "*Sí*, true. But nothing like the fabled riches *Don* Simeón Santiago sent out. The first load we took to Alpine assayed some twenty dollars the ton. The next, fifteen. The third, nine. Gato's men are miners, Elgera. They have worked on veins that pinched before. Perhaps this vein will get better. They do, sometimes. But I keep asking myself why *Don* Simeón and George Douglas only dug back so far and no farther? The men are beginning to ask that, too."

"Do you need to ask that any more?" said the huge Mexican standing between two scrub oaks at the edge of the clearing.

Elgera turned sharply, realizing the miners had come down through the trees from where the string of mules stood loaded by the mine above. Gato was the one who had spoken. He was called Cat for his claim that he could see in the dark. His eyes did look feline, somehow, gleaming, opaque and milky, from beneath a heavy black brow, pupils oblong rather than round. He wore tremendous mustaches that hung, long and greasy, over the brutal jut of his unshaven chin. The girl took in the pair of black-handled Colts strapped about his thick hips.

"Like Avarillo says," growled Gato, "we have worked veins that pinched out before, señorita. We would like our pay now."

The girl clenched her fists. "Your contract isn't up. You'll get paid when you deliver that load of ore to Alpine."

Gato grinned balefully. "We will get paid when we deliver the worthless ore to Alpine, did you hear that, compadres?"

The dozen Mexican peónes began to move restlessly behind him. The one on his right was Enrique, great bull shoulders straining at his dirty white shirt with the bulged knotty muscle that comes to a man who swings a pick for his living. His calloused hands held a heavy pickaxe almost tenderly, and the way his flat-nosed face was scarred made Elgera think he had used the axe for more than mining, against other men who used theirs the same way, and whose faces were scarred like his.

Gato stopped grinning. "I said we would like our pay now. You keep your money in the house, *señorita*, no? Who gets it from there . . . you or us?"

Señorita Scorpion flushed, lips opening to say something. She saw the men behind Gato begin to shift. Enrique moved to one side, caressing his axe. The girl realized their intent, and suddenly a strange excitement swept the anger from her. Sunlight caught the gleaming ripple of blonde hair as she threw her head back, and there was something wild in her ringing laugh.

"Gato," she called, spreading her legs, "if you think you'd like to try and get the money in my house, go ahead! I swear I'll shoot the first man who takes another step down that hill!"

Enrique stopped moving to her side for a moment, scarred face surprised. Gato's grin faded; there was a certain hesitation in his milky eyes as they swung down to Elgera's Army Colt. Then he laughed, too.

"Down at Boquillos they say you can throw a gun faster than the Negro Caballero himself. I don't think so. I don't think any *muchacha* could be that *maravillosa.*"

Enrique began moving aside once more. She couldn't keep both him and Gato in her line of vision now. Avarillo took out his *cigarro.*

"*Dios*, Gato, you wouldn't do anything with a woman . . . ?"

"I'm taking a step down the hill." Gato grinned, and took the step, and pulled at both his guns.

The girl knew what a mistake it would be to divide her attention. Ignoring Enrique, her whole concentration was on Gato, and her reaction was instinctive. She didn't know she'd drawn till the gun bucked upward in her hand. Gato's left hand weapon slipped back into its holster as he let go to claw at his right shoulder, and his other six-gun dropped to the ground from the spasmodically stiffening fingers of his right hand, and he reeled back with more surprise on his face than pain.

"*¡Dios!*" he cried. "You've killed me with your diamond speed."

Enrique had been too far to the side of Elgera for her to see him move; she heard the pounding *thud* of his feet. She was thumbing desperately at her hammer and whirling toward the man with the scarred face as he charged down on her with that axe above his head.

"*Santiago*, you black *borrachón!*" bellowed someone. "Saint James and clear out Spain . . ."

The yell ended in a prodigious grunt as another bulk hurtled in between Elgera and Enrique. The girl saw Enrique fly into the air suddenly, axe jumping from his hands. He came down in a big arc with the momentum of his own rush, striking the ground with a solid *thud*, lying still after that. Avarillo stood with his post-oak legs spread wide in the position he had assumed to meet Enrique's rush and throw him over one fat shoulder. The men in the crowd behind the wounded Gato were still shifting, and one of them had a gun out.

"No," said Elgera.

The *peón* looked at her blankly, then he let his revolver drop to his side. Gato stood there, looking from his own six-shooter on the ground to the Army Colt in Elgera's hand.

"*Dios*," he said huskily. "*Dios . . .*"

"I'll shoot the first of you to move a finger," Elgera said.

Avarillo chuckled, flourished ashes from his *cigarro*. "She throws it around pretty fast, Gato, no? *Sí*. Did you think those were idle rumors about her in Boquillos?"

Blood was beginning to seep through the fingers Gato held tightly around his wounded right arm; he shook his head dazedly. "*Por supuesto*, not a woman, not a woman . . ."

"She isn't a woman." Avarillo laughed. "She's a wildcat."

"I'm riding the pack train with you," said *Señorita* Scorpion flatly. "And what I said still goes . . . you get paid when you deliver that ore safely to Alpine!"

CHAPTER
TWO

The double-rigged Porter saddle creaked a little as Chisos Owens idly swung off his big claybank and stood there a moment, letting the sleepy afternoon sounds of Alpine creep in through the double doors of Si Samson's livery stable. Owens's gray eyes had the squinted look that comes to a man much in the outdoors. Beneath the brim of his Texas-creased Stetson, the strong flat planes of his face were caked thickly with the dust of the long ride behind him. He was taller than average, with a heavy bulk to his shoulders beneath a faded denim jumper. His calloused, rope-scarred hands were fitting, somehow, with the indifferent way his ponderous Bisley .44 hung against the slick leather of old apron chaps, its holster scarred and stiff with little use.

Samson came from the gloom of the rear, a bent oldster with a mop of white hair that stood up like the roached mane of an Army jack. Owens slapped the claybank's hot flank.

"Give you double to take special care of her, Si. I pushed it all the way from the Río."

"Sure thing, Chisos." Samson grinned. "By the by, that Douglas gal's in town with a load of her ore."

Owens stiffened perceptibly. "Elgera?" Then he grinned almost wistfully. It seemed a long time since he had seen her. Fifteen years ago the Douglases had finally managed to reach the outside world from the hidden valley in which their clan had lived for so many generations. But it had taken the outside world over twelve years after that to discover where the Santiago Valley was. It had been Chisos Owens, a little more than two years before, who had followed the half-wild Elgera Douglas back into her valley after one of her infrequent trips to the outside. He had been the first man from the outer world to see the Santiago in 200 years. They had been drawn to one another from the first, Elgera and Chisos Owens, and each succeeding meeting had strengthened that bond.

Owens caught Si watching him, and realized he had been reminiscing. His grin turned wry, and he touched the brim of his hat, turning out into Main Street. It was a broad, wheel-rutted way, running north and south through Alpine, with the S.P. cattle chutes and brick depot squatting at its upper end along the tracks.

Tawny dust puffed up beneath Owens's boots as he crossed toward the line of cow ponies at the hitch rack in front of the Alpine Lodge, a two-story hotel with a long porch shaded by a wooden overhang that slanted down from the blank row of windows on its second floor. Owens bent forward a little to walk — a square, heavy man who was neither graceful nor awkward in his movements, whose every deliberate step seemed to hold an intrinsic purpose within itself.

The boards rattled beneath his weight as he mounted the sidewalk and went on up the front steps and into the Alpine Lodge. The clerk behind the desk was as drab and faded as the pink carpets on the floor of the lobby. Owens got a dim impression of glasses and a bald pate when he swiveled the dog-eared register. He found the name he was looking for, and his lips thinned distastefully, then he saw another name below it.

"Miss Douglas in?"

The clerk shook his gleaming head. "Went out with her engineer. Mentioned the assayer's office."

Owens nodded and turned to the stairway that climbed the back wall above the desk to the second floor. Going up the stairs, he turned right at their head, halted before a dirty white door with **205** in tarnished metal letters on the casing. It was the room registered to Carry Tuttle, and Carry Tuttle was the name Clay Thomas had said he would use. The door opened to Owens's knock and he walked in and stopped with his legs spread a little, trying to hide the dislike from his voice.

"It had better be good, Clay. I started from the Río as soon as your *cholo* boy brought the note, and it was a long ride."

Thomas almost slammed the door shut, turning the key in its lock with shaking fingers. When Anse Hawkman had owned everything from Persimmon Gap on down to the Río Grande, Clay Thomas had been Anse's lawyer. He might have been tall once; he looked shriveled and old now somehow, his black frock coat hanging slack from stooped shoulders, his legs bent slightly at the knees in what looked like an habitual cringe. His face was seamed and furrowed like an old satchel, gaunt hollows beneath his bony cheeks, watery eyes trying to hide in deep sockets.

"Don't say it that way, Chisos," quavered the man, turning from the door and clutching at Owens's arm with a claw-like hand. "It's all over now. Anse is dead. I'm disbarred. It's all done."

"What else did you expect?" asked Owens, distaste in his tone as he shrugged the hand off. "Did you think they'd let you keep your power of attorney over the AH when they found you'd stolen every acre of it? You stole Delcazar's Rosillos, Clay, and just as good as stole my Smoky Blue. I'm glad you tried to grab the Santiago, I'm glad Anse saw it squatting there right in the middle of the Dead Horses and had to try and get it. The Santiago finished him proper, didn't it?"

"You finished him, Chisos," said Thomas. "The girl couldn't have done anything without you. That's why I asked you here. You're the only man in the Big Bend who can save me."

Late afternoon sunlight was dying in the room and Owens turned toward the lamp on the round, marble-topped table, fishing in his hip pocket for a match. "What do you mean . . . save you?"

Thomas clutched his arm again. "Don't strike a light, Chisos. They'd kill me if they knew I was here with you. That's why I had to meet you at Alpine, why I registered under another name. They'd kill me if they found me, Chisos . . ."

Owens noticed the green shades had been lowered; he turned to Thomas. "Kill you? Who?"

A wild light had come into Thomas's eyes. He spoke swiftly, gripping Owens's arm with a growing desperation. "It's the Santiago again, Chisos. It'll always be the Santiago. You know what happens when something as rich and famous as that is discovered. Elgera won't ever be safe with it, Chisos. There'll always be someone trying to get it from her. Anse was the biggest man in the Bend, but he was willing to stake all he had on getting the Santiago. And now it's the secret, Chisos, the secret of the Santiago. I've got a third of it in my wallet, see, a third. That's what they're after. They'll kill me for it."

He was trembling and there was a shrill hysteria in his voice. Owens grabbed him by the shoulders. "Third of what? Quit puling like a sick dogie, Clay. Who's going to kill you?"

Thomas panted, collar dark with sweat. "Remember how I got hold of Delcazar's Rosillos spread for Anse?"

"Del thought his old Spanish grant was good," said Owens disgustedly. "Never took out homestead papers."

Clay nodded, almost eagerly. "That's right, that's right. Del never filed on his land. Anse hired him for fall roundup, kept him away from the Rosillos long enough for one of our AH hands to squat there and take out homestead papers. There wasn't anything Del could do when he got back. His family had their papers down in Mexico City. That old Spanish *sitio* didn't hold water, but I went down there to make sure the grant

134

was clear. That's where I found this third of the *derrotero*, among those papers. Delcazar was descended from Pío Delcazar, captain of *Don* Simeón Santiago's muleteers in Sixteen Eighty-One. That's how they got this piece of the *derrotero*, see, handed down from Pío. They didn't know what it was. They couldn't read. But I do. It's a third of it, see, this piece of the *derrotero*'s a third of it."

"Third of what?" Owens almost yelled.

"Third of the secret," babbled Thomas. "*Derrotero*. Third of the secret of the Santiago. They know they can't do anything without the whole. That's why they're after me. They know I have a third. They think the girl's got a third, too . . ."

Owens grabbed him, face twisting. "The girl?"

Clay Thomas cringed beneath his grip. "Yes, Elgera Douglas. That's why I called you, Chisos. I knew you'd do anything to save her. I'll give you my third of the *derrotero* and tell you all I know, if you'll only help me, Chisos, if you'll only take me down to your Smoky Blue . . ."

He broke down, sagging across Owens's arm till his face was on the table, sobbing uncontrollably. Owens tried to lift him. Finally, supporting the man with one hand, he reached around behind him and got a chair and lowered Thomas into it.

"I'm an old man, Chisos," babbled Thomas, clinging to him. "You're the only one can save me now. I've got no place to go. If anybody connected with the old AH showed up in Boquillos now, his life wouldn't be worth a plugged *peso*. Nowhere to go, Chisos, and they'll kill

135

me. If you only knew what kind they are, Chisos. Hawkman's games were penny ante beside this . . ."

Over the man's hysterical babbling, Owens caught the slight scraping noise behind him. He was turning when the room suddenly became lighter. Whirling on around, Owens saw that the shade had been shoved aside, and that the last fading afternoon light was streaming into the room. He was pawing for his Bisley when the gun blazed from the window.

He threw himself aside with the terrific thunder of that single shot filling the room. He heard Clay Thomas scream. Owens had his .44 out by then. He snapped a shot at the bulk of a man skylighted against the open window. The curtain flapped back into place and there was a sharp, sliding sound. Owens scrambled around the table and lurched to claw the shade aside. A shed roof slanted down into the narrow alley behind the Alpine. He heard the diminishing sound of feet from down there. Impulsively he raised a boot to climb out, then he halted, turned back.

"Thomas!" he called. "Thomas!"

The Mescal Saloon squatted in ugly iniquity on the north-west corner of Main and Second. From Second Street, a covered stairway led up the west side of the Mescal to the assayer's office on the top floor. *Señorita* Scorpion was coming down the stairs when the first shot drummed out from across the way. She clattered on down the shaky steps, Colt flopping against the big silver *conchas* sewn down the seams of the buckskin *charro* leggings she had worn for the long ride north from the Santiago.

Men were already shoving through the batwings of the Mescal by the time she reached the sidewalk. Si Samson legged it from his livery stable at the intersection of Main and Second, shouting something.

The Alpine Lodge stood directly across Second from the stairway Elgera had taken down, its side toward her, its front facing the livery stable across Main. A narrow alley separated the Lodge from the Alamo saddlery just behind it on Second. Charlie Done came out of the saddlery and turned up the sidewalk at a run, when the second shot crashed over the other sounds. Charlie crossed the mouth of the alley in time to collide with a man plunging from its shadowed darkness — a squat little man with greasy black hair done up in a queue and a six-gun stuck nakedly in the waistband of his *chivarras* in the middle of his belly.

"Thomas has just been shot!" he yelled. "Chisos Owens just shot Clay Thomas in the Alpine!"

"Chisos?" gasped the girl.

Sheriff Hagar clattered onto the walk from his office on the same side of Second as the Mescal, and out into the street. Elgera was running then, shouting over her shoulder at Avarillo where he stood by her line of loaded mules at the curb.

"Stay there and watch the mules . . . and Bruce-Douglas!"

She passed the man who had run into the street from the alley, and reached the opposite walk before the sheriff caught up with her. In the two years Johnny

137

Hagar had held office, fame for his inimitable style on the twin, ivory-handled Peacemakers bobbing at his hips had spread far and beyond the confines of Brewster County where he held jurisdiction. He was a tall young man in his middle twenties with black hair close-cropped beneath the jaunty line of his center-creased John B. Even in high-heeled Justins his long-legged run held a certain easy grace. Elgera caught the reckless smile spreading his mouth as he came up beside her.

"What's that about Chisos Owens?" he shouted.

She shook her head, not wanting to answer. There was already a crowd gathered on the sidewalk and porch of the hotel, blocking the way in like a mill of thirsty steers. But Nevada Wallace had come across from Samson's livery and reached the porch about the time Elgera and Johnny Hagar did. Nevada was one of the deputy sheriffs, and, although Hagar was six feet or more, the deputy topped him by a big head. He had to send to St. Louis for custom-made shirts because no store in Alpine had ready-mades large enough to fit him. His tan cowhide vest had an extra piece fitted into the back so he wouldn't split it across the shoulders every time he bent over or reached for something. He went through the crowd like a man swimming the breast-stroke, making a broad lane for Elgera and Hagar to follow through. The bald clerk stood in the middle of the lobby.

"Shooting," he gulped. "Shooting upstairs."

"Yeah?" said Hagar, and went on by.

He left Nevada on the second floor at the head of the stairs to keep the crowd down in the lobby. Elgera saw George Kaye come across the pink carpet below; he was Hagar's other deputy, a lanky boy from Kentucky. Then she proceeded on down the hall after the sheriff. A derby-hatted whiskey drummer stood discreetly in the open door of **203.** Other men stood farther down the hall; none of them had made a move toward the closed door. Hagar banged on **205.**

"Owens, you in there?"

The voice was muffled. "Lighting the lamp. Minute."

Elgera felt her breath coming faster as she heard the dull, metallic sound from within the room, then the *thud* of footsteps. A key rattled in the lock, then the door opened and he stood there, a big heavy-bodied man blocking off whatever was in the room.

"Chisos . . . " almost whispered Elgera.

He looked past Hagar to the girl. His rope-scarred hand raised in some small, nameless gesture. Hagar nodded his head forward, and Owens moved back into the room without speaking, still looking at the girl. Elgera saw the Bisley lying on the table beside the oil lamp, and then the body of Clay Thomas sprawled grotesquely over the chair he had knocked down when he had fallen.

The sight of death drew Hagar's lips back against his teeth. "Well. And Clay never packed an iron, either."

Patently Chisos realized how it looked.

"You know Chisos isn't that kind," said the girl hotly, stepping around the sheriff.

"I know what kind Chisos is," said Hagar. "I know that next to Anse Hawkman, he hated Clay Thomas worse than any man in the world. Remember they took his Smoky Blue, Elgera."

"Hagar," said Owens heavily, "I'm not going to argue. Thomas sent me word to meet him here at Alpine. He was afraid of something. Whoever shot him did it through the window."

Hagar's black eyes went to the Bisley on the table. "Your gun, Chisos?"

"I said I wasn't going to argue," said Owens, and a grim purpose slid into his weathered face. He seemed to settle forward slightly; a dogged line entered the hunch of his big shoulders. The signs were easily readable. Most men who knew Owens wouldn't have been able to go on smiling. Johnny Hagar knew Owens. He kept on smiling.

"I'm not going to argue, either," said the sheriff. "Let me see your gun."

Owens picked up his Bisley; he didn't hand it to Hagar. "It's got one bullet gone, if that's what you want to know."

"I heard two shots," said the girl.

"I didn't," said Hagar. "I asked for your gun, Chisos."

Owens's rope-scarred fist clenched around the gun, and he hardly moved his lips when he spoke. "I know what's on your mind, Hagar. Do you think I'll be taken in for a killing I didn't do? Do you think I could prove my innocence behind your bars?"

Si Samson appeared at the door, a sour-looking man in a black fustian behind him. Samson spoke to Hagar. "Coroner's here."

Hagar didn't seem to hear him — he was still watching Owens. "I've got to hold you, Chisos. It's what they call circumstantial evidence. Everybody knows how you hated Clay. One slug gone from your gun, one slug through him. Nothing to show for your man at the window. Give me your gun and come easy. That's the way it has to be."

"Don't be a fool, Hagar," snapped the girl. "That man who ran from the alley. What about him?"

"There were lots of men running around," said Hagar. "Give me your gun, Chisos."

Owens shifted the Bisley till it bore on Hagar. "If you want my gun, come and get it."

It must have struck Si Samson then just what he had stepped into. He took a stumbling step back into the coroner. "Judas!" he said.

Hagar laughed easily. "I'll come and get it all right, Chisos. Think you have what it takes to shoot me cold like that?"

"Maybe not," said Owens, and holstered the gun. "Try it now."

Elgera turned pale. She knew Owens was no gunman; he had always been the first to admit that. Hagar's brilliant skill was recognized throughout the Big Bend. And Owens was facing him like that.

Hagar's eyes dropped to the battered .44 hanging so indifferently at Owens's hip; the momentary expression that came into the sheriff's face might have been admiration.

"You don't want it that way, do you?"

"I told you," said Owens with a heavy deliberation.

Gunman or not, Owens wasn't the kind to pull his .44 without using it. Hagar lived by the same code. The girl could see the tacit understanding that had settled between the two men now. It was in the way Hagar's lips pulled back flatly against his teeth still in that grin, in the way Owens took a careful breath and leaned forward a little — the next move by either man would start both of them for their guns.

"Hagar!" cried the girl. "Chisos! Don't! I won't let you do it, Hagar, I won't let you take him . . ."

"I'm coming, Chisos," said Johnny Hagar.

He was still grinning when he shifted his boot on the carpet. It snapped both men into movement. But Elgera moved, too. With a wild cry she sprang toward Hagar, her big Army Colt flashing upward in her hand. From the corner of her eye she saw how clumsy Owens's draw was. Ahead of her she caught the glint of Hagar's Peacemakers leaping out of leather. Then she felt the cold shock of her blow striking him and saw his hands stiffen spasmodically on his guns.

Hagar's sick grunt was lost in the detonation of his right Peacemaker. It sent a futile slug into the door. Then he was lying in a heap at Elgera's feet. She stood there above him, panting, eyes flashing. Owens didn't even have his Bisley out. He was bent forward, with it half drawn, surprise just leaving his face.

The girl grabbed him and shoved him over Hagar and out the door. The coroner made a jerky move down the hall, then stopped, mouth open. Si Samson was backed up against the opposite wall; he grinned at them as they ran by. The girl and Owens were halfway to the stairs when Hagar lurched out of the door behind them, holding his head in one hand, a Peacemaker in the other.

"Nevada's down there!" he shouted. "You'll never get through him! Nevada, stop 'em! Stop Chisos Owens!"

Then Elgera saw why he hadn't shot. Nevada Wallace had come into the hallway off the stairs where Hagar had left him, and would have been in the line of fire. His gigantic bulk filled the whole hall, and he pulled his gun, bellowing: "Stop, Chisos! I'll shoot!"

George Kaye, the other deputy, came pounding up behind Nevada.

"Chisos," choked Elgera hopelessly, because she was still running behind him and she saw how completely the two huge deputies blocked the hall, and she didn't think even Owens could get through a giant like Nevada Wallace. But Owens just bent forward a little in his stride, his denim jumper flapping away from his square block of a torso. He didn't even go for his gun. He just shouted only once: "Get out of my way, Nevada!"

"I'll shoot, damn you!" roared the tremendous man.

But he couldn't shoot for fear of hitting Hagar and the others in the hall farther down. With a yell, he raised his gun, and Owens crashed into him, knocking

143

him on back into Kaye. Elgera ran head-on into all three of them, expecting to be stopped abruptly. To her surprise, she felt herself stumbling on forward. Owens's legs were driving into the carpet so hard that his boots ripped the rug with each pounding step, and his right arm was working back and forth like a piston. Every time it jerked forward, Nevada gave a sick grunt.

Stumbling back behind Nevada, Kaye raised his gun to slash at Owens. The girl struck at him over Owens's shoulder with her Army. His face twisted with pain and he reeled backward. Nevada tried to hit Owens with his gun. Owens reached up his big-knuckled fist and grabbed the giant's wrist, and kept on slugging him in the belly, driving forward inexorably. Nevada's feet made a final, desperate scuffle against the floor as he tried to set himself and stop Owens. Then he collapsed backward and fell. As he went down, Owens rammed a shoulder against him, knocking him on into Kaye. Both the men stumbled sideways and crashed into the wall.

Owens pulled Elgera roughly over the kicking feet of the two men, and around the corner of the stairs. Hagar stumbled across Nevada as he came running after them, cursing.

Pulled on down the stairs by Owens, Elgera had to keep going at a headlong run or fall on her face. Nevada and Kaye had been quieting the crowd in the lobby below. One or two townsmen stood on the stairway, faces turned up toward the sounds of the fight. A man shouted and threw himself aside as Owens and the girl pounded down the stairs.

"It's Chisos!" one of the crowd shouted, and a pathway melted for them toward the door.

Hagar clattered into view at the head of the stairs behind, and still couldn't fire for fear of hitting someone. Then Elgera and Owens were out of the front door and across the porch and down the steps.

"The palomino," panted the girl.

Owens was ahead of her and he cut toward the hitch rack at the corner where Elgera's Morgan palomino stood, a golden horse with a mane and tail as blond as the girl's own hair. He ducked beneath the rack and knocked the palomino's reins loose, and the reins of a *trigueño* horse. A man ran out onto the porch of the Alpine Lodge, yelling.

Elgera jumped the rack from the high curb, caught her reins up, carried them back over the palomino's head as she vaulted into the saddle with her free hand slapping the horn for leverage. She wheeled the startled horse in a full circle before she could drive it into the open, then she whirled it to follow Owens on the *trigueño* on south down Main. She had a fleeting glimpse of Avarillo, standing in the middle of Second as she swept past the intersection.

Señorita Scorpion felt a sudden savage joy in their escape. The swift tattoo of drumming hoofs and the wind whipping through her long blonde hair filled the girl with a heady exhilaration. She threw her head back to let her laugh echo down Main Street behind her, infinitely feminine, wild, triumphant.

CHAPTER
THREE

Ignacio Avarillo stood in the middle of Second, watching the dust settle into the wheel ruts of Main after Elgera had passed. Sheriff Hagar appeared at the corner of the hotel, having difficulty mounting a strange horse. Avarillo felt a hand on his sleeve.

"You're not just going to stand here?" asked Bruce-Douglas. "You're not going to let them go without you?"

Avarillo chuckled complacently. "You mean I'm not going to let them go without *us*, don't you? *Señor* Bruce-Douglas, that was Chisos Owens and Elgera. If you think you can follow them, go ahead."

"Chisos Owens?" said the Englishman. "What do you mean?"

Avarillo took his time about answering. He removed his inevitable *cigarro*, blew a smoke ring. Bruce-Douglas had insisted on accompanying them north to Alpine. Avarillo had no particular liking for the man. He twirled his *cigarro* in fat fingers, studying it.

"I said what do you mean?"

No, reflected Avarillo, he had no particular liking. In fact, he felt a certain aversion. *Sí*, an aversion. He took a slow puff on his smoke. "What I mean," he said finally, "is that there isn't an Indian in Texas you could hire to track Chisos Owens. That is what I mean."

Hagar had managed to mount the horse now. He gigged it across Second, shaking his head groggily, bent forward in the saddle. Suddenly he wheeled it back and turned to look for a long moment at Avarillo and the Englishman. Then he wheeled it again and booted its flank. The horse broke into a gallop down Main Street after Owens and the girl.

Avarillo stood there a few moments before he sensed that Bruce-Douglas was no longer by his side and realized the man had been gone since Hagar had halted and looked at them. Avarillo turned to see the Englishman back by the lead mule at the other end of the pack train, talking with Gato and his miners. There was something tense in the way Bruce-Douglas stood that started the fat Mexican back toward him. Avarillo got close enough to hear Bruce-Douglas speaking. The man's voice was no longer testy or disdaining. It held a thin, feral menace in its cold tones. It stopped Avarillo in his tracks.

"You played the fool with Elgera back at the Santiago once already, Gato," said Bruce-Douglas, "and once is enough, I think. You'll put that pack saddle back on the mule."

Avarillo could see the *aparejo* lying on the ground beside the lead animal; Enrique was still bent over its hitches, his axe lying on the ground, his scarred face turned up to watch the Englishman. Gato stood a little to one side of him, and he made a jerky gesture with his hand, speaking viciously.

"We haven't got any money yet or anything else. We're taking what we can get right now, *Señor* Bruce-Douglas, we're taking the mules. They'll bring ten *pesos* apiece at the border, and that's —"

"Put the pack saddle back on the mule," said Bruce-Douglas without raising his voice.

Avarillo moved sideways and forward till he was almost at the curb and could see Bruce-Douglas's face. Avarillo stopped again there. The perpetual smile faded from his moon face. His *cigarro* sagged, forgotten in one corner of his mouth.

The Englishman stood bent forward a little with both hands in the pockets of his blue greatcoat. His thin lips were compressed till the flesh above them was white. He was looking at Gato with a terrific intensity; his eyes were the chill blue of shadowed ice, and whatever they held was as indefinable as it was deadly. For a long moment there was no sound. Gato and Bruce-Douglas seemed locked in some silent struggle.

Suddenly Gato's eyes fell and he turned, snarling at Enrique: "*Pongase el aparejo en el burro!*"

Enrique looked at him blankly. Then he stooped to heave the pack saddle upon the flop-eared jack again. Avarillo became aware that his *cigarro* had collected a long ash. With a jerky motion, he took it out, tapped it.

"You seem to have some hold over Gato, *señor*," he said.

Bruce-Douglas turned toward him sharply, as if coming out of a daze. He shrugged, and Avarillo could see the effort it took him to make his voice indifferent.

"My property, after all, you know. Just protecting my interests."

"*Sí*," chuckled Avarillo, "*sí*. I'm glad you feel that way. You can take care of the pack train for me."

"I thought you said you weren't going to follow Chisos Owens."

"That is right," said Avarillo. "It is also right that I don't think you know what the secret of the Santiago is. You know of its existence, perhaps, but not what it is."

"I don't care much," said Bruce-Douglas, "what you think I know or don't know."

Avarillo went on as if he hadn't heard. "I do not know what the secret is, either. However, when there are things to be found out, there are usually places at which one can do the finding out, if you understand what I mean. No? *Sí*."

Bruce-Douglas seemed to bend forward. "Monclava?"

Avarillo laughed softly. "You seem to know, *señor*."

"You mentioned it to Elgera," muttered the Englishman.

"Did I now?" said Avarillo. "Did I? *Bueno*. When Spain owned this country, Monclava was the capital of the combined provinces of Texas and Coahuila. All the official business of the province went through there, including the gold shipments from the northern mines, of which the Santiago was one. *Así*, when Mexico broke away from Spain, the official documents of the old Spanish government were handed over to the Church. I have had access to the archives at the Cappella del Santo down at Monclava. Perhaps I missed something that I shouldn't have missed. Perhaps it would behoove me to seek access again."

"I'll get my horse," said Bruce-Douglas.

Avarillo turned to him in mock surprise. "But, señor, you already know the secret."

"I'll get my horse."

Avarillo studied his *cigarro*, laughing in that soft way. "It is summer, señor. Why do you wear such a large coat?"

"My health requires it," replied the Englishman testily.

"And the snuff, does your health require that?" asked Avarillo, still looking at his *cigarro* — then he turned to the man. "No, I don't think you are as anemic as you appear, señor. In fact, I think you are a man who could do a lot to get what he wants and to go where he wants. Perhaps it would be foolish to antagonize you unnecessarily, no? *Sí*. If you wish to accompany me to Monclava, that is your affair. *Pues*, you'd better fill up your snuffbox. It is a long ride."

The day after Owens and Elgera had escaped, Sheriff John Hagar came wearily back into Alpine and left the horse he had ridden into the ground at Si Samson's livery stable. He got a breakfast of ham and eggs at the Mescal. While he was eating, his two deputies came in.

Hagar took his coffee in a gulp, clapped the cup onto the table. "He and the gal headed into the Del Nortes. From there on, it was like trying to follow a bald eagle. No wonder you can't hire the Indians to track Owens.

150

He led me the wildest trail I ever want to ride. Finally I lost his sign completely."

"I thought you was a better tracker than that," grumbled Nevada.

Hagar glanced at him sharply, then he grinned and pointed his finger at the tremendous deputy. "Whenever you start talking like that, just remember you were the ranny who couldn't stop Chisos Owens, Nevada. I would have stacked you against ten Brahma bulls in a horse-high corral. I thought there wasn't a man in the world could throw you. Just remember sometimes. Chisos Owens did."

Nevada sunk his massive head into his chest, growling sullenly.

Kaye laughed softly, turned to Hagar. "You ain't going out again?"

Hagar took a last bite of ham, shoved his chair back. "Think I'll let 'em get away with that? I had to come back for a fresh horse and some grub, that's all. There's other ways of trailing a man besides the prints he leaves. What kind of horse did you say Chisos took?"

"Coroner's horse," said Kaye. "The brown kind the Mexicans call a *trigueño*."

"He'll have to switch it somewhere," said Hagar. "It isn't a range horse like that gal's palomino."

"But those are his hills down there, the Chisos, the Santiagos," said Nevada. "People couldn't find the Lost Santiago for two hundred years, and it was standing still. Chisos Owens isn't going to let any ground get warm beneath his hocks."

Hagar laughed, and it sounded reckless. "I won't give him a chance to set his hocks down, much less warm any ground with 'em. If he murdered Clay Thomas, I'll get him for it. That's my job, isn't it?"

"That part is," said Nevada. "The girl?"

"Why not?" said Hagar.

Kaye stood up, punched Hagar playfully in the shoulder. "Better not let the county board hear that one. They didn't hire you to chase a blonde *bandida* all over Texas."

"I'm chasing a murderer," said Hagar. "Can I help it if he took a pretty girl along? While we're talking about Elgera, did you nab her bunch like I told you to?"

Kaye shook his head. "Time we got around to it, Avarillo and the Englishman had vamoosed. They left the jackasses at Si's livery. That Gato and his *amigos* had taken a *pasear*, too."

Hagar shook his head disappointedly. "I had a talk with the Englishman. Bruce-Douglas. Name's familiar from some place. Face, too."

Kaye was fishing something from his pocket. "Couldn't be this *hombre*?"

He handed a crumpled Reward dodger to Hagar. There was no picture; there never had been one of the Negro Caballero. There was not much description, either. The people who might have gotten a good look at him were generally found in no condition to do any describing. The single paragraph on the paper said he wore black clothes and rode a black stallion, full Arabian.

"Got it on the morning train from Austin," said Kaye. "His latest was over at Marathon and they're hot to have him caught."

"'The Negro Caballero,'" read Hagar, "'the Black Horseman, wanted for bank robbery and murder in Marathon, Texas, June Three, Eighteen Ninety-Four, wanted for train robbery in Austin, January Tenth, Eighteen Ninety-Four, wanted for murder in Tucson . . .'" Hagar stuffed it in his pocket, grinned. "Gets around, doesn't he. Wonder what brings him down this way?"

Hagar got his own horse, fresh, and bacon and flour and coffee, and he didn't mean to come back till the chase was over, one way or the other. He struck the Comanche Trail on the second day south, riding toward the lower Big Bend where Chisos Owens's Smoky Blue spread was. When Geronimo had been defeated and gathered in, Army life had become tame for Johnny Hagar. When his enlistment was up, he took his discharge papers and began hunting the excitement that had lured him over the next hill since he was old enough to ride a horse and carry a gun. Brewster County was in the wildest, toughest, deadliest section of Texas, and two predecessors had died with their boots on in office, and the good citizens of Brewster were hard put to find a man to replace the last deceased sheriff, when Johnny Hagar hit town. On his second day there, a pair of drunken gunnies had begun tearing the Mescal apart, and Hagar had handled them with his usual inimitable style, and that was all it took to put him behind Brewster County's five-pointed star.

His center-creased Stetson was set at a jaunty angle on his bandaged head; there was a rakish swagger to his long figure, swaying in the saddle. He couldn't help thinking of the girl, and remembering how he had run out of the Alpine Lodge to hear that ringing, taunting laugh echo down Main behind her as she rode out of town. Some said it was that laugh which had first drawn Chisos Owens into the unknown Dead Horses after Elgera. Hagar didn't doubt it. Her wildness drew him, too — like a magnet. Suddenly a reckless grin spread his lips and he began humming "Stable Call".

Oh, go to the stable, all you who are able,
And give your poor horses some hay and some corn.
For if you don't do it, the captain will know it . . .

He rode a weary mount into Ramón Delcazar's spread on the east fringe of the Rosillos Basin. Ramón was a young Mexican who wore his white cotton shirt tails outside his buckskin leggings and a pair of .45s buckled on around that. He came out of his two-room mud *jacal* and stood watching Hagar dismount.

"See you still pack those irons, Ramón."

The boy shrugged almost sullenly. "Habit I picked up when Anse Hawkman was grabbing things down here."

"You worked for Anse, didn't you?"

"*Sí*," said Ramón bitterly. "Many *pobres* down this way thought the old Spanish land grants, the old *sitios*, were all they needed for title to their spreads. Like me and my father, they didn't file any homestead papers.

154

That's how Clay Thomas got hold of more than one spread for Hawkman. After I lost the Rosillos, it was work for the AH or buck him. There was only one man who ever bucked him and stayed alive."

"Chisos Owens?" asked Hagar, and he was looking at the horses in the ocotillo corral behind the house. There was a *bayo coyote* in it, with a black stripe down its back, and a gray mare.

"*Sí*, Chisos Owens," said Ramón. "And I am not Chisos Owens. That is why I worked for Anse Hawkman. Is it Chisos you are hunting?"

Hagar glanced at him, then grinned. "That's right. You're a pretty good *amigo* of his. How about it?"

The boy rubbed a dark hand across his leggings. "I heard Chisos is accused of murdering Clay Thomas. He wouldn't do anything like that, Hagar. If Thomas is dead, it will make everybody in this part of the Big Bend that much happier. But Chisos wouldn't do it. Like you say, I'm a pretty good *amigo* of his down here. It's his country. How about that?"

Hagar was still grinning. "I didn't expect you to answer, Ramón. I won't ask you to. Prospector up by Nine Point Mesa said he thought there was a powerful lot of *pasear* going on down here during the last week. All south, he said. What's down south, Ramón? Boquillos . . . ?"

"Mariscal," continued Ramón indifferently, going on south, "then Santa Helena . . ."

"Monclava?" asked Hagar.

There were other towns farther south, but he stopped at that one because he had been watching the ocotillo corral all the time, and the mare and the other horse had shifted so that he could see the one standing behind them that he hadn't spotted before. It was a brown animal. It was a *trigueño*.

CHAPTER
FOUR

Monclava was across the Río Grande and on down past the purple bulk of the Sierra Mojada, its huddled cluster of tawny adobe *jacales* flanking a dusty main street that led to the ancient Cappella del Santo — Chapel of the Saint. Owens had tried to make Elgera leave him, once they were out of Alpine, but she refused to do so till she had helped him prove his innocence in Thomas's murder. Owens told her why he had taken so long to open the door, then — he had been hunting for Thomas's wallet. He had found it, but neither the girl nor Owens could find anything in the pockets that could be connected with the Santiago.

Elgera had heard Avarillo tell how the *presidio* at Monclava had been the capital of the province when Spain had ruled Texas, and how the gold shipments had gone through there. The official documents had all been given into the keeping of the Church when Mexico overthrew Spain, and Avarillo had found much of his amazing knowledge concerning the history of the Santiago in the archives of the Cappella del Santo. Patently Thomas's death was mixed up somehow with the mine and south of the Río was out of Sheriff Johnny

157

Hagar's official jurisdiction. Monclava was the original destination for Owens and the girl.

With more than two weeks of the weary trail behind them, they ate breakfast at the ramshackle *posada* that passed for Monclava's inn, left their horses to be fed by the sleepy hostler, and went across the sunlit plaza and down the winding cart road to the chapel at the edge of town. Framed by tall poplars, the ancient doorway of oak was sunk deeply into a recess formed by massive adobe buttresses; a niche on the right hand contained a tarnished bronze bell. Owens gave it a shove, and its brazen *clang* shook the sleepy silence. Elgera glanced backward down the cart road.

"Nervous?" asked Owens.

"I can't get over the feeling we're followed," she said.

"That's natural" — he laughed — "for a couple of fugitives."

A sudden, violent screech stiffened Elgera — she whirled, hand grabbing at her gun. Then she leaned back against the adobe, laughing shakily. The noise had come from a creaking *carretta* being hauled into the plaza by a ponderous speckled bull. The cart's great solid wheels squeaked raucously on dry axles, and a dozing *peón* sat on top of the onions piled high in the bed. A couple of bawling children ran across the street; a hen *clucked*, scratching the yellow earth. Elgera turned back to the door, relaxing a little.

Then the heavy hand-carved portal of ancient oak was swung open on its beaten iron hasps, and a lay brother stood there, tall and gaunt in a simple cassock of brown wool. There was something ethereal about him, as if he could release his earthly bonds almost at will. He was completely bald, and the faint glow emanating from his dome-like skull seemed to come from within. His thin, bloodless lips hardly moved when he spoke; his voice held the dry, sibilant rattle of a wind through the summer aspens.

"*Los benediciones de Dios en usted, mis niños,*" he said.

Owens cleared his throat. "We . . ."

"*Ai*" — the man held up a pale hand — "*americanos.* You will pardon me, *señor.* I thought you were one of my flock. You are welcome to our humble *cappella.*"

The Franciscan wore smoked glasses, and Elgera suddenly realized that he was blind. Ushering them in, he allowed his hand to brush the girl slightly. She drew away instinctively. It was thin and spidery, that hand, with soft flesh lying in slack pink folds; it revolted the girl strangely.

"*Perdón,*" murmured the brother, "but touch, you see, is my substitute."

Coming in from the outside, the interior had been only a myriad of candles winking in a velvet gloom for Elgera, but now her eyes were becoming accustomed to the cloistered darkness. She could make out the hand-hewn corbels supporting the *viga* poles that formed the beams and rafters for the steeply slanted roof. Light came meagerly through the leaded, stained glass of the slot-like windows, casting pale stripes across the earthen floor in front of the girl. In the shadowed niches beneath the windows were many ancient *bultos,* statuettes of saints that might have been carved two centuries before by some reverent *peón*. Gradually the girl became aware of the other man in the room, silhouetted by the candles set beneath the high back of the altar.

"You have come a long way," the blind brother was saying. "The smell of dust is still heavy on your clothes."

"*Sí,*" said the man by the altar. "All the way from Alpine. You should have given them a more royal welcome, Brother Katopaxi. It is not often that such personages as Chisos Owens and Elgera Douglas honor Monclava."

The girl's voice was high. "Avarillo!"

"*Buenos días, mis compadres.*" The fat Mexican chuckled. "You spent too much time running around in the Del Nortes, trying to throw Sheriff Hagar off your trail. Bruce-Douglas and I beat you there by a *día*. Such an interesting place, too. Belongs to one of the oldest dioceses in the Americas . . . the sacristy is part of the ancient *parroquia* in the original monastery, which was founded in Sixteen Hundred. *Correcto, Hermano* Katopaxi?"

The blind man's voice was no more than a whisper. "*Sí, señor,* that is correct."

"What did you find?" asked the girl impatiently.

"*Sí.*" The fat Mexican chuckled again. "Founded in Sixteen Hundred. The archives contain such fascinating documents. Ancient land grants from the King of Spain . . . a fine old map of Tejas. Brother Katopaxi was kind enough to help us in our perusal. We have been supping

160

in the *padres'* garden while I studied at my leisure. If you would care to join me in a bite of tortilla, a sip of *pulque* . . ."

Chuckling secretively, he led them out into the flagstoned garden. Beneath a pair of weeping willows a large oak table was set with clay *ollas* of grape wine and a big wooden bowl of steaming tortillas. There were a few pieces of ancient parchment to one side, and a pile of stiff sheepskins on the white cotton cloth. The sun fell warmly over the thick adobe wall, but the man sitting languidly on one of the peg-legged benches had the collar of his blue greatcoat pulled up around his narrow chin. His thin face betrayed no surprise at the sight of Elgera.

"It looks," said Bruce-Douglas casually, "as if we all had the identical idea."

"*Sí, sí,*" agreed Avarillo, walking over to the table and putting one foot on the bench, and reaching for the parchments. "And now, *señores y señorita,* from the innumerable documents and papers in the archives, we have sifted out a few that might be indicative, if you understand what I mean. This one, for instance, was among the *papeles* from the *presidio,* transcribed by a government clerk. It is dated July the Fourth, Sixteen Hundred and Eighty-One. '*Recibimiendo esta día, veintes cargas del oro desde la Mina de Santiago . . .* '"

"English, please," said Bruce-Douglas testily.

Avarillo shrugged, chuckling. "'Received this day, twenty *cargas*' . . . a *carga* is a mule load, understand . . . 'twenty *cargas* of gold from the Santiago Mine, each *carga* consisting of twelve round bars bullion, each

161

bar measuring one *metro* long, one *decímetro* in diameter . . . ' "

Owens's voice was impatient. "We already know Santiago shipped his gold through here . . . it was a government depot."

"*Paciencia,*" said Avarillo, holding up a fat hand, "patience. If you will allow me, I will read from another paper. In the Sixteen Hundreds, understand, the Spaniards had many other mines north of the Río Grande besides the Santiago. This second document is another receipt transcribed by a clerk, recording a shipment from one of the fourteen San Saba diggings. *Ahora,* I will read. 'March Tenth, Sixteen Eighty-Three . . . received this day, twenty-two *cargas* of gold, each *carga* consisting of six square bars bullion, each bar measuring two *metros* long, one and one-half *decímetros* in diameter.' "

Avarillo stopped, looked up inquiringly. Bruce-Douglas made a bored gesture with one slender hand.

"From that, I take it, we are to gather that Santiago's gold came in round bars and the San Saba's gold in square ones. Brilliant, Avarillo, positively brilliant."

Avarillo chuckled. "You have made the deduction, but you fail to draw the correct conclusion from it. The standard mold set by royal decree at that time was for square bars, two *metros* long, one and one half *decímetros* thick. All the shipments from the other mines are in bars of that size and shape. Yet, without fail, the receipts for bullion from the Santiago register shipments of round bars."

"Really," said Bruce-Douglas. "Could it just be conceivable that *Don* Simeón Santiago was using a different mold?"

"No," said Elgera, shaking her head, trying to form something in her mind now. "No. *Don* Simeón was *adelantado,* entrusted with the visitation of mines in New Spain. He, of all men, would have the proper equipment, the standard molds. No, it's something else . . ."

Avarillo flourished ash from his *cigarro,* poked it at the girl with a chuckle. "You are beginning to understand, aren't you, *chiquita?* I will give you aid. When I was working your mine, Elgera, I found a large boulder about a quarter mile above the mouth of the main shaft, hidden in a thick clump of chapote trees. Did you ever see it?"

The girl was frowning. "No."

"I didn't think so," said Avarillo. "It was almost impossible to penetrate the brush under those persimmons. It looked as if nobody had been there for a long time. The boulder was hollowed out on top as are *metates* the *peón* women use to grind their maize in. But this was no *metate.* The hollowed-out portion was blackened as by the smoke of many fires. The dirt around its foot did not contain signs of grain . . . it was hard and slick like a slag heap. I did not attach much importance to it at the time. *Pues,* now . . ."

"A smelter," said the girl excitedly. "The Indians had worked the mine for centuries before *Don* Santiago found it. That boulder must have been the smelter they refined their ore in. And the round bars, Avarillo. I've seen gold molded like that before. The Indians use hollow canes from a canebrake when they haven't anything better. It's an old way. They pour the refined molten gold into a section of cane. When it cools, they break off the cane. It leaves a round bar."

She was breathing faster because she was beginning to sense what it meant. Watching her, Avarillo chuckled.

"You have arrived, *señorita,* you have arrived," he said. "Do you wonder now, Elgera, why the tunnels *Don* Santiago dug from that vertical shaft only went back so far, no farther? *Don* Simeón found out the same thing we did. The veins pinched out too soon for any use. The mountains had been worked clean of paying ore by the Indians long before Santiago discovered the mine. He wasn't getting his gold from the Santiago Mine at all!"

For a long moment, the little garden was silent. *Señorita* Scorpion noticed dully how Bruce-Douglas had leaned forward suddenly, unable to keep the surprise from his face. Brother Katopaxi's spidery hand was running up and down the slim golden chain that held a cross around his neck. Finally Elgera spoke.

"Then . . . how . . . where . . . ?"

Avarillo took his foot off the bench and plumped himself down, reaching for an *olla* of wine. "In the old days, Coronado and Pizarro and Cortés were all hunting it. Call it the Seven Cities of Cibola or the Gran Quivaro or the Treasure of the Incas, call it whatever you like. It is all the same thing. Gold. The Spaniards who found the New World knew the Indians possessed great riches. They saw irrefutable evidences of that. But few ever found those riches. Perhaps *Don* Santiago was luckier. The mine had obviously been worked out long before he discovered it . . . yet he sent gold through Monclava as fast as Pío Delcazar could drive his mule trains, gold enough to be the basis for the fable of the richest mine in the Southwest. Round bars of it, *señores*, one *metro* long . . ."

"You are redundantly expository," said Bruce-Douglas, having recovered his composure. "What you are saying, in so many words, is that the Indians who worked the mine prior to Santiago's discovery of it refined their ore and molded it into round bars and stored it somewhere, and that *Don* Simeón found where they had stored it. All right. Where?"

Laughing, Avarillo poured grape *pulque* from the clay jug. "I admit I am a remarkable man, *señores*, but not that remarkable. We knew the secret of the Santiago existed before, but not *what* it was. Now we know what it is, but not *where*. That third part is going to be the hardest, I think."

"The whole thing seems divided into thirds," muttered Elgera. "How about the *derrotero*, Chisos? Don't you think it's time?"

Owens shrugged, took Clay Thomas's black wallet from beneath his shirt. He put it on the table and told Avarillo how the lawyer had come to him with it. "He babbled something about a *derrotero*. We couldn't find anything that looked like a third of the secret, or a *derrotero*, whatever that is."

Avarillo took the wallet with an air of suppressed excitement. He dumped the contents on the table,

165

sorting through them. "A *derrotero,* Chisos, literally means a route. But in the old days, it meant a map, a chart. Don't you see the possibility therein . . . a map . . . ?" He picked up a bunch of cards, shook his head, scanned an old will and testament of some long deceased *peón,* shook his head again, then he fingered the wallet. "I see you slit the lining. This is a Mexican *hato,* this wallet, Chisos. Clay Thomas probably picked it up in Mexico City. You said he was there. No? *Sí.* It contains all the love of intrigue so characteristic of a Latin. One lining? Two, three, or five. *Así . . .*"

The knife that had suddenly appeared in his corpulent hand might have come from his broad red sash. Elgera had seen other surprising things come from it. He did something with his thumb on the golden-chased haft; a gleaming blade leapt into view. Then he was touching the point to the wallet. The outside, which Owens had already cut away, gaped open, then the blade slipped lengthwise beneath it, and another layer of soft leather suddenly dropped away from the blade. Avarillo slipped an exploring finger in. A smile spread his fat face. He took out a thin piece of ancient, yellowed parchment almost reverently.

Elgera bent over his shoulder, spelling out parts of words at the bottom of the paper: "'El . . . *ondido de los Indios . . . de Santiago.*'"

"It is only a part, you see." Avarillo chuckled. "One third of a *derrotero . . .*"

Elgera jerked away suddenly as a pale, bloodless hand slipped down beside her on the table. It was Brother Katopaxi's. There was something almost ghastly in the way his bony fingers groped blindly till they encountered the jagged edge of the paper. She saw his hand tremble slightly. He reached inside his cassock and pulled out a buckskin *maleta*. From this pouch he removed another piece of paper. His voice was hardly audible. "Would this fit, *señores?*"

Avarillo accepted the second piece. The girl knew it would fit before he put it down. The two jagged edges came together, forming the sides and bottom of a large square, leaving a gap torn out of the top in the form of a rough triangle.

"*Dios* is kind," said the blind brother. "Do you know how many years I have been waiting here with that piece of paper, *señores?* When I was young, and still had the blessing of sight, I was called to give benediction to a *peón* near Saltillo. Pedro Tovar, dying of the plague. He told me he had been the personal *mozo* to *Don* Rodriguez Santiago, the last of the Santiagos whose ancestor discovered the Santiago Mine. When Mexico overthrew Spain, remember, the ruling classes lost everything. *Don* Rodriguez was reduced to a penniless wanderer. The only one of his myriad retainers who stayed with him was this Pedro Tovar. When *Don* Rodriguez died, he had nothing to give the faithful Pedro but the sword of his house, and this piece of parchment."

With the two pieces together like that, the words took form, and Avarillo read them. "'*El Derrotero del Tesoro Escondido de los Indios de la Mina de Santiago.*'"

167

"The chart of the hidden treasure of the Indians of the Santiago Mine," Elgera said breathlessly.

"According to this Pedro Tovar," said Katopaxi, looking blindly straight ahead, "the piece of paper I gave you was sent from the Santiago Mine in Sixteen Eighty-One by *Don* Simeón Santiago, carried to his son in Mexico by a faithful Tlascan slave. The Tlascan died from the hardships of the journey, before the mine was lost. And when *Don* Simeón and his Santiago Mine disappeared so suddenly, the only clue to its whereabouts was this third of the *derrotero*. *Don* Simeón's son never found the mine, and the piece of the map was handed down in the Santiago family till it reached *Don* Rodriguez, who gave it to Pedro Tovar, who in turn gave it to the Church on his deathbed. I knew the other portions of the chart would come, if I but had patience. If you find the *tesoro, señores,* you will see that the Church gets its share . . ."

"*Naturalmente,*" said Avarillo, "*naturalmente.*"

A strange, secretive smile caught at Katopaxi's bloodless lips for a moment, and his hand seemed to run up and down the chain around his neck a little faster. Elgera couldn't help shivering a little. She looked up — sunlight fell across the wall and lighted her face warmly. Still she felt cold.

Chisos Owens put a blunt finger on a spot at the bottom of the page marked with an X and bearing the name, Monclava. Avarillo nodded, and began tracing a dotted line that ran from the spot marked Monclava on up the page.

"Zaragosa," he said. "That was a *posada* on the old trail from Texas. Farther on, the Comanche Crossing . . . we are at the Río Grande now. The line turns east up the Río to Boquillos. A turn northward from that town and we have another landmark. Los Dos Dedos de Dios . . . The Two Fingers of God. And finally . . . La Ciénega Embrujada . . ." He trailed off as his fat finger had reached the jagged edge of the paper.

Elgera looked at the last spot. "La Ciénega Embrujada," she muttered. "The Haunted Swamp? I never heard of that, but, if you turned northward from Boquillos like this, you'd be . . ."

"Right in the middle of the Dead Horse Mountains," finished Avarillo, then he shrugged. "Why not, Elgera? The Indians wouldn't have gone too far away from the Santiago Valley to store their treasure. *¿Quién sabe?* If we had the other third of this *derrotero*, it might lead us right back to your house."

The *padres* kept Indian *mozos* to serve the Church, and the one who slipped in from the garden door was dressed in white doeskin leggings and a hand-tooled vest of calfskin over the smooth bronze slope of his shoulders. He whispered something to Katopaxi.

"Someone is outside who would like to see you," said the blind brother, turning to the group.

"Really," said Bruce-Douglas indifferently.

"*¿Quién es?*" asked Avarillo.

"He says," answered Katopaxi, "that he is Sheriff John Hagar."

"Yes," said the lean young man who stepped through the garden door, "Sheriff John Hagar."

Elgera whirled about the same time Chisos Owens did, and both of them started to do the same thing. Then they stopped, and let their hands fall away from their guns. Johnny Hagar stood with his Justins spread apart on the flagstones and his John B. shoved back on his close-cropped black hair and his two ivory-handled Peacemakers steady in his fists. He moved forward in that lithe, effortless walk.

"I spotted your *trigueño* at Delcazar's."

"Did you?" said Owens. "It was no range hoss. The palomino's the only one lasted down here."

"You should've left that with Del, too," said Hagar. "Nobody could miss that animal in a thousand miles . . . no, don't move any more . . . every Mex I asked had seen it go by. Unbuckle your gun, Chisos. If you try anything funny, I'll shoot you in the legs and take you back behind my saddle like a sick dogie."

"Before we go any further with this little drama, you might disburden yourself of your own weapons, Mister Hagar," said Bruce-Douglas's arrogant voice, whirling Elgera toward him.

The Englishman still sat at the table, face depicting utter boredom. His pale hand rested on the cloth. It held the dueling pistol with GD inscribed in the plate over its old-fashioned firing pin.

Elgera didn't see Hagar shoot because she was still turned toward Bruce-Douglas. She heard the deafening sound, and saw pain twist the Englishman's face as his hand jumped upward suddenly, the ancient pistol flying from smashed fingers. But it had taken Hagar's attention for that instant, and, as the pistol hit the

170

flagstones with a dull, metallic sound, Owens threw himself at the sheriff. The girl whirled back and jumped at Hagar, too. The young man's other Peacemaker bellowed. Then Owens struck him, and Elgera struck him, and Avarillo's resilient bulk smashed in behind her, and all four of them went to the ground in a kicking, cursing, slugging mass.

Elgera saw Avarillo's English riding boot come from somewhere and catch Hagar neatly across the right wrist, knocking his gun from that hand. The girl had his other arm, and she rolled on it so her body pinned his forearm against the ground. She caught the hand, twisted viciously. Hagar cried out, let go of the other Peacemaker. Elgera got to her knees, grabbing the gun.

With her weight off his arm, Hagar rolled over and jammed a shoulder into Owens, shoving him sideways. Then the sheriff got to his hands and knees and threw Owens clear off of him and rose, whirling to grapple with the powerful man before he could get fully erect.

Elgera jumped them, clawed at Hagar. The sheriff jerked his arm back to slug Owens and his elbow struck the girl in the stomach. Breath knocked out of her, she clung grimly to his shoulder, trying to pull him off Owens. She raised the Peacemaker to hit him.

"Elgera," gasped Owens, rearing up beneath Hagar, "not that way . . ."

Fat arms were suddenly around Elgera, yanking her off of Hagar, and Avarillo's chuckle was bland in her ear. "*Señorita*, that would not be ethical. Let them fight it out, man to man, now. Let it be fair. This has been coming a long time and might as well be settled once and for all. No? *Sí . . .*"

She sagged in his grip, realizing he was right. It had been coming a long time and it had to do with more than the issues involved in Clay Thomas's murder. Chisos Owens was battling to stay free and prove his innocence, and Hagar was fighting for his right to arrest Owens — but both of them went at it with a terrible savagery that came from something deeper, something far more primitive, something that needed no words to bring them together fighting like this whenever they met. Elgera had sensed what it was back in the room at Alpine. She could see it plainer here. There was an eager ferocity in the way they met, like two wild stallions battling over a mare.

Hagar's lean frame was lighter by twenty pounds, and Elgera knew Owens, and she expected the sheriff to be completely outmatched. What he lacked in bulk, however, he made up with skill. For a long terrible time the two of them stood there slugging it out, and Hagar's feet moved in a swift, skilled shuffle, too fast for Elgera to follow, and his bony fists landed three blows for every one Owens got in.

That flat-lipped grin spread on Hagar's mouth as he danced in and out, not allowing Owens to set himself, cutting the bigger man's face to ribbons. He ducked in and rolled Owens's right off a shoulder and drove his own right into Owens's square belly and his left into Owens's face, and danced out again.

Owens tried to spread his legs, and that dogged hump came into his shoulders. But Hagar moved in again before Owens could get his balance, pounding the man's face with a tattoo of lefts, jumping back before Owens could strike. Again Hagar weaved in, grinning. Then, while he was bent low in there, Elgera saw him jerk suddenly, saw the sudden look of pain that crossed his face. She knew Owens had landed a blow.

Quickly Hagar retreated, covering up, head ducked into his shoulders, elbows hugged in tightly. It gave Owens his chance. His square torso bent forward a bit, and he spread his legs and started moving forward, and the girl had seen it like that before.

"*Nombre de Dios*," muttered the blind priest, his head moving helplessly from side to side. "Stop this, my sons . . ."

Hagar had recovered. The grin was back as he stepped in again, hooking a sharp right over Owens's heart. Owens grunted sickly. He bent forward a little farther. His boots made a relentless scraping against the flagstones, coming on. Johnny Hagar warded off his left and ducked in under his right to smash a straight-arm blow fully into Owens's mouth. Owens gasped and spat blood and didn't stop.

The girl couldn't help her choked cry. "Chisos . . ."

Desperately Hagar struck Owens again, trying to stop him. But an adamantine cast had settled into the flat planes of Owens's bloody face; he slogged into Hagar, moving with his heavy deliberation that was neither graceful nor awkward. His square torso jerked from one side to the other as he threw his patient, driving blows.

173

Hagar danced in and pounded three lefts into Owens's face and countered Owens's swing and threw a right into the heavy man's stomach. Then Elgera saw the sheriff's body jerk again, and saw the agony twist his face suddenly. The pale, set look hadn't left him when he danced backward this time, hugging his elbows in, shaking his head, blinking his eyes.

"Let me go!" sobbed Elgera, fighting Avarillo's fat arms. "They'll kill each other. Let me go!"

"Si," said Avarillo, holding her without much apparent effort. "They'll probably kill each other, but you can't stop them. That is Johnny Hagar and Chisos Owens, Elgera, and nobody could stop them now, I think."

The grin was fixed and ghastly on Hagar's face. There was a desperation in the way he slashed back in, bending forward and driving his swift blows from clear down at his boots. The grunting sounds of pain Owens made were hardly human. He leaned forward to take the blows and kept on walking, and his boots still moved across the flagstones with that inexorable, scraping sound, and nothing Hagar could do would stop him.

Hagar blocked one, sunk his fist into Owens's belly. He rolled another off his shoulder, came in with an uppercut that jerked Owens's head back with a snapping motion. He drove a third back into Owens's belly that doubled the big man over. And with that last one, he dropped his guard. Before he could step back, Owens caught him. Elgera saw Hagar stiffen suddenly, and his spasmodic grunt slapped against the garden wall. He staggered back, trying to cover up. Owens was still almost doubled-up as he plodded into Hagar, and his head went against the man's hugged-in elbows. One of his big, rope-scarred fists smashed up from below and knocked the elbows apart and ripped Hagar's shirt from waist to neck as it howled on up to crash into his chin.

Hagar's head snapped up, Owens's own head against the sheriff's body now, and he kept on hitting from there. His right fist thudded into Hagar's belly with a sickening, fleshy sound. Hagar stiffened. Owens slugged him in the ribs. Hagar spun halfway around, tottering there. Owens slugged him again, and Hagar jerked around the other way. Again. Again. Again. Hagar went over on his back as stiff as a board and stretched his length on the flagstones.

Owens stumbled on over his body, hands pawing out, and for a moment Elgera thought he would fall, too. Then he caught himself and turned around. He stood there a moment; he drew a hoarse, sobbing breath, then held it, waiting. Avarillo's arms slackened, and the girl bent forward, lips open slightly, waiting. But Hagar didn't move. He lay there with his shirt almost ripped off, blood leaking from one corner of his split lips, one eye closed and beginning to swell already. There were big, red, beefy spots on his lean torso as if he had been slapped with the flat of a board. His breathing was hardly audible.

Finally Owens dabbed at his battered face. He began walking around in little circles, one hand held out in front of him. His face was even worse than Hagar's. His brow was laid open from one temple to the other, bleeding profusely, and his cheeks were lacerated and torn till they looked like freshly ground beef. He was bleeding at the mouth, too. He spat out a tooth, and kept dabbing feebly at his eyes, and walking around in circles. Elgera realized he couldn't see, and she broke free of Avarillo with a sharp cry, running to Owens. She caught his arm and led him to the bench.

"I didn't think . . ." he gasped, sagging to the seat, "I didn't think there was a man that tough in Texas . . ."

He put his head into his arms and drew a great sobbing breath, shaking and quivering like a wind-broken horse. The Indian *mozo* had brought in a silver bowl of warm water and some clean cotton. Elgera went to Hagar, knelt beside him.

"Oh, Chisos," she said, "did you have to do it this way?"

From the corner of her eye she saw Avarillo pick up the Adams dueling pistol that Hagar had shot from Bruce-Douglas's hand. The fat Mexican started to slip it into the voluminous folds of his amazing sash. Bruce-Douglas walked over with one hand inside his coat; he held out his other hand. Shrugging, Avarillo handed him the pistol.

"What did you expect to do with it against Hagar's guns, anyway?" Avarillo grinned. "You know it won't work."

Elgera's head raised sharply, and for a moment she forgot the sheriff's wounds. She had wondered what it was Bruce-Douglas hid beneath his affected hauteur.

176

She knew now. Owens and Hagar weren't the only deadly men in that little garden.

Hagar regained consciousness finally, and they half carried him to the bench. Brother Katopaxi had ordered the *mozo* to boil some live-oak bark and mix it with pounded charcoal and maize. From this, the brother made poultices. He put some on Bruce-Douglas's hand and sewed a piece of bull hide around it. Then he applied it to the other men's faces, holding a poultice on Owens's wrecked brow by a strip of cotton around his forehead, bandaging them in other places where it was possible. Speaking with difficulty through mashed lips, Owens told Hagar about the *derrotero*, and showed him how the route on the map led back to Boquillos and on to La Ciénega Embrujada.

"Clay Thomas's murder is hitched up with the secret of the Santiago somehow," said Owens. "And we have two-thirds of the secret. Find that other third, and where it leads, and we're just as likely to find out who shot Clay. I'll give you your choice, Hagar. You can come with us and give me your word you'll let me have a chance to clear myself. Or I can take your guns and your horse and leave you stranded here. This is out of your jurisdiction. You aren't known down here. It'd take you a long time to get back."

Hagar shook his head groggily. He looked around at the girl. Suddenly she saw him grin.

"All right," he said. "I give my word I'll let you try and clear yourself."

Owens gave him back the Peacemakers — then he stood up. "The way I feel now, you'll probably have to tie me on Del's horse, but we might as well hit for Boquillos."

"What good will that do?" asked Bruce-Douglas. "We have only two-thirds of the map. Perhaps you think you'll get the other piece by asking the first *peón* you see in Boquillos to hand it over."

Avarillo's chuckle was sly. "*Pues,* it might be almost that easy. I think we better go to Boquillos, all right."

The girl glanced sharply at him. "You know something."

"I think we better go to Boquillos, all right." He grinned.

The *mozo* had brought their horses from the *posada.* Although Owens and Hagar could hardly stand up, they insisted on starting at once. The girl helped Owens into his saddle and mounted her palomino, kneeing it in close so she could catch Owens's arm. Avarillo hoisted Hagar onto his horse. The girl watched the fat Mexican narrowly, almost angrily.

"*Vaya con Dios . . .*"

Katopaxi's dry rattle whirled *Señorita* Scorpion. He stood in the small, arched doorway piercing the wall, his spidery hand running up and down the slender chain supporting his cross. Elgera murmured goodbye — then a strange expression came into her face, almost a fear, and she gigged her palomino forward suddenly to reach Owens. She caught his arm.

"Did you see that brother?" she asked in a strained voice.

Owens was trying very hard not to be sick. He swayed forward in the saddle, one rope-scarred fist gripping the horn tightly. "Katopaxi? What about him?"

"The cross he wears around his neck," said Elgera. "It was hanging upside down!"

CHAPTER
FIVE

When Anse Hawkman had controlled all the land from the Río Grande north to Persimmon Gap, he had made his headquarters at the border town of Boquillos. But the AH empire was crumbled in the dust now, and Boquillos was already slipping back into the obscurity and peace it had known before Anse had put his greedy hands on it. With the long ride from Monclava behind them, Elgera and the four men entered Boquillos from the west, turning into the main street that had been known as Pasadizo Hawkman. They passed the big adobe *cantina* Anse had run. Elgera glanced for a long moment at the idlers by the hitch rack in front of that saloon, and under the cottonwoods at the corner of the building. Chisos Owens rubbed his healing face gently, grinning.

"You won't find any AH hands," he said. "They mostly drifted up to Alpine and Marathon where the air's a little healthier for the men who worked for Anse."

They passed the adobe stables across from the *cantina*, a large, squat building with the *viga* poles that formed rafters extending on out through the yellow walls and casting an uneven shadow pattern across

180

them. Under two persimmon trees in front, the gnarled smithy was shoeing a huge black horse. A heavy-set Mexican rose from where he had been hunkered down against the water butt. Elgera reined in her palomino.

"Gato!"

The man known as Cat came on from the cool shade into the bright sunlight and shoved his roll-brim sombrero back and stood, squinting up at them, grinning maliciously. "You left Alpine in a big hurry, *señorita*," he said. "You forgot to pay us. Perhaps you would like to do that now."

Avarillo bent forward in his saddle as far as his prodigious girth would allow, and spoke ironically: "*Muy afortunado*, Gato, that you just happened to be here when we rode by, very fortunate."

Gato glanced at him. "This is my town, *Señor* Avarillo. Why shouldn't I be here?"

From the corner of her eye, Elgera caught the shift of men across the street. Enrique had come down the alley between the *cantina* and the adobe hovel next door. His scarred face was turned toward the riders, and he shifted the inevitable pickaxe from his shoulder to across his belly where he held it with both hands.

"You know you'd have gotten paid by going back to the Santiago," snapped the girl. "My brother's there."

"Go back through those Dead Horses?" Gato grinned. "Even I couldn't find my way through them to the mine shaft, *señorita*. You Douglases are the only ones who could ever follow that trail. A man would be a fool to try it alone."

"Chisos did," said the girl.

181

Gato looked at Owens, spat. "Sometimes I think maybe he is not all-man, like the Indians say. We would like our money now, *señorita*."

One of the idlers in front of the *cantina* turned and called softly through the open door. A man appeared there then, moving out.

Elgera spoke angrily: "You know I don't carry that much money around in my saddlebags, Gato. I can't pay you now."

Gato moved toward her. "Can't you? Can't you, *señorita*?"

Quills were pureblooded Indians of Mexico. The man who had come from the door of the *cantina* was a Quill. He was short and squat with his greasy black hair done up in a queue and buckskin *chivarras* serving for leggings. He had his hand on the butt of a gun stuck through the waistband of his trousers in the very middle of his belly. Elgera couldn't help wondering where she had seen him before. Then Gato reached up and grabbed the cheek piece of her bridle. The palomino jerked his head up. Gato pulled it down with a brutal grunt.

"Can't you, *señorita*?" he repeated. "My town. Can't you pay me now?"

"Gato!" shouted Hagar, wheeling his horse and trying to get around Owens.

Owens tried to turn his animal, too, and got in the sheriff's way. Bruce-Douglas spurred his animal in between them and to the head of the palomino, turning till he was broadside there. He bent forward as if to speak, but *Señorita* Scorpion had already turned in her saddle and dropped one hand to the cantle near enough to the butt of her big Army Colt. Facing Gato that way, there was a wild look in her flashing eyes.

"I don't have to remind you what happened before, do I, Gato?" she said. "We're just passing through Boquillos. You'll get paid and you know it. Right now we're just passing through. Better let us."

The baleful grin slipped off Gato's dark face. For a moment, his strange opaque eyes met Elgera's, then they dropped to her hand where it rested so near her gun. Enrique had come around behind the palomino, hefting his axe. The Quill followed him, face impassive. Another man was walking across from the *cantina*, shifting a holstered gun around in front of him a little.

Bruce-Douglas was leaning forward, and his voice wasn't arrogant now, or testy, or supercilious. It was strangely flat and cold. "Gato. What are you doing?"

The Mexican's head turned toward him momentarily. For a moment their glances locked. Elgera could see how the Englishman's thin lips were compressed till the flesh showed white around them; his eyes were as cold as his voice.

Gato's own eyes dropped before them suddenly. He looked at the girl's hand again. The palomino's head jerked up as he let go of the cheek piece. A dull flush crept into his thick neck as he took a step back, raising his eyes again to Elgera.

Avarillo suddenly took his *cigarro* from his mouth and laughed. "*Sí*, Gato, Elgera doesn't have to remind you of what happened before, does she? You remember well enough, *caracoles*."

But Elgera was watching the Englishman, and she was wondering if Gato had taken his hand off because of her — or because of Harold Bruce-Douglas. She wheeled her palomino away and broke it into a canter up the street. Bruce-Douglas was next after her, then Hagar. They were close enough for the girl to hear what they said when the sheriff caught up with the Englishman. Hagar spoke first.

"What did you mean by that back there?"

The Englishman sounded supremely bored. "By what?"

"You asked Gato what he was doing?"

"Could you suggest," asked Bruce-Douglas, "a better way of finding out?"

Hagar was unperturbed. "It meant more than it sounded like. When did you meet Gato?"

"Really, now," said Bruce-Douglas. "Really."

Elgera knew Hagar was grinning without turning to look at him. She dropped her palomino back beside them.

"You ride like Army," Hagar told the Englishman.

Bruce-Douglas took his snuffbox out, pinching the powder disdainfully between thumb and forefinger. The way he tilted his head back was eloquent. He put the box back, dabbed at his nose with the silk handkerchief.

"Posting, old boy," he condescended. "Posting."

Hagar shook his head. "That isn't posting . . . not the way they do in England, anyway. You ride like Army. I was in the Army, Bruce-Douglas. I'll remember sometime."

Hawkman had built a two-story frame hotel on the south side of the little plaza, and they decided to rest a day there. Elgera took a front lower, overlooking the sunlit square. She had finished bathing and was combing her long, gleaming hair by the cracked mirror over the rickety bed table, when someone rapped on her door. Hagar came in to her call.

"Thought you'd be about ready," he said, rubbing a freshly shaved jaw. "Want to eat?"

She nodded, buckling on her gun. "Why do you think Avarillo was so insistent we come to Boquillos?"

"Don't know exactly," said Hagar. "Now he's talking about heading toward La Ciénega Embrujada as marked on that *derrotero*. I think he knows a lot he doesn't tell."

"Maybe we shouldn't have let him keep those two pieces of the document," she said, frowning.

Hagar shrugged, coming closer, and he was grinning, and it wasn't so brash now, somehow. "Elgera, how do you feel about Chisos?"

She drew a breath. "I like him very much."

"I heard it was more than that. I heard he was sweet on you," said Hagar — and her fingers were suddenly caught up in his strong hand. "You know it wouldn't work that way, Elgera. It would be like hitching a thoroughbred with a plow horse."

"I wouldn't say that," remarked Chisos Owens from the open door.

Hagar let go of Elgera's hand, and turned. They stood looking at each other for a moment, the two men.

Owens's shoulders stooped forward a little as he moved on into the room.

"You got your cows in the wrong pasture, Hagar," he said heavily.

"I didn't see any fence around it," replied the sheriff.

"I figure you're the kind who'd climb over the fence if there was one," said Owens.

The girl was looking from one to another, and she realized what it was that had lain between them all along. Her lips twisted a little. She had known it, really; she had just been reluctant to admit it. She had sensed it lying between them back there at the Alpine Lodge, had seen it at Monclava. It was a new thing to *her*, but not really a new thing. It was as old as Adam and Eve. "This is what the fight was about at Monclava, then," she said in a low voice.

"I came to take Owens back for a murder," insisted Hagar, grinning.

"You know what I mean," said the girl.

Hagar's grin faded slightly. "Yeah, I know what you mean. I came to take Owens back, but the fight wasn't really about that. She's right, isn't she, Chisos? This is what the fight was about."

"I guess so," said Owens.

"You know so," said Hagar.

Owens bent forward a little. Hagar's grin spread again, but his lips had flattened against his teeth. The girl stepped between them swiftly.

"Didn't you settle it once?" she said. "Don't start in again."

"We didn't settle anything," said Hagar.

"So you're just going to keep on fighting every time you meet," said the girl hotly. "If you do it that way, I promise I won't have anything more to do with either of you. Now, are we going out and eat like intelligent adults, or am I saddling up for the Santiago?"

Hagar seemed to relax, and Owens shrugged. Elgera turned to smile at the sheriff. "That's better. Avarillo has the map . . . I think you'd better get him and Bruce-Douglas, Hagar."

Hagar left reluctantly. Owens turned to Elgera, speaking slowly. "He was right, in a way, Elgera. It'd be like hitching a thoroughbred to a plow horse. But that's the kind I am. I can't help it. You know how I've felt about you all along."

She patted his thick forearm. "Don't talk that way. I know."

"And Hagar . . . ?"

"A young man who can be very nice or very deadly, and who can smile just as pleasantly when he's being beaten to a pulp as when he's making love," she said.

"He means more to you than that," Owens grumbled. "But I guess I'm acting like a kid."

"Both of you are." She laughed. "Maybe that's why I like you."

Hagar came back down the hall and into the room. "Not in their rooms. Funny, too. Bruce-Douglas was in our room when I left."

"Avarillo shared mine," said Owens. "He was in, too."

Elgera saw something cross his face then. Her hand slipped off his arm as he turned to walk toward the window. He put his hands on the sill and bent to look out toward the hitch rack in the plaza. *Señorita* Scorpion saw his calloused fingers tighten on the sill.

"Avarillo's horse is gone," he said. "So's Bruce-Douglas's. They're both gone."

The Sierra del Caballo Muerto rose, jagged and mysterious, northward from Boquillos, and their very name bespoke the death that lay in their unknown fastness. There was not enough water in the Mountains of the Dead Horse to maintain human life. A few stands of skeleton timber clung to the barren slopes and rattled in the wind and mocked the three riders heading down the dark cañon that led deeper into the terrible range. Shadowy mesquite squirmed down the barrancas, and the prickly pear sought fissures in the rocks, as if hiding from the malignant spirit that hovered over the whole region.

The golden coat of Elgera's palomino was turned gray with dust; she sat the horse with a dull weariness, legs slack against sweat-darkened stirrup leathers, both hands holding the pommel of her three-quarter rig. Behind the cantle were slung a pair of Army canteens; the water sloshed in them continually with a hollow, tinny sound, reminding Elgera how little was left. Three days of the grueling ride had passed beneath their horses' plodding hoofs, yet Hagar still rode with that marvelous insouciance in the easy slouch of his long body, his grin splitting an unshaven chin. He hummed idly at the "Stable Call":

188

Oh, go to the stable, all you who are able,
And give your poor horses some hay and some corn.
For if you don't . . .

He sat erect suddenly, snapping his fingers. "That's where he was. Troop A of the Fourth. I knew I'd remember it."

"Who was in Troop A?" asked Elgera uncaringly.

"Bruce-Douglas," said Hagar. "Corporal Bruce-Douglas. Court-martialed in Eighteen Ninety-One for letting one of Geronimo's Apaches escape while we were taking them to Florida."

Elgera turned farther toward him, eyes darkening. "Then he isn't an Englishman, he isn't . . . ?"

Hagar shrugged. "Might be English, all right. Might even be the rightful heir to your mine. I don't know. I do know he was in the Fourth, though. Drummed out for letting that Indian get away. That was about a year before my own discharge."

Owens halted the horse he had taken from Delcazar. Ahead, the cañon spread out. Flanking it on either slope, two spires of reddish sandstone stood in fantastically eroded majesty.

"Los Dos Dedos de Dios," said Owens.

"The Two Fingers of God?"

Owens nodded. "We made our mistake letting Avarillo keep the map. But I remember the route we traced down there at Monclava. You been wondering why I cut back and forth so much? From Boquillos, remember, the dotted line turned north to La Ciénega Embrujada . . . the Haunted Swamp. That was the last spot before the route ran off the jagged edge of the *derrotero*. The landmark nearest the Ciénega was called The Two Fingers of God. I figured they'd be easier to spot from a distance, and, if we could find them, we could find the swamp. And if these ain't the fingers, I'm not a Texican."

Hagar spat. "Swamp! We've come a hundred miles without seeing enough water to wet a sidewinder's last rattle."

"He's right," said the girl. "In four hundred years, the Santiago's the only place in the Dead Horses where men have found water like that."

Owens hiked a boot over his saddle horn, reached for the makings in his jumper pocket. "Right. So, if there is a swamp, it must be fairly near the Santiago. And like Avarillo says, the Indians wouldn't go very far away from the valley to store their gold . . . no farther than the length of time the water they could carry would last. Which brings us to what?"

Hagar wasn't enthusiastic. "The gold and the swamp are close to each other."

Owens rolled himself a wheat straw, thick fingers amazingly deft. "One more. The gold and the swamp *and* the Santiago are close to each other."

Hagar slapped his canteen; it emitted a hollow sound. "If you're wrong about that swamp, we'll be slitting our own throats by going ahead. As it is, we'll be lucky to make it back out. And even supposing there is a swamp, if you miss it by one hair, you might as well miss it entirely."

190

Owens glanced at Elgera. Elgera looked at Hagar. Hagar grinned, gigged his horse. "All right," he said. "I don't have a back door, anyway."

As they rode on toward the Dedos de Dios, Elgera noticed how Owens kept bending from side to side in the saddle. Finally, in the shadow cast by the twin spires of sandstone, he halted. They were standing beside a hollow sink, its clay bottom slick and hard, criss-crossed by deep cracks and fissures. Elgera thought the mesquite here seemed darker than the growth they had been passing. Owens climbed from his horse. He dropped the stub of his cigarette, ground it out with a heel.

"We'll stop here."

Night fell slowly through the blinding heat of afternoon. Finally the shadows had turned to darkness. A lizard made a sibilant scraping sound in the silence. The thirsty horses fiddled nervously. At last the moon yellowed the blackness, casting an eerie light over the weird peaks surrounding them. Elgera saw why Owens had stopped here.

The bottom of the sink was wet already; the horses bent weary necks to muzzle the dampness eagerly. Owens grunted in a satisfied way.

"If there's water at all, it seeps up this way at night," he said. "The mesquite looked healthier than most we passed. It's usually the sign. Let's go."

From the sink led several gullies. Owens took each one in turn, following it a few yards, squatting down to feel the earth with his hands. Finally he came back and picked up his reins and led them into the gully that turned northward between the needles of sandstone. Elgera followed, leading her palomino. At first, her boots made a soft, shuffling sound in the damp sand, then they began passing through slush, and farther on the slush turned to ooze that popped and sucked with each step. The mesquite on the banks of the gully gave way to intermittent hummocks of toboso grass that sighed eerily in the light breeze. Elgera's hand tightened on her reins. Ahead of her, Owens swung aboard his horse, and Elgera could see why — the animal was sloshing through muddy water to its knees. Elgera mounted, turning to see Hagar coming up behind her, and behind him, the Dedos de Dios towering into an ominous sky. Then, from ahead came the unmistakable boom of a bullfrog.

As they moved forward, more slowly now, a strange assibilation entered Elgera's consciousness, an insidious rattling, not as loud as the croaking of the frog, yet more intense. She wiped a perspiring palm against her *charro* leggings, unable to recognize the sound. Then the first spread of canebrake rose against the low moon in a tall, ghostly pattern, rattling incessantly in the breeze. And she remembered the round bars that might have been molded in canes from a brake like this.

"La Ciénega Embrujada," said Owens. "The Haunted Swamp."

Elgera's palomino started at a sudden movement on the bank of the gully above.

Hagar's voice rang sharply from behind. "Watch it, Elgera, watch it . . ."

The thunder of a shot cut him off. The palomino reared, squealing. Fighting it around, Elgera could see Hagar bent forward in his saddle. He held his right shoulder with his left hand; his right holster was empty.

"Please don't continue acting so foolish," said someone from the bank. "We really don't want to kill you."

CHAPTER
SIX

The flickering campfire turned Elgera's blonde hair to a ruddy cascade where she sat with her back against the gnarled bole of a post oak. Beside her, Hagar lay full length on the soggy ground, his reckless grin forced against the pain of his wounded shoulder, hands bound behind him, ankles tied together. Owens was at Elgera's other side, rawhide lashings gathering his denim jumper into folds about his blocky torso. She could hear his heavy breathing, and an occasional grunt; already he was beginning to strain at his bonds.

Bruce-Douglas stood farther out, firelight throwing sinister shadows across his thin face. It had been the Englishman and Gato and Gato's men on the bank of the gully. Under the threat of their guns, Elgera and Owens and Hagar had been disarmed, then taken across the bog and through the canebrake to this clearing of salt grass and post oaks. The Englishman was toying with the Adams dueling pistol he carried with him, studying the GD inscribed over the pin, apparently enjoying the strain that the lengthening silence caused Elgera and the others. His thin smile was turned toward the man lying at his feet. It had surprised Elgera at first; she had thought all along that

Avarillo had conspired with Bruce-Douglas, had left Boquillos willingly. There was nothing willing about the corpulent Mexican, lying there with his arms spread-eagled by the stakes they had thrust into the ground and tied his hands to. He lay so that his bare feet would have been in the fire if his legs hadn't been curled up beneath him; the reddened, blistered look to those feet held its own grim significance. Bruce-Douglas caught Elgera's horrified eyes on them.

"This little exercise on his pedal extremities isn't the only persuasion we have tried," he said. "Gato worked all the way up from Boquillos, but so far his handicraft has failed miserably. We thought, like you, Elgera, that Avarillo knew more about that third piece of the *derrotero* than he told us at Monclava. We spirited him out of the Hawkman Hotel while Chisos and Hagar were in your room."

"I am dying, *señores*," panted Avarillo. "Tender me one more *cigarro* before I pass on. Just one. It's all I ask."

"We'll give you something more *caliente* than a *cigarro*," grunted Gato viciously.

He wasn't the Gato Elgera had known. His magnificent black Arabian stood tethered apart from the other horses, Spanish rig the same color as the animal, heavy with silver plating. His big Colts were thonged low around the legs of shiny black *mitajas* leggings; his white shirt had been replaced by a black one, and over that was a black *charro* jacket hemmed in gold.

Elgera hadn't been surprised, somehow, at Gato's being the Negro Caballero. What had caused her real shock was to see the blind man, Brother Katopaxi, and his Indian *mozo* from Monclava. Katopaxi stood just outside the circle of firelight, one bloodless hand running up and down the slender chain holding his inverted cross, like a spider on its web. The husky, sibilant rattle of his voice held a sinister note for the girl now.

"Why not give our dying *hermano* this last consideration?" he said mockingly. "We are all *hermanos* in the sight of our Majesty. Give him a *cigarro*, Gato, my son."

Gato squatted beside Avarillo, shoving his tremendous black sombrero back on his head. He took two *cigarros* from the pocket of Avarillo's silk shirt, lit them in the fire. He jammed one in the fat Mexican's mouth, put the other into his own. Avarillo sucked gratefully on the smoke. Finally he spoke.

"Why do you always play with that Rodriguez, *Señor* Bruce-Douglas?"

Elgera saw the surprise in the Englishman's face for a moment, then he covered it with a careful indifference. "The gun is an Adams. London, you know, Sixteen Seventies."

"No," said Avarillo. "It is a Rodriguez, made in Toledo by the Rodriguez brothers, much later than your Sixteen Seventy."

Hagar was watching the Englishman, and maybe he had caught that momentary surprise, and maybe he saw the game. "Perhaps he's right, Corporal Bruce-Douglas."

196

Bruce-Douglas turned toward him sharply, then he tilted his head back slightly. "Really, gentlemen. Really."

"Then you aren't English," said Elgera swiftly. "You aren't . . . ?"

"I'm not descended from your infamous George Douglas, if that's what you're going to say," shrugged the man resignedly. "And as far as the other . . . I owe no especial allegiance to any one country. I was born in the Bahamas. I was sent to Eton. Served in the French Foreign Legion as well as your stupid U.S. cavalry. What would that make me?"

"Do you really want us to tell you," inquired Avarillo chuckling, then he grimaced with pain. "Where did you get the dueling pistol, señor, where did you really get the Rodriguez?"

Bruce-Douglas condescended. "On a detail transferring some of Geronimo's chaps to Florida. One of the Indians promised to give me the key to the secret of the Santiago. That was before the outside world had become aware of the Santiago, naturally. I thought the secret was the knowledge of its whereabouts. I helped him get away. This dueling piece was all I could get for my trouble. The Indian said it was a tribal fetish . . . said it had been taken by one of his ancestors who raided the Santiago Mine over two hundred years ago. Said Don Simeón Santiago ran out of the house with this gun when he heard the Indians. It misfired. He threw it into a Comanche's face. The bounder then killed Don Simeón and took the gun as well as his hair. That is how the Indian I helped escape came by it."

"Why the Adams business, then?" asked the girl.

"I passed it off as an Adams only to enhance my rôle as Bruce-Douglas recently from England, who was the legal heir to George Douglas's estate," he replied. "I had found out by then that the gun was no key to the secret . . . had found out, in fact, what the secret really was. We had one-third of it. We thought, naturally, that Elgera would have a third, being George Douglas's descendant."

"We?"

"Gato, Katopaxi, and I." The Englishman smiled thinly. "I was drummed out of the service for letting the Indian escape. The gun wasn't what I'd expected, but it had whetted my curiosity. Eventually I drifted to Mexico City, hunting some other clue to the secret. There I found out that in the Cappella del Santo were all the old official documents of the Spanish government during the time Santiago had shipped his gold through Monclava. It was how Katopaxi and I met. He had that third of the *derrotero* he got from Pedro Tovar. And when he saw this dueling piece . . ."

"Saw!" cried the girl.

Bruce-Douglas glanced at Katopaxi, and his laugh held a veiled contempt. "Our bogus Franciscan is a complete hypocrite, being neither a priest nor blind. Gato is his son. Long ago, Katopaxi became too decrepit for the kind of life led by the Negro Caballero. He took the cloth as an easier way to spend his last years. It has proven very beneficial to all."

"But the cross, the friars . . . ?"

"Do you think I let them see my cross?" cackled the old man. "No, my dear, for ten years I have been the

198

blind brother Katopaxi, tending his flock of ignorant *peónes*, waiting for the riches of the Santiago to come to me. It was in my first year at Monclava, you see, that Pedro Tovar called me for benediction and gave his third of the *derrotero* to the Church. I knew what that piece of parchment meant. I knew I only had to be patient and I would get the treasure men have been hunting for two hundred years. Soon I heard the Santiago had been found again, owned by a half-wild girl descended from George Douglas. When Bruce-Douglas came to Monclava with the dueling pistol, and the same name as the girl, it gave me the idea. Gato wanted to try and find the girl's portion of the *derrotero* by means of force. The other way was more intelligent, don't you think?"

"Not especially," said the girl. "You didn't get anything."

"If you had possessed a third of the chart," said Bruce-Douglas coldly, "I would have found it, believe me."

"What does it matter?" Katopaxi laughed shrilly. "You have been delivered into our hands by his Satanic Majesty . . ."

"*Dios*, a devil-worshipper!" gasped Avarillo. "Cross me, quick, somebody cross me."

Gato's laugh was ugly. Elgera shifted her bound wrists uncomfortably behind her; the hemp was rasping them. Hemp? Yes, not rawhide. Owens and Hagar had been tied with rawhide dallies, but Gato had used a spare piece of rope on the girl. She caught the sudden bright glow of Avarillo's *cigarro*.

"It was you following Clay Thomas, then?" said Owens.

The firelight caught opaquely the green in Gato's eyes as he turned toward Chisos Owens. "When Clay Thomas got Delcazar's spread for Anse, he went to Mexico City for the papers they had with a law firm there, and to clear the old Spanish grant. I have connections down there. Clay had been in Mexico City about a week when I heard that he was pestering the government officials for the old maps of the border states."

"*Sí*," hissed Katopaxi. "We knew that Ramón Delcazar was descended from Pío Delcazar, *capitán* of *Don* Santiago's muleteers in Sixteen Eighty-One. It wasn't hard for us to guess what Clay Thomas had found among the Delcazar papers that made him so suddenly interested in the old maps. We tried to get him in Mexico City, but he got away."

Enrique had come with Gato; he stood at the fringe of light, scarred face fantastic in the glow of red flames, axe over his shoulder. Another man had come with the Negro Caballero, too. He was the Quill who had walked across the street there in Boquillos when Gato had stopped Elgera. A squat little man in buckskin *chivarras*, greasy black hair queued, gunstock carried nakedly through his waistband in the middle of his belly. His appearance had struck a familiar chord in Elgera at Boquillos; she knew why now.

Gato caught her intent gaze on the Quill, and laughed. "*Sí, señorita*, that is Torres. Torres is the man you saw run from the alley behind the Alpine Lodge,

200

remember? As my *padre* says, we missed Clay Thomas in Mexico City. While Enrique and I hired on as miners to Avarillo, we sent Torres to follow Thomas and get what he had. Torres didn't know Chisos Owens was in that room at Alpine. I'm afraid it surprised him a little. He really shouldn't have run till he got the *derrotero*, should he?"

"I told you, Hagar," said the girl grimly.

She saw Hagar's face turn toward Owens a moment. The sheriff grinned suddenly; Owens grinned. Gato suddenly squatted again beside Avarillo and grabbed a leg, snarling: "I'm tired of this talk. I'll give you something more *caliente* than that *cigarro* if you don't tell us where that last piece is . . ."

"Gato!" said Bruce-Douglas imperviously. "I think we have a superior stimulus, now that everyone has arrived. I wondered why our fat Mexican has been so obdurate about telling. Perhaps I see . . ." He turned to Elgera. "You're such a fascinating creature, Elgera, you draw men like moths to a flame. Other than his amplified waistline and his amazingly diversified accomplishments, Avarillo isn't much different from other men, is he? Perhaps he's undergone our tender ministrations so stoically because of an unavowed devotion to you. Yes, I think that might be it."

Still holding the dueling piece in one hand, he went to the fire. Grasping the unburned end of a glowing stake in his free hand, he straightened and moved toward the girl. Her breath gagged in her throat suddenly. There was a sharp ripping sound to her left. She saw that Owens's jumper had torn across the bulge

201

of muscle humped up on either side of his big neck as he writhed madly at his bonds.

"*'Por Dios,'*" gasped Avarillo. "Not that, Bruce-Douglas . . ."

Bruce-Douglas bent almost languidly. Elgera drew back from the glowing heat as the brand was brought closer to her face by that slim, pale hand. She could see the strange, feral light in the Englishman's icy eyes. She jerked spasmodically as a burning ash fell on her leg.

"You have but a moment, Avarillo," said Bruce-Douglas in that bored voice. "Such a lovely soft face, too. The other third of that *derrotero*, please."

Avarillo made a choked sound. With a sudden hoarse roar, Chisos Owens jerked onto his knees and drove upward and threw himself on Bruce-Douglas, bound hand and foot as he was. With Owens's big head in his stomach, Bruce-Douglas grunted sickly and went over backward, burning stick flying from his hand.

Gato let go of Avarillo's leg and jumped erect, pawing for one of his guns. Avarillo snaked out one of his burned feet and slammed Gato across the back of his knees with a postoak calf. Gato's legs snapped shut like a pair of hinges, and he stumbled forward, falling to his hands and knees as his gun went off into the ground. The Quill named Torres tried to get around from behind Katopaxi, but the old man got in his way, shouting maledictions in Spanish.

Owens rolled over the Englishman and flopped onto his knees again and then onto his tied feet, throwing himself forward toward the horses before he fell onto his face once more.

"Stop him!" yelled Bruce-Douglas, rolling onto his belly.

Hemp, hemp, hemp. It ran through the girl's mind as she rolled toward Avarillo. Torres shoved Katopaxi so hard the old man fell, and then the Quill was free to snap a shot at Owens. But the big man had already jerked to his feet again, and the slug kicked up dirt behind him as he heaved his tied body in another prodigious jumping hop toward the horses. Enrique was running toward him with the axe upraised. Bruce-Douglas was on his hands and knees; he still held the dueling pistol, his free hand fumbling beneath his coat for something.

"Stop him, you fools!" he called.

Sheriff Hagar's lean body suddenly flopped into the Englishman, knocking him over again. Elgera was half-lying on Avarillo now, her bound hands by his head.

"Hemp on my hands," she panted. "Your *cigarro*, quickly."

He had a nimble wit, Avarillo, and he needed no more than that. She stiffened with the pain as the glowing *cigarro* was jammed against the rope on her wrists. Gato was running after Chisos Owens, and so were Enrique and Torres, and they were all getting in each other's way, and Hagar's body had rolled on over Bruce-Douglas and right into the fire. Owens took a last heaving jump and crashed in among the horses, sending them into a kicking, squealing, whinnying mill.

Hagar bounced around on his back in the fire, kicking embers and burning wood and coals every which way. Gato turned back toward him with a shout, pointing his gun at the sheriff. But the fire was scattered already, and the moon hadn't yet risen above the tall cane, and the darkness that settled over the clearing so suddenly was solid and intense after the ruddy glare of the flames.

Writhing with the pain of the burning *cigarro*, Elgera saw Gato's gun stab in the gloom. A horse must have broken free; it galloped across the clearing. Someone shouted, stumbling out of the animal's way and toward Elgera. She was sobbing now, but she could smell the rope beginning to burn. Two more horses came thundering across the soggy grass. Then the man coming toward her stumbled over her legs.

Elgera caught the shadowy movement that might have been his hand, and she knew she had to do it now. Throwing herself upward with a strange cry, she wrenched desperately at her bindings. She felt the burned rope around her wrists give, then break. She went into the man with her freed arms jerking around in front. The thick wool of Bruce-Douglas's greatcoat was suffocating against her nose and mouth.

She caught him around the legs. As he fell, he slashed at her viciously with a gun. She stopped his arm coming down, let go of his legs to grab the weapon and twist it from his hand. Then they hit the ground, and she rolled free of him. More horses clattered across the clearing, one of them galloping between Bruce-Douglas and Elgera. She got to her knees, but couldn't see the Englishman. She heard someone fighting on the other side of the clearing.

"Gato!" shouted a man.

Elgera turned toward the noise, tripped, and fell over a body. She still held the gun she had taken from Bruce-Douglas. She raised it to strike.

"Elgera," panted Johnny Hagar.

She halted, the gun above her head. Then she was tearing at his bonds, feeling him stiffen with the pain of burns he had taken in the fire. Finally she had him free.

"¡Caracoles!" shouted Avarillo. "Either give me another cigarro or untie my hands, somebody."

She found him, and yanked up the stakes holding his hands spread-eagled. A shot bellowed, another.

"Gato?" yelled that man across the way again.

She realized Chisos Owens was over there somewhere and once more scrambled to her feet and turned that way, running. Suddenly she slid off the solid ground into the mud. Floundering around, she half fell into the canes. She held the gun in one hand, pawed with her other, trying to feel her way back to the clearing. The canes kept rattling against her; she thought she had become turned around. She whirled the other way, plunging through the rattling madness. Panic caught at her when she didn't emerge. She turned back, panting. It took her that long to realize what had happened. She couldn't hear the sounds from the clearing. No sounds. Nothing.

Then the sibilant rattle of canes jerked her around. Her voice sounded small. "Avarillo?"

"Really, now," said someone. "Really."

CHAPTER
SEVEN

Just before Hagar had scattered the fire and thrown everything into the darkness, Owens had cast himself in among the horses with Gato's bullets kicking up mud behind him. Still tearing at his bonds, Owens heaved up under the stake ropes, tearing the stakes from the ground and freeing the animals. He got to his knees, tearing bloody wrists finally from the loosened bindings. He was stooping to untie his feet when Gato dodged in through the frenzied horses. Gato had his gun ready. Elgera's palomino wheeled to gallop away and its rump knocked the weapon aside. Owens threw himself at the man, catching the gun and twisting it between them before it went off again.

"¡Cabrón!" snarled Gato, fighting for balance.

Someone else came running in, shouting: "Gato!"

Owens bellied up to Gato, holding the right hand gun in one fist. Gato tried to pull away and free his left arm from between their bodies so he could draw his other gun. He got the arm out. Owens slugged him in the face. The man coming in heard Gato's grunt, and fired twice at the sound.

"Stop that, you *necio!*" Gato swore. "It's me. You'll hit me."

"Gato?" yelled the man again.

Gato had his other gun halfway out now. Owens turned suddenly and rammed a hip into the man's belly and grabbed that right hand gun with both big hands, twisting viciously. Gato screamed and let go. Owens bent low and slugged him; at the same time he pushed him back into the other man. Both Gato and the man who had run in among the horses went to the ground in a kicking heap. Avarillo's fat mare ran in between Owens and them. By the time it had passed, one of the men had regained his feet, and was farther away. Owens jumped past the mare's flying hind hoofs and slugged the second man with Gato's gun as he tried to rise. The man sank back with a groan. Owens bent to feel his face. No mustaches.

He turned toward the other figure, farther across the clearing. He made the man out dimly in the dark, bent over, apparently reloading. The man straightened suddenly, shouting: "Do you know why they call me Cat, you *borrachón*? They call me the Negro Caballero because I ride a black horse and wear black clothes. But I like Cat better. I can see in the dark, *Señor* Chisos. Come on and get me. I can see you. Come on . . ."

He fired, and the slug clipped at Owens's jumper. He began to move forward, lips pulled back in a half grin, half snarl. He couldn't see Gato very well and he knew it would be useless to fire till he had a better target. His feet made a solid, dogged sound against the soggy salt grass.

"¡Asno, burro, diablo!" bellowed Gato, and fired with each word.

207

Owens was bent forward in that slogging advance and the first bullet caught his arm from wrist to elbow, jerking it up, and still he didn't fire. The second one took a hunk from his neck and he felt the hot pump of blood over his collar. He was almost running when the third one burned through his side and threw him halfway around. He lurched on forward, twisted sideways like that, almost falling till he finally squared himself. Still he didn't fire. His boots made that inexorable pound against the wet ground.

"¡Madre de Dios!" screamed the man who could see in the dark, and pulled on his last shot.

Chisos Owens didn't even know if that final one had hit him and he didn't care if the flame of the shot blinded him for that instant, because he had caught the dark bulk of Gato over his sights and he squeezed his trigger on a sure thing and kept squeezing out one deliberate shot after another as he ran on into the man.

The clearing was ominously quiet when Johnny Hagar clawed his way up out of the muck surrounding it, dragging Katopaxi's Indian *mozo* behind him. After Elgera had untied Hagar, he had gotten to his feet in time to meet the rush of Katopaxi's servant, running from the stampeding horses. The Indian had bowled Hagar over and both men had rolled off the ground into the bog.

Hagar didn't know how long it had lasted there in the mud. He only knew everything had stopped out in the open when he finished it with that last blow. He had broken his hand on the blow, too. He wouldn't have bothered taking the Indian out, but the man had confiscated Hagar's Peacemakers when Gato had stopped them in the gully. Hagar wanted his guns. He had them unbuckled off the man and was strapping the belt around his hips when the silence and the darkness were suddenly filled with the pound of someone's feet.

"Hagar!" a man shouted.

The sheriff whirled. The man coming at him wasn't the one who had shouted. It was Enrique. Moonlight sifted through the canes now, and yellowed the man's contorted, scarred face, and flashed on the great pickaxe he swung above his head. Hagar wasn't fully turned and he knew anything he did would be futile and he had time for nothing but the thought that this was it, this was it.

Then a great square-bodied bulk hurtled out of nowhere and blocked Enrique off from Hagar's sight, and knocked him aside as he went into Hagar. Hagar stumbled back, Enrique's axe falling on one side of him, Enrique and the other man going to the other side. The sheriff saw who had shouted then.

Chisos Owens came up on top of Enrique as they rolled and stopped their momentum by straddling out his legs. Enrique clawed at Owens's mouth, gouged at his eye with a thumb. Owens raised up and drew a great rope-scarred fist back. Terror was in Enrique's widening eyes; he tried to jerk aside, voice breaking.

"*Dios . . .*"

Owens lay there a long moment after that blow. Finally he got to his hands and knees above the limp Mexican.

"That axe would've been in my skull right now," observed Hagar. "I thought you were my rival?"

"You've got it wrong," groaned Owens. "You're *my* rival. But not that way."

"Gato?" asked Hagar.

Owens nodded his head across the clearing. "Taken care of."

Hagar saw the blood soaking Owens's jumper then and got to him, stooping to try and help him off the unconscious Enrique. Then he stopped trying to help him, and stood straight again, and turned toward the canes rattling at the edge of the clearing.

"Gato?" asked the man who had just come out of the brakes.

It was the Quill who had murdered Clay Thomas. It was Torres. The moon had risen above the tops of the canes now, and it caught the glint of Torres's gun stuck nakedly through his waistband in the middle of his belly. His hand hung stiffly over it.

"No, Torres," said Hagar, and his body bent into a little crouch, and the moonlight glinted on his guns, too. "No, not Gato."

"Oh," said Torres.

Hagar's hands curled slightly. Pain shot through the one he had broken hitting the *mozo*. There was a reckless grin on his face. His voice was almost amiable.

"You've got an even go, Torres. Shall we count it off?"

There was no expression in Torres's voice. "You count it."

210

Hagar's grin spread. "I'll count to three. Have your go at the last one or anything in between. All right? Uno . . ."

Torres stiffened a little there at the edge of solid ground. Hagar was still grinning. The slight bend in his body was easy.

"Dos . . ."

Owens's labored breathing stopped suddenly as he caught and held his breath.

"Tres . . ."

Torres dove and Hagar dove and the thunder of their guns rolled on through La Ciénega Embrujada, and the canes rattled in ghostly answer.

Elgera stood stiffly there in the darkness after Bruce-Douglas had answered. She still held the dueling pistol she had torn from him at the clearing. The weight of it in her hand only accentuated her feeling of helplessness. From the first she had sensed the corrosive menace hovering beneath the man's affected arrogance. She remembered now the strange control he had over Gato, remembered how coldly he had faced Hagar's fabulous Peacemakers back there at Monclava — with this same useless dueling pistol.

"Perhaps I should have done this like Gato wanted to at first," called Bruce-Douglas thinly. "But killing a woman is a sordid business. Such a beautiful woman, too."

The soft, popping gurgle of mud around the man's feet came to her. She felt a little vein begin to pound in her throat. He had been fishing for something beneath his coat back there in the clearing when Owens had knocked him over — he had another gun.

Fighting panic, Elgera stooped, feeling around for the clumps of toboso grass growing in the muck. She felt the sticky growth, grasped a handful of it, pulled. The clump came up with a dripping gob of sand on its roots. She swung her arm in an arc and the mud-weighted toboso slapped into the bog far to her right.

She heard a sudden rattle in the canes, as if a man had turned sharply in them. "Elgera?"

She didn't answer. She was seeking another clump of grass. She pulled it up, throwing it far to her other side this time. Again there was that sudden rattle in the brakes — as a man would make turning sharply toward the sound of the grass striking the swamp.

"Elgera?"

She thought his voice sounded higher this time. Sweating, trying to keep her breathing silent, she pulled up another bunch.

"It's no use moving, Elgera!" he called. "No use trying to get away. I have a gun. I know you haven't. I'm going to kill you, Elgera. No use trying to get away."

It sounded as if he were trying to convince himself more than her. Suddenly she wanted to laugh because she knew he was afraid, too. She threw the next hunk of grass far to the right and lurched forward under the cover of its sound. There was that rattle in the canes ahead of her, then a gun blared, stabbing toward the noise of that last toboso grass falling into the swamp.

The flame revealed his position. It was a shock to realize how close he stood. She began pulling frantically at the grass now, throwing clump after clump all around her, lurching forward.

"Elgera!" he called shrilly. "Elgera . . ."

He fired to her right, to her left, to her right again, as each clump of grass struck. She drew a final breath, waited till his gun flamed again, then leaped into the canes at him. Brakes slapping at her face and rattling against her body, she struck Bruce-Douglas. She beat at his pale thin face with the dueling pistol. She caught his gun and twisted it away as they both fell into the mud. The strength in her grasp must have surprised him; for that instant there was no resistance in his wrist as she twisted it. Then his arm stiffened and his body arched against her. The gun exploded between them.

She felt the hot burn of powder against her ribs. Bruce-Douglas remained stiff like that for another moment. Then he collapsed in the Ciénega.

Dazedly she got up off of him, ooze dripping from her *charro* leggings. She saw how the gun was turned in on his body. She felt nauseated and had to force herself to stoop and fumble beneath his blue greatcoat for the two pieces of the *derrotero* he had taken from Avarillo. Someone came stumbling through the bog. A man called her name. It was Hagar.

Together they found their way back to the clearing where Chisos Owens sat, propped up against a tree. Enrique was tied up and so was the Indian *mozo*, and the fire was beginning to blaze again.

"Avarillo?" she asked.

"*Madre de Dios*," said an amiable voice from the edge of the canebrake, "this mud feels so good on my feet I hate to leave it."

The moon was above the canes; its light fell on the familiar corpulence of Ignacio Avarillo at the fringe of the brakes, and on the glittering object he held in one fat hand. It was a cross on a golden chain. It hung upright.

He chuckled. "I see you still have the dueling piece."

The girl looked at the gun she held gripped in one hand, realizing only then how tightly her fingers were clamped around its ancient butt. Avarillo came reluctantly from the Ciénega.

"The politics of New Spain in Sixteen Eighty-One were so rotten," he began, "that any man finding such riches as the Santiago boasted would be the fair prey of every greedy government official in the province, and would undoubtedly be ruined in the mad scramble to get his discovery. How deep a secret *Don* Simeón wanted to keep his find is evidenced by the manner in which he cut this map into three parts, each part going to a man he trusted implicitly. One to Pío Delcazar, *capitán* of his muleteers. The second sent by a faithful Tlascan to *Don* Simeón's son in Mexico . . ."

"The third . . . ?" began Hagar.

"*Sí*, the third." Avarillo chuckled. "This dueling piece, as you know, is not an Adams, but a Rodriguez, made by those famous brothers in Toledo. At Monclava, there is a transcript of an order sent by *Don* Simeón Santiago from the mine to Rodriguez, for a pair of gold-mounted dueling pieces inscribed with GD above their firing pin. What else could they be, but a gift from *Don* Simeón to George Douglas? Undoubtedly Douglas had by that time won *Don* Simeón's friendship by his invaluable service in the mine. And if Santiago thought enough of Douglas to give him such a handsome gift, wouldn't he go a little further and trust his friend with the third portion of the *derrotero*?"

The girl raised the pistol, and Avarillo saw the look in her eyes, and chuckled again. "*Sí*, Elgera, why do you think it misfired when *Don* Simeón ran out of the house and shot at the Indian¿ Douglas, you remember, escaped the massacre because he was in the bottom level of the mine where the Comanches couldn't find him. Would he take such a valuable pair of guns with him down there? No. Perhaps they were on the very mantel that holds the one pistol you retained. *Don* Simeón grabbed the first weapon at hand when the Indians came. Unfortunately for him he should take the gun in which Douglas had hidden his part of the map. Why do you think I tried to get the *pistola* down at Monclava when Bruce-Douglas had it shot from his hand? In the butt, Elgera, rolled up in the butt."

The girl smashed the handle against a rock, felt the dry, harsh paper rolled there in the hollow frame. It tore as she pulled it out. She took the other pieces of the map, fitted them all together on the ground.

"The secret of the Santiago," announced Avarillo, "and Bruce-Douglas had it all the time and didn't know it."

★ ★ ★

215

Chisos Owens's neck wound was superficial, as was the wound down his forearm. They tied his ribs up tightly in strips of his own ducking jacket so the ride wouldn't jar the bullet hole through his side. They filled their canteens with boiled water from La Ciénega Embrujada. And with their two bound prisoners, they set out next morning to follow the last leg of the route marked on the third portion of the *derrotero*. As Chisos Owens had said, La Ciénega Embrujada wasn't very far from the Santiago Valley, and it was still afternoon of the same day when they topped the last ridge and looked down into the green valley with the Río Santiago rising from under the ground at its northern end.

"What did I tell you." Avarillo chuckled. "This is the way Santiago shipped his gold down to Monclava, instead of out through the mine. We took the back door into your valley, Elgera."

She shook her head, unbelieving. "For two hundred years, the Douglases have thought that route through the mine was the only way out."

"Natural enough," said Owens, "when the map to the other route was scattered all over Texas and half of Mexico."

Elgera's people watched them joyously, and, as soon as they were fed and had rested, they followed the secret to its end. The mouth of the main shaft was clearly marked on the third piece of ancient parchment; from there, the dotted line led straight back up the mountain, measuring off 50 *pasos*. 500 double steps back of the shaft took them to the grove of chapote trees and the huge boulder that Avarillo had found before — the boulder which the Indians had used to refine their ore in, the dirt around its foot slick and hard.

From this rock, directions on the *derrotero* led them ten *pasos* north, where the growth of chapote and mesquite was so thick they had to hack their way through with machetes and shovels. Avarillo was in the lead, and suddenly Elgera saw his feet kick up into the air as he burst through the stubborn brush.

"*Caracoles*, there is a hole here!" he cursed — then he stopped a moment, and, when it came again, his voice sounded strangely hollow. "This is it, *señores*, the *tesoro*. Bring your *entraña*, Natividad. It is one of the old shafts dug by the Indians."

Natividad lit one of his buckthorn torches and preceded Elgera into the tunnel. Chisos Owens had insisted on coming, and the girl and Hagar helped him down the crumbling incline. Natividad's light fell across Avarillo, standing farther down. In front of the Mexican was a pile of what looked like the rawhide kaks used to pack ore on the burros. Avarillo stooped and grabbed a hitch on one, tugged at it.

"Received this day," repeated Avarillo, "one round bar bullion, one half *metro* long, one *decímetro* in diameter. And a thousand more where that came from. You're *rico*, Elgera!"

The girl looked at the round golden bar a long time without speaking, unable to believe it somehow. Finally she smiled at Avarillo, dazedly.

"We're all rich, you mean. Whatever it is, we'll divide evenly."

Avarillo flourished his *cigarro*, grinning. "*Bueno, bueno*. I always wanted to be a fat old miser. I guess that settles about everything."

"There's a lot that isn't settled," said Owens.

The sheriff nodded. "How about it, Elgera? Was Chisos right down there at Boquillos? Did I put my cows in the wrong pasture?"

"You can't ask me to decide that now." She smiled. "Give me time to get over all this first. Then, maybe . . ."

Her blonde hair rippled suddenly as *Señorita* Scorpion threw back her head, and there was something wild in her laugh, and the three men looked at each other as if they knew how long it would be before any of them ever tamed a girl like that.

Trail of the Silver Saddle

Les Savage, Jr.'s title for this short novel, when he completed it in March, 1946, was "Six-Gun Stalk". It was submitted to Malcolm Reiss at Fiction House who bought the story for $420 on April 10, 1946. When it appeared in *Action Stories* (Fall, 1946), the title had been changed to the more intriguing "Trail of the Silver Saddle". That title has been retained for the story's first book appearance.

CHAPTER
ONE

Kelly Grenard could see they were getting nervous now. He did not move, standing there in the center of the sumptuous San Antonio apartment, a big man in his black tailcoat, his dark trousers stuffed into the tops of polished, black, flat-heeled boots that came almost to his knees. His black hair was worn long down the back of his neck, and his eyes, set deeply beneath a heavy, level brow, held a searching, calculating quality.

David Bederley rose sharply from the wing chair. "What are you doing, Mister Grenard? You've been standing there for ten minutes now. When you wanted to see Joseph Iderland's apartments, I supposed it was to search for some hidden personals, something we had overlooked. But this . . ."

"Joseph Iderland had a predilection for monte," said Kelly Grenard deliberately. "He was a heavy, if not habitual, drinker who remained a connoisseur even in his cups, and a linguist of singular merit. His taste in both literature and liquor was discriminating and he had but one real friend in his life, a Mexican he had known in his youth."

Bederley was staring at Grenard in amazement. "I thought you didn't know Joseph Iderland."

"I know him now," said Grenard. He moved across the Daghistan rug to the table beside the wing chair, choosing a Caliente Puro from the cigar box. He pointed with this to a pack of cards spread out on the table. "That's a Spanish deck, for monte. It hasn't got any eights, nines, or tens. They've been worn down with handling. A man doesn't usually like a game that much unless he's pretty good." He bit off the end of the cigar, pointing it to the decanter beside the cards. "Smells like Old Kentucky. The quality of that would indicate a refined approach, but the quantity of the liquor in the cabinet over there would indicate more than mere discrimination. As for the linguistics, a man who can read a language can usually speak it. Those books on the shelves are mostly in the original. The top of the binding on that Goethe, where a man would put his finger to pull it off the shelf, has been worn down farther than the majority of books. A man who pursues a poet to that extent can usually quote him." He lit the Puro, blew out the match, pointed it at the worn book of poetry lying beside the cards and whiskey on the table. "And isn't that Baudelaire's *Fleurs du Mal?*"

There were half a dozen members of the board of directors of Iderland, Incorporated in the room, and they shifted about with a nervous incredulity. Bederley shook his head in open admiration.

"Pinkerton's told me you were an excellent man. They are masters of understatement."

Grenard shrugged. "My job."

"Iderland's taste for monte was known to a very limited group of his acquaintances," said Bederley. "But that Mexican friend. You must be mistaken. I never heard of it. Did you, Harold?"

Harold Moss shook his head impatiently, but Grenard motioned to the fancy saddle hung on the wall, its silver-mounted cantle high and old-fashioned, the stirrups covered with laced *tapaderos*. "You don't find many white men sitting a Mexican tree kak by choice. *Compadre* signifies more than just a friend to a Mexican. There is no English equivalent of the word, really. A Mexican would give his life for a *compadre*. Or his saddle. It's not uncommon. That name carved into the leather beneath the horn. Modesto. I don't think it's the maker."

"This is so much poppycock," said Moss, unbuttoning his gray, single-breasted to stuff a hand impatiently in his pants pocket. "You have a detailed description of Iderland."

"Perhaps it will be necessary to recognize him by other means than physical appearance," said Grenard.

"A man doesn't change that radically in three months," said Bederley.

"Not without reasons," said Grenard.

Moss flushed angrily. "You're not following a criminal, Grenard. Iderland would have no reason to change his appearance. He did not go of his own free will."

"You admit you don't know why he disappeared," said Grenard.

"He was the president of Iderland, Incorporated," said Moss hotly. "The richest man in Texas. He had just consummated one of the biggest deals of his life and was in high spirits about it. On the day of his disappearance he had called a meeting of the board for the next Tuesday to complete plans for a vast expansion of the corporation. There was utterly no reason for a man in that position to wilfully drop out of sight. I dislike your implications, Grenard."

"I am merely considering a possibility, gentlemen," said Grenard. "When was he last seen?"

"In this room, by his manservant, reading the book you see on that table, at ten o'clock of the evening before he disappeared. When his valet came at nine the next morning with his coffee, Iderland was gone. His bed had not been slept in."

"Yet there was no sign of struggle," said Grenard.

"Are you still trying to . . . ?"

"Business." It came softly. "Iderland, Incorporated is a big corporation. Could there be some ramification . . . ?"

"We opened our books to you," said Bederley, containing a growing irritation with effort. "You had access to any files you needed. Our legal firm was at your disposal. You admit yourself you found nothing to indicate business trouble in any way. The corporation is running like a clock. Every subsidiary is doing better than anyone could expect. The whole organization, financially and industrially, is in the best shape it has known since it started."

"I had access to what files you wanted me to have access to," said Grenard. "As to the legal firm, why wasn't I allowed to interview Judge Forman?"

"He is no longer officially attached to the staff," said Moss. "Besides, he's a sick man."

"Is he?"

224

"What are you driving at, Grenard?" said Moss.

"That there is something here you have not told me," said Grenard, studying his cigar, "something so big and so bad it scares even you."

San Antonio in 1890 was becoming one of Texas' growing industrial centers. High turrets of the breweries loomed up over the riverbank, and the first cement factory west of the Mississippi was raising its smokestack north of town. To a man who had known it as a vivid, brawling, lusty cattle capital, this change was depressing, somehow. Or perhaps the session with the board of directors had affected Grenard more than he realized. Their strange, secretive attitude left a deep-seated irritation in him.

He turned his horse through the growing evening crowd of the Alamo Plaza into the livery stable across from the Menger Hotel where he was staying and stepped off the animal in the cool gloom of the great frame barn.

"Cartier?" His voice boomed in hollow echo through the building. A horse snorted somewhere back in the stalls. "Cartier?" he called again. Then he heard the movement behind him, and turned toward it.

"Cartier went over for a beer," said the woman. Then she bent forward, inhaling perceptibly. "Caliente Puro?"

"A Mexican cigar," he said. "You know it?"

A strange expression came into her face, and she did not answer the question. In the gloom, he got but a vague impression of her. Big, for a woman, almost as

225

tall as he was, with a rich abundance of hair in an upswept coiffure that added to her stature and a white moiré evening gown that outlined the Junoesque proportions of her figure.

"How much is Iderland, Incorporated paying you to find Joseph Iderland?" she said.

He managed to hide his surprise. "You have the wrong party," he said. "Insurance is my line. Occidental Life. I have a nice medium-income policy . . ."

"I haven't got the wrong party," she said. "You are Kelly Grenard, from the Pinkerton Agency."

"In that case," he said, "you should know that Iderland, Incorporated's fees goes to the agency, not me. I work on salary."

"They offered you a bonus if you found him. How much was it?"

"May I inquire as to your line?"

"I'll double Iderland, Incorporated's offer . . . if you see to it that you don't find him," she said.

"I thought there was a cocklebur under the saddle," Grenard told her, tapping ash from his Puro.

"Did they tell you two other men have already been killed trying to locate Iderland?" she asked.

He studied that a moment. "Perhaps the agency was informed. It never reached me."

"You have a reputation for singular mental attributes, Grenard," she said. "Use them now. No intelligent man would go into this thing so blindly."

"I also have professional ethics," he said. "I have yet to back out on any case assigned to me."

"Three times what they offered you."

He moved his head forward to get a look at her face, but she took a swift, surprised step back, and stood there ready to move farther. At first, he had thought the faint sound behind him was his horse. But it held something more deliberate than the restless movement of an animal. He put the cigar in his mouth and shifted his right elbow across in front of him so the movement of his arm would not be apparent from behind.

"Monte," said the woman.

"Don't pull anything," said a man from behind Grenard.

The detective had his hand beneath the lapel of his coat, and his fingers twitched in reflex action against the rosewood grips of his Smith & Wesson where it hung under his armpit in a shoulder sling.

"I'll give you a chance to reconsider," she said. "At four times what Iderland, Incorporated offered you."

"Why don't you want Joseph Iderland found?" he asked.

"You must realize your alternative," she said.

"Those other two men?"

"Whatever is necessary to render you incapable of going any further with your job will be done," she said.

She stood there a moment, waiting. He could see the moiré gleaming dully across the faint rise and fall of her breast. Then she turned and walked out.

For a moment, after she had left, Grenard seemed in a void. The swish of her skirt was swallowed in the dim, sporadic sounds of the plaza, and, although he had been aware of these sounds before, he could not hear them now. He had the sense of being suspended in a vacuum, waiting. All his involuntary functions had ceased.

Then it all came at once. The sounds from outside and the sounds from inside all burst upon his consciousness with the explosion of his movement. It started with the hissing, indrawn breath behind him. He threw himself forward and to one side bodily and the babble inundated him. The rattle of a carriage crossing the plaza and the muffled ring of a tinny piano in the lobby of the Menger Hotel and the clatter of a galloping horse coming in off Crockett Street. The grunt the man gave from missing his blow and the shrill whinny of Grenard's own horse as it reared up, spooked by the sudden violent movement.

"Get him, Six Beans. I missed him. Get him . . ."

Grenard had struck the ground rolling, and he came up against the clapboard wall of the office so hard the whole structure shuddered. He tried to rise and reach beneath his coat at the same time, but a blurred figure appeared above him, and a viciously swung kick caught him in the crook of his elbow, the boot's pointed toe tearing his arm away from beneath the coat. He saw the man shift his weight to bring the other foot into play, and flickering torchlight from the porch of the Menger Hotel across the plaza caught momentarily on gleaming spurs.

Forgetting his gun, Grenard rolled away from the wall onto his side and caught the man's leg, lurching on into it with all his weight. It upset the man, and he went backward with a shout. The one the woman had called Monte struck Grenard then, carrying him off Six Beans and back against the wall once more. He let himself go, with his knee up between them, and, when he struck the wall, Monte crashed in against him, fully catching that knee in the groin.

Grenard twisted violently from beneath the writhing man and lurched to his feet, stumbling away from the office wall. If he had come erect facing the opposite way, it would have caught him. But he had that glimpse of it coming at his head in a great, lethal arc, and once more threw himself to the ground, toward the other side of the aisle. It caught at his coat, ripping it, and then was gone. Crouched there in the shock of realizing how close he had missed being struck, he saw what it was. In order to get his baled hay into the loft, Cartier had rigged a hoist from an overhead rafter, a heavy hawser run through a pulley that ran along steel tracks. At the bottom end of the hawser was a huge cast iron hook, and it was what Six Beans had swung at him. The man had seen how it missed Grenard, and was jumping at him now. Grenard could not see what it was Six Beans held till the man dodged the back swing of the hook. Then dim light from those torches across the plaza ran in quick, silvery lines down the tines of the pitchfork. Grenard lurched with his body to the left.

"There!" roared Six Beans viciously, and lunged.

Grenard's move had been a feint. He had kept enough of his weight beneath him to shift back the other way from that lunge. He heard the tines plunge into the side of a stall with a ringing, metallic sound, and heard the man cry in pain as the force of meeting drove his hands down the splintery handle. Before Six

229

Beans had released his grip, Grenard whirled to catch him. He grasped the man's shirt with one hand, tearing him away from the stall in a half circle, his arm drawn back to strike. At that moment, Monte came in from behind. The man must have still been weak from that knee in his groin, for his flailing arms caught Grenard about the knees, knocking the detective into Six Beans, his head against the man's sweaty shirt front. Monte's weight carried all three of them out into the middle of the barn in a staggering, floundering bunch. Grenard was still up against Six Beans's chest with his face, when he felt the man shudder, and heard his scream of utter agony.

Six Beans's body went limp in Grenard's arms. He let go the man, fighting for his own balance, and Six Beans fell back, and Grenard saw what had happened. The hoist hook was no longer swinging. Six Beans had stopped it with his face.

Monte was still feebly clinging to Grenard's legs. Grenard took the man by his hair and tore him away. Then, standing there in the settling sawdust, his coat torn, breathing in a hoarse, gusty way, and still holding the man by his hair, Grenard panted.

"Now you tell me one thing, or I'll start that hook swinging again and hold you in front of it, too."

"I don't know," gasped Monte. "I just work for her. I don't know why she doesn't want Iderland found."

"Forget that," said Grenard. "All I want to find out is who that gorgeous creature was!"

230

CHAPTER
TWO

Georges Cartier was a huge, shuffling Frenchman, spilling over his belt a little, the soil of his trade on his blue jeans. He had groomed the best horses in America, and the effort of maintaining such a reputation in this hot, sleepy land left him in a grumbling, irascible mood most of the day.

"Ha, you lazy *pou!*" he was shouting at one of his Mexican stable boys. "Get back there and clean up number four. I never saw a more useless bunch of *lourdauds.* I don't know why I pay you. I have to do all the work myself anyway. I have . . ." — he looked up as Kelly Grenard came into the barn, and the mutation from scowl to beaming smile was made with an effort so distinct his whole body seemed to jerk with it — "ah, *M'sieur* Grenard. *Bonjour.* What a fine day for a ride." The smile faded a little, and he inclined himself toward the detective. "What was that last night, *m'sieur?* I heard something . . ."

"Nothing." Grenard dismissed it with a movement of his hand. "A mistake. You went out for a beer?"

"Not beer, *m'sieur!*" exclaimed Cartier in a hurt tone. "*Vin.* Always, before closing, I slip across to the Menger for one glass. Just a touch." He measured it with a thick, dirty thumb and forefinger. "I always leave Portola to watch. But he is such an irresponsible *pou*. He must have left early. If I could only . . ."

"Never mind," said Grenard, moving back to the stall in which they kept his animal. "You've been here a good many years, Cartier. Know the town pretty well."

"*Oui*," said Cartier, shambling along beside him. "A hostler is like a bartender. He is brought into contact with a very representative cross-section of a town. The great and the small, the good and the bad, the politicians, the professional men, the ranchers. If they don't stable their horses here regularly, they bring them here when they're staying overnight in town. If they don't stable them, they rent them. You see?"

"Ever stable any of Forman's animals?"

"The judge. Oh, *mais oui*. Ten, twelve years ago, when he was not so rich and did not have his own stables here in town. Steady now, Sable, steady . . ."

Cartier slipped in beside Grenard's black mare to unhitch her and lead her out. Grenard took a cigar from inside his coat, biting off the end, spitting it out.

"You wouldn't know him well enough to get me an *entrée?*" he said.

Cartier looked at him across the gleaming back of the mare, put his tongue in his cheek meditatively, shook his head. "Getting *entrée* to Judge Forman is like trying to take the vinegar out of a roan."

"I know," said Grenard. "I've tried."

Cartier shrugged, reaching for the saddle blanket. "He is exclusive, to say the least. Like Joseph Iderland. They are two of a kind. Or were. Was it important?"

232

Grenard put a ten-dollar bill on the animal's rump. "Rather."

Something sly was in Cartier's smile. "There might be a way," he said, looking at the money. "Not many people would know about it, of course."

"Of course," said Grenard. "A hostler is like a bartender."

"*Oui*," said the man. He slung Grenard's custom-made kak onto the horse. "This mare has Quarter blood in her, *non*? Have you ever raced her?"

"Never seen anything could beat her on a quarter mile yet," said Grenard.

"I'm not telling you this, of course. If it were to be heard, that I used my professional offices in this way, certain pressures might be brought to bear ..." He bent to pull the hair cinch beneath Sable's belly. "However, through my association with Judge Forman in earlier years, it came to my attention that he had a passion for horses the way some men have a passion for women. For the past years he has been breeding Quarter horses out on his ranch in Bandera County. It has also come to my attention that, once a week, he and a few other of the gentry who are interested in Quarter racing meet to match their animals. The *canaille* are not at all welcome, of course. No one but the elite are even supposed to know where these races take place. However, if one of the *canaille* should happen to be riding in Bexar County at the northern tip of Medina Lake, where the Comanche Hills and the Greens run parallel for several miles, and he had a horse with as much Quarter blood in it as this one ..." He tugged the latigo tight with a grunt, dropped the stirrup leather to look across the saddle at Grenard. "I am not telling you this, of course."

The Mexicans called the bluebonnet *el conejo* because its white tip looked like a rabbit's tail. And in early spring like this, they carpeted the fields west of San Antonio. Grenard had taken it easy in his ride from the city to Lake Medina, and had camped in a fold of Comanche Hills two nights before the men appeared in the flats below. He knew where Forman's ranch was from here, but had tried twice before, unsuccessfully, to see the judge.

That second morning in the Comanches he was dropping down the slope to the creek to get water for his coffee when, through a break in the timber, he saw movement in the valley below. He went on back with the water and boiled his coffee and fried his bacon, knowing that, if they were racing, it would last several hours. Then he saddled up and dropped his rested black down into the flats. It was a small crowd, with perhaps two dozen horses, gathered near a shack that looked like a line cabin. A small cedar-post corral stood behind it.

He halted in some hackberries growing on the lip of a gully behind the shack and, hidden by them, waited. There were a bunch of dusty hands scattered through the horses, one man holding four saddled animals, another sitting a bronco that was obviously not going to race. As Grenard watched, a group of gentlemen in frock coats and clean hats came from the cabin, several of them still holding cups of coffee, laughing and talking. One portly figure in a black-tailed coat and a pair of cream-colored trousers tucked into jackboots that held a careful, gleaming polish dominated the group. His spurs rattled ostentatiously and there was something cultivated about the sonorous geniality of his voice. Grenard decided this was Judge Felix Forman.

"I tell you, gentlemen," he was saying, "Running Red is the horse I been looking for all my life. There ain't anything in the world can match him on the quarter. He's got more vinegar than a roan and more getaway than a jack rabbit and more bottom than my old colored mammy herself . . ."

The laugh this brought was polite and genteel, and drew a small, satisfied grin to the judge's mouth. *Touché*, thought Grenard, *you pompous old* . . . But never mind. There were weaknesses in a man you worked on. Already they were beginning to catalogue themselves in Grenard's mind. The pomposity. The smugness. It probably hadn't been pricked in a long time. It would undoubtedly be ripe for it.

They were gathered at a spot between two hackberries that was apparently the starting line. The judge mounted a big bay as fat and pompous as he was and, followed by the majority of other gentlemen, trotted off down the flats. Then four of the cowhands came over from the larger group of horses held at the corrals, each of them leading a saddled animal. Grenard spotted a small, short-coupled chestnut with a ruddy tinge to the coat across its prodigiously muscled rump, and decided that was Running Red. One of the hands was picking up the empty coffee cups the men had set down; several of the gentlemen had remained behind to oversee the mounting of the four Quarter animals. The judge and his retinue had reached the finish line now, still visible a quarter mile down the flats. Grenard began tensing up purposefully, and Sable felt it, and he could see the excitement prick her ears up.

"All right, Toby?" asked one of the men out there.

"All right," said the man on Running Red, and the four Quarter animals were standing in a line.

"All right, Sable," said Grenard, and gave her the hardest boot in the flanks that she had felt in a long time.

He was halfway to the four horses before the gun went off. Running Red was a jack rabbit, sure enough. The chestnut seemed to bounce out ahead of the other three. But Grenard was already in a headlong gallop, and he quartered in across the starting line that way, through the surprised, shouting group of men, leaving them standing behind in an instant. One of the Quarter horses had made a bad start, and Sable overtook and passed it before the animal had reached its full run. Then Grenard was after the other three, bunched ahead, with Running Red in the lead. The one invariable distinction of these horses bred for the quarter mile was the heavily muscled rump, which gave them their incredible getaway and their driving power for that short distance. Grenard could see the churning, writhing ripple of rump and quarters ahead of him, slowly drawing closer as Sable narrowed the gap. There was nothing like an excited horse to run away with a man, and he shouted wildly to excite his own horse as well as the others. Grenard drew up to those rumps. Running Red was in the lead now, and the other two were neck and neck, directly behind, with a ten-foot space between them. Grenard booted Sable right down that space.

"Sable!" he bellowed. "Sable!" He made it look as if he were fighting to pull her down. The man on either side of him looked around in surprise, and it caused them to be thrown off their rhythm. Grenard was aware of a definite break in their speed as he pulled through between them. He was directly behind Running Red now, and the finish line was ahead. Grenard got a blurred impression of the sweated red hide ahead of him and the deafening clatter of hoofs and the vague group of figures sitting their animals to one side of the finish line. He didn't try to pull around Running Red. He let Sable pound right up on the animal's rump till her nose bobbled into the chestnut's quarters. It was just a touch, on the off side, where the other men couldn't see, but it was enough to throw the red horse out of stride. When they went over the finish line, they were neck and neck.

"Whoa, Sable, whoa!" shouted Grenard, loud enough for them to hear him, fighting the black mare down. It took longer for the men to halt Running Red, and by that time Judge Forman and the other men had cantered up to the detective. "Couldn't stop her." Grenard grinned, patting the neck of his fretting mare, still excited and hard to hold from the run. "Get her near a race like that and you just can't hold her down. I was coming off the slope when that fellow shot the gun off. I hope I didn't break up anything. She's just too much horse, sometimes . . ."

"Break up anything!" Forman's face was flushed excitedly. "How much do you want for her?"

"What do you mean?" said Grenard.

"What do I mean? You came in from behind those four horses, man, we saw you from here. You came in behind, after they'd already started, and yet you passed the three and caught up with Running Red to boot!"

"He nosed me from behind." The rider had finally pulled Running Red down and cantered back and he spoke angrily. "He nudged Red in the rump and threw him off . . ."

"What does it matter?" shouted Forman. "The black would have passed Red anyway in another ten yards."

"He was yelling and shouting all the time," offered another Quarter rider. "It threw us all off."

"Of course, he was," said Forman. "We heard him. Trying to hold her down. Imagine that. Pulling her down and still she almost matched Red. Coming up from behind and trying to stop her all the way and still she almost won. I've got to have that horse, young man. How much?"

Grenard pulled a handkerchief from his pocket, mopping at his dusty face. "You take me by surprise, sir. I'll have to think it over."

"Of course, of course." The excitement had settled in the judge now and his officious condescension was returning. "We'll go back and have a drink in the lodge and talk it over. Judge Forman's my name. Felix Forman."

"Kelly's mine."

When they got inside the cabin, Grenard saw why the judge had alluded to it as a lodge. It was no line shack. It was furnished sumptuously with a lush Empire Ambusson on the pegged floor and a white bear rug before a great stone fireplace. The walls were hung with heads of bear and elk and deer and a great cabriole-legged walnut dinner table stood in the middle of the room. One of the cowhands had even donned a starched apron to serve the gentlemen. Forman took a silver-inlaid cigar box off the mantel, passing it around.

"No, thanks," Grenard told him. "Have my own."

Forman started to turn away, but his glance caught on the cigar Grenard produced. He took his time about biting off the end, spitting it into the fireplace, lighting up. Then he allowed himself to notice the judge's attention.

"Haven't seen one of them in a long time," said Forman. There was a strained look to his lips.

"Caliente Puros?" said Grenard casually. "I guess you're right. Not many smoke them. Friend of mine got me going on them. You ought to try one. Odd bite, but good when you get used to it."

"A friend of yours?" Forman's tone was hollow.

"Felix Forman. *Judge* Felix Forman?" It just seemed to have crossed Grenard's mind, and he looked up in mild surprise. "You must know him. He spoke of you. Joe Iderland."

Grenard found himself standing in a silence so abrupt and so complete it held the shock of a blow. One of the men had been in the act of lighting his cigar, and he stood there staring at the detective till the match burned his fingers, and he dropped it with a curse. Forman's face had the pale, nauseous texture of white dough.

"Gentlemen." It was the judge, bringing himself to speak, holding out his arms in an inclusive, paternal gesture. "Gentlemen, for the first time in my life, I'm forced to be inhospitable. If you will excuse me. Perhaps . . . the horses. I'll have George serve the liquor out there. Whatever you want. Just ask for it. If you will only excuse me . . ."

"Of course, Felix," said someone, and the others murmured politely, passing around Grenard uncomfortably. When they were outside, Forman closed the door and stood there a moment with his back to it, looking at Grenard.

"He sent you?" said the judge finally.

"Joe?" said Grenard. He smiled deprecatingly. "You know, a lot of people might think he had gone to that place in Colorado he was supposed to have bought. Nobody knew exactly where it was, but the rumor . . ."

The snort came out of Forman spasmodically. "Of course, they think that. Why do you think we started the rumor? Nobody knows he came from New Mexico. Nobody would ever guess he . . ."

The judge raised himself with distinct effort. Suspicion narrowed his little eyes. The floridity was returning to his face now, the pomposity coming back.

Sticking his belly out, he paced stiffly to the fireplace. Turning from there to face Grenard, he spoke gruffly. "I don't think you came from Joe, Kelly. The cigars mean nothing. I think I'll have you arrested."

"He could have sent Modesto," said Grenard.

Again it was that way. Like a pricked balloon. Forman's smug ostentation left him in a palpable flood. "Modesto?" It held a vague, frightened awe.

Grenard's faint smile was lopsided. "Not many men know of him, do they, Felix? When Joe and I and Modesto broke up, Modesto had a hard time deciding whether to give me that saddle, or Joe. I finally got Modesto's horse. A black stud."

Forman made an obscene gesture with one fat hand. "Then . . . Sable . . . ?"

"Yes. The stud's get. Bred the stud to a Quarter mare in Abilene. Modesto always ran a good horse."

Grenard was seeing the judge with a new understanding now. He had known a weakness lay beneath the man's ostentation. But with all the smug, condescending haughtiness wiped away, the man's true character was revealed to a greater extent than Grenard had hoped for. The lines of his face were soft and flaccid. His mouth worked abortively. His eyes shifted before the detective's gaze. From the beginning now, a picture of Joseph Iderland had been forming in Grenard's mind, and, looking at Judge Forman, he realized something he had only guessed at before.

"It's funny you knew about Modesto," Grenard told him. "You weren't really close to Joe. You knew him better than his other business associates, you probably spent more time with him than anyone did, yet you weren't really his friend."

"I was the closest friend Iderland ever had," flamed Forman. "Modesto? He was nothing but a saddlemate Joe rode with a couple of years in his youth. You? What do you know of friendship . . . ?"

"Did he ever throw monte with you?"

Again it stopped Forman. The flaring return of the bombastic pomposity had been a synthetic effort anyway. He moved to the table and sat down heavily. His hand trembled as he poured himself a drink.

"All right," he said defeatedly. "So Joe never played cards with me. Who *did* he play cards with? Always shuffling and dealing and working with them that way. You'd think he was an old short card man just in off the *Mississippi Queen*. But whoever saw him play?"

"He threw monte with his friends."

Forman struck the table. "He didn't have any friends."

"Then why did you try to convince everybody you were his friend?"

Forman didn't answer. He tried to toss his drink off neatly. It caused him to cough and spew the liquor all over the table.

"The reflected glory, maybe?" said Grenard. "Quite a distinction, being the only intimate of a man as rich and influential as that."

"What do you want?" Forman had turned to him in a dull desperation. "What did Joe send you for? How much does he want?"

Grenard saw he had him on the run, and set out to pump as much as he could from the man while it lasted. "He wants to know just where you stand in this thing, Judge."

"What thing?"

"You know."

"I don't, I don't. All I know is one of those maps Joe made in Eighteen Seventy-Six has showed up again. We didn't know where it was. We would have destroyed it if we had. Perry Curdar escaped jail last March. Joe thinks it's him."

"Eighteen Seventy-Six," mused Grenard, tapping ash from his cigar to give his mind time to bring up the history of that year, and then he had it. "How many acres did the state of Texas appropriate for the building of a new capitol in Austin? Three million?"

"Yes," said Forman. "When they adopted the constitution of Eighteen Seventy-Six, the people appropriated three million acres of Public Domain to be used for building a new state capitol. Provision was made under this law for the surveying of the land. When the survey was approved, the Legislature by the Act of April Eighteenth, Eighteen Seventy-Nine authorized the appointment of commissioners to advertise for bids for the construction of the capitol building. The Eldorado Syndicate by their bid proposed to build the capitol for the three million acres of land, and in Eighteen Eighty won the contract, and the land was signed over to them in payment."

"Judge, Judge!" The hoarse shout came from outside, and the door shook with the violence of someone opening it. The man framed in the portal had to bend his shaggy red head to get through. The judge whirled angrily at the giant.

"Yellowstone . . ."

"That's him, that's him," the huge man interrupted Forman.

"Kelly?"

"Is that what he said his name was?" thundered Yellowstone. "Kelly. Sure. That's his name, all right. Kelly Grenard. He's the one I kicked off your place twice before when he tried to reach you at the house. He's the Pinkerton man they hired to find Joseph Iderland!"

CHAPTER
THREE

The last light of sunset silhouetted the scrub oaks, marching up the ridge of the hogback like a line of gnarled little old men, and somewhere to the west of the road, in the marshes formed by the northern tip of Medina Lake, a cinnamon teal was calling in his soft, husky squawk. The peace of it did not touch Kelly Grenard, however, as he sat Sable's easy kak. He was still filled with the tension of that scene back there in the lodge, and the sense that it was not yet finished. And there were the other considerations in his mind. Perry Curdar. The 1876 survey. One of those maps. Things to be fitted into the puzzle.

"Sable!" he hissed, catching himself as the black mare shied to one side. He drew her up, staring at the horseman sitting in the middle of the road ahead. He must have come down the slope and just appeared from the trees.

"This ain't the way to San Antonio," said Yellowstone.

Grenard moved in a little closer, his glance dropping to the man's hands. They were big, gnarled hands, trap scars marking their hairy backs, and they lay quiescent on the pommel, making no move toward the pair of huge Sharps dropping-block pistols thrust nakedly through the broad black belt about the giant's thick waist.

"Maybe I'm not going to San Antonio," said Grenard.

"Then I'll ride with you a piece," said Yellowstone, pulling his gelding about till it faced the same way Sable did. The horse hadn't yet shed its winter coat and was as shaggy as the man. "Lucky you wasn't killed back there," said Yellowstone.

"Is the judge capable of that?" said Grenard dryly.

That amused Yellowstone, and he emitted a guttural chuckle. "I was expecting him to ask me. He was that mad."

"Do you think you could?"

"Ain't never met a man yet I couldn't."

"Apparently."

Yellowstone chuckled again. "You're a purty edgy varmint. Wormed a lot of news out of the judge, didn't you? I could see you'd worked on him. Not many men would be able to prick Felix that way."

"How long have you been his personal bodyguard?"

"What makes you think I am?" said Yellowstone.

"I'd say it's been ten years since you skinned a beaver."

The giant looked involuntarily at his hands. "You read sign like an Indian. Them trap scars is pretty old, ain't they? Maybe I'm retired."

"From trapping, anyway," said Grenard. Yellowstone let those little blue eyes shift around beneath his shaggy red brows till they settled on Grenard, bright and gleaming with the suspicious wariness of a trapped animal. "Haven't seen anything like those pistols since I was a kid," said Grenard. "Got Lawrence pellet primers on them?"

Grenard felt a dim satisfaction at the surprise the abrupt transition caused in Yellowstone. The giant's eyes were stupidly blank for a moment, then they followed Grenard's gaze down to the pistols in his belt. Grenard could almost see the thought working in Yellowstone's mind. Then the man must have decided this could bear no possible relation to what Grenard had been pumping Forman about.

"Yeah. They have at that. Breech-loading. Nobody'd trust 'em when they first came out in Eighteen Forty-Eight. Operating the breech block with an underlever like that on a rifle didn't seem right in a handgun, somehow." Yellowstone raised his head sharply. That angry suspicion was in his eyes again, like a child who thought he was being laughed at but could not be sure.

They rode in silence for a while. Finally they reached the end of Comanche Hills and crossed some flats that dropped down to the sluggish Comanche Creek that flowed on past them into Medina Lake. Grenard halted Sable in the sand near the water, swinging down.

"I'm camping here."

"How about we make some coffee before I go on?" said Yellowstone.

Grenard looked at those bright little eyes again. He was facing Yellowstone across the back of his horse, and he unlashed his sougan and dropped it, and pulled the latigo free of the cinch ring, hearing the soft *click* of the dropping cinch. Then he lifted the kak off and lowered it to the ground.

"You build a fire," he said. "I'll water my mare and fill the pot."

Going down to the creek, he walked directly in front of Sable, keeping the horse back of him all the time. There was a deep cut bank that dropped him below the surface of the sand upon which Yellowstone was gathering wood for the fire. He could hardly see above the bank while he dipped the rusty coffee pot into the water.

Yellowstone had begun kicking around amid the dry underbrush of mesquite. When he had gathered enough wood, he piled it in the sand. Grenard saw the flare of the match. Anyone lighting the fire from this side would have been silhouetted by the blaze. Yellowstone lit it from the far side. It drew that lopsided smile vagrantly across Grenard's lips.

He walked back with Sable. The fire blinded him to any detail of Yellowstone, sitting back of the blaze, but he could have seen what movement the man made. He unrolled his sougan and took out a paper sack of coffee. Then he put the pot on the fire. He picketed Sable off to the left.

Now he had become accustomed to the flames enough to see Yellowstone's face. Firelight glinted in the giant's green eyes, watching Grenard. He realized those eyes watching must have been watching him like that from the time they dismounted. It gave Grenard a faint, constricted feeling in his chest. It was the first tension he had felt.

He lowered himself opposite Yellowstone, sitting cross-legged in the sand the way the mountain man sat. It was an effort to keep his eyes from dropping to Yellowstone's great hands where they lay in his lap, hairy and scarred against the greasy buckskin of his leggings. Water began to hiss in the pot. Yellowstone's face was impassive. Only his eyes moved, glittering. A wolf started to howl from some yonder ridge. Then it stopped again. The hiss became more audible as the water came to a boil.

"We drink it from the pot?"

Yellowstone's voice startled Grenard. He realized how tense he had become. *Might as well have it now*, he thought, *as any time*. He got up and turned toward his sougan as if to get the tin cup lying partly revealed in the duffle. He was faced fully away from the man. He bent over and reached slowly for the cup with his left hand.

There would be a sound; they were so close. He knew there would be some kind of sound. He stayed that way, feeling the flesh tighten about his eyes as the little muscles of his face drew up with tension. *All right, damn you, all right*, he thought, and then could stand it no longer, and whirled back with the cup in his hand.

Yellowstone sat without expression, his big hands in his lap.

Grenard took the two steps back to the fire and lowered himself over the pot, watching the giant. He got a bandanna from his pocket and folded it several times to protect his hand. Then he took the pot off the fire and allowed it to stop boiling before pouring the coffee. The spout of the pot touched the tin cup, and Grenard was surprised to hear it rattle from the trembling of his hand. He jerked the pot away from the contact.

He caught the faint flicker in Yellowstone's eyes. It filled him with a stab of anger. With a bitter deliberation, he set the pot down and handed the cup across the low flames to the giant. Yellowstone took it, eyes meeting Grenard's over the top.

"So black it stains the cup," he said, and then threw it in Grenard's face.

After expecting the man to do it while his back was turned, Grenard was taken completely off guard. Both of them still had their hands stretched out. With the scalding coffee blinding him, and his own shout of pain ringing in his ears, he did the only thing possible. He threw himself aside.

The deafening boom of a gun drowned all other sounds, and then he was rolling through the sand and coming up on his back with the hand already beneath his coat. He pawed at his eyes with his free hand and yanked the Smith & Wesson free of its sling and opened up all at once. He only had a blurred impression of Yellowstone beyond the fire, and he had fired the third time before he heard the heavy grunt and the solid, fleshy sound of a falling body. He got to his hands and knees, panting hoarsely with the violent action and with the pain of his scalded face. Blinking his eyes, he rose and stumbled past the fire, dropping to his knees beside the gigantic frame stretched in the sand.

Yellowstone must have drawn one pistol at a time. The first one lay in the sand a few feet away, fired. The second gun was still gripped in the man's huge paw, cocked. Grenard had thought, at first, that it was his last bullet that had hit Yellowstone. He saw now that all three of them had struck the man squarely, one after the other, and realized it took that much to drop the trapper. Then he became aware the man's eyes were open.

"Why didn't you do it that first time, damn you?" he said. "I gave you the chance."

"You expected it then," said the man huskily. "I knowed you did. You turned your back deliberate to give me the chance. That coffee took you by surprise. I would 'a' had you if you'd waited one more second before you rolled . . ."

"Wait a minute, you can't die yet!" Grenard shouted at him, jerking him by the shoulder. "Not till you tell me why Judge Forman sent you after me."

"I couldn't do it back at the lodge, with all them men there."

"I don't mean that. Why doesn't Forman want Iderland found?"

"Curdar," said Yellowstone. "He's out of jail."

"Who is Curdar?" Grenard asked him.

Yellowstone's great shaggy head rocked back and forth deliriously. "Curdar? Sure. It wasn't really murder. Curdar had his gun out and three slugs into Moran before Moran could take a breath. But Moran drew first. Curdar was going to petition the Supreme Court of the United States about the Deaf Smith Strip. They couldn't have that. It had already caused too big a smell. So they sent Moran. Moran failed, but Curdar got murder. Twenty years."

"They?" said Grenard, shaking him. "Who are they?"

"The money!" Yellowstone reared up against him spasmodically, then dropped back, breathing heavily. "He was supposed to establish a trust fund for the boy." The giant's voice was barely audible now. "Instead, he thought he'd feather his own nest first. Invested in Ojibway Oil. Didn't know Iderland, Incorporated was going to buy it out. Now Ojibway belongs to Iderland, Incorporated, and it'll crash with all the rest."

"Boy? What boy? Yellowstone? Can you hear me? You haven't told me yet. Why didn't Forman want me to find Joseph Iderland?"

CHAPTER
FOUR

It was spring in New Mexico. White-stemmed aspens were budding into new leaves along cut banks turned to chocolate mud by the roaring yellow freshets. Hummingbirds sucked at horsemint along the trails and beaver emerged from their lodges to wet their timber slides. Above the aspens, cottonwoods turned their greening foliage to the sun, and the vagrant gleam of white sheep was visible momentarily on the high peaks.

Some of the sleek tallow on Sable's flanks had melted off with the long ride, but she looked the better for losing the weight as she dropped down from higher timber to Ute Creek. It was several weeks since Grenard had left Yellowstone back there in a shallow grave on Comanche Creek. Now he was following the doubtful lead Judge Forman had given him.

It had been a discouraging quest. He did not want to ask any direct questions, or brand himself as a man seeking Iderland, and nowhere had he been able to unearth any information regarding any past connections Iderland might have had in this section. His discouragement was tempered by the soaring sense of well-being that filled him. His face was ruddy with sunburn, and, like Sable, he had been fined down by the long ride. As he turned the black mare parallel with the swollen creek, seeking a ford, a dim sound came from the trees on the opposite slope. At first he took it for the wind. Then, as it grew, the caution his profession had bred in him caused Grenard to rein the horse back into the white-stemmed aspens, and, screened by them, he waited there.

The noise became distinguishable now — the rattling crash of chokeberry brush burst by the passage of a heavy body. It came on, and the ground began to shudder faintly. Sable stirred restlessly, raising her head. Grenard gave a yank on the reins that arched her neck and shoved her nose down against her chest, aborting her whinny.

The first one crashed through the greening brush on the opposite bank, shaggy mane flying, eyes white and spooked. It was a big roan shedding his winter coat, and he plunged without hesitation into the roaring creek, disappearing completely for a moment beneath the yellow, churning water, his head bobbing up finally, swept downstream in his struggle to swim across. Others followed him, bursting from the aspens and running headlong into the creek. Then a rider appeared on the tail of the last one, rearing his horse up in the air on the very edge of the cut bank.

A second rider appeared, and they milled around on the bank, shouting at each other and gesticulating. Over the roar of the creek, Grenard could not hear their voices. They wheeled their animals and mushed down the opposite bank through that chocolate mud, following the horses that were being swept downstream. The roan had managed finally to reach the near bank, and, as he heaved up out of the water, Grenard saw the brand on his shaggy hip. Lazy M. It catalogued itself in his mind with no volition from himself. A man got that way in this business.

Then a third rider burst from the trees across the swollen creek. He had a Winchester in his hand, and, as soon as he saw the other two men farther down, he turned his horse and broke into a sloshing run down the muddy bank after them. As the horse wheeled, its rump was brought into view. Grenard saw the brand there matched that of the other horses.

The pair of riders had halted at a spot where the creek turned, sweeping the swimming horses into the bank there on the same side that they had left. Then he saw one of the men pull a saddle gun from its boot and begin levering. The gushing clatter of the creek drowned the sound of the shots, but the puffs of smoke were plainly visible. It must have been the third or fourth one that caught the horse of the third rider. The animal stumbled in its run and then went down on its forelegs, pitching the man over its head as he plunged into the dirty, brawling water.

Most of the horses had been swept back onto solid ground at that turn now, and the other two riders had wheeled to drive them on down the cañon in a wild run. Grenard saw the man who had been pitched into the river bob up in the middle of the current, his hat following him on the yellow turbulence twenty feet behind. He was fighting crazily, and Grenard booted

Sable out in the open, running her along the bank till she was parallel to the man.

"Don't fight!" he screamed. "Let it sweep you onto that neck the way it did the horses. Fighting will keep you right out in the middle. Don't fight it, you fool . . ."

He could not make himself heard over the roaring water, and the man was wild with panic anyway, flailing at the mucky surface with his arms. The neck of mud reached out toward him, but he was too far gone to let himself be swept into it. Choking and gasping, his open-mouthed, white face turned upward in spasmodic panic, he was swept on by.

Grenard touched Sable's flanks with his heels again, sending her into a gallop on down the bank till he was ahead of the drowning man. He rode on till he came to the trunk of a small aspen that had been uprooted somewhere on the upper slopes and had been swept down to lodge on the bank here. He jumped off Sable, dropping the reins over her head, and shoved the aspen out into the current, sweeping his flat-topped Stetson off onto the ground as he surged out after the tree trunk. Kicking and flailing, he managed to get himself out into the powerful suction of that middle current. He felt a terrible panic clutch at him.

Fighting it with all his will, he turned to stare at the saffron turbulence behind him. The man was not in sight, and for a moment Grenard knew an awful fear that the fellow had gone on by. Then something resilient was thrown heavily against him by the current, and he felt hands clawing his legs. Still clinging to the aspen trunk with one arm, he reached down and pawed blindly in the water, finally getting a handful of the man's hair. He yanked up and pulled a face into view, more boy than man, the smooth cheeks dead white. He was close enough now to hear dimly the hoarse retching sounds the boy made trying to get his breath.

Then he began fighting Grenard again. Grenard tried to stop his struggles and hold him at the same time, and it caused him to lose his grip on the aspen. He was underwater, gasping and choking in a spasm he had no control over. His lungs were filled with water and he bobbed to the surface, filled with that awful, suffocating panic. Fighting for air, Grenard struck wildly at the boy as he fought to throw his arms around the detective's neck. Grenard could get no leverage for the blow, and the clutching hands were on him again, the boy's weight pulling him under. A rage swept in with his panic, and he sucked in all the air he could before going under again, and, without fighting the boy beneath the water, pulled out his Smith & Wesson. Then, as deliberately as he could, he set about freeing himself before his air gave out.

With the water in his lungs, he wanted to cough, and it was hell fighting that. Finally he got his left arm levered across the boy's neck, shoving him back till the boy had to release him. Tumbled and twisted by the current, smashing into rocks, buffeted by branches and débris, Grenard finally found the surface. He let his breath out in an explosive gasp, coughing desperately, trying to breathe again. Then, in that last instant before he went down again, as the boy clawed once more for a hold, Grenard lifted the gun and struck with all his strength.

The boy's body collapsed, swept limply into him by the current. Grenard put his gun away, placed one arm beneath the boy's armpits, and then quit the fight. He let the current sweep the two of them on down, only coming to the surface when he had to breathe. Even that would not have lasted very long. There were some moments when the suction carried him so far under he thought he would never come back up. Time and time again it held him down and the desire to breathe almost won out.

Then they were swept into another branch, and Grenard caught at that. It was large enough to hold the two of them on the surface. Finally the creek made another turn that took them close enough to shore for Grenard to battle his way in. He staggered across the viscid mud onto solid earth, half carrying the boy, half dragging him, then threw himself down in utter exhaustion.

When he could hardly find the strength to rise, he stumbled around till he found a large boulder, and dragged the boy over to it, laying him across, belly down, and rolling the water out of him the way he would have on a barrel. Dripping water off his hair, shirt soggy and mucky, panting in a weak, hoarse way, Grenard worked over the boy for half an hour before he saw signs of life. The young man rolled off the boulder and retched, then he lay, face down, a long time before turning his eyes up to Grenard.

"Thanks," he said weakly.

Grenard made a vague motion downstream. "Those bad hats. Running off your horses?"

"Yes." Even in his exhaustion, the boy's voice held a clipped precision that did not fit with this country, somehow. "They've been working on our herds quite a while now. Thought we had them trapped." He sighed heavily. "At least, I got close enough to see who it was this time. Now we don't have to wait around for them to make another raid on our horses before chasing them. We can swear out a posse and make New Mexico the hottest place they ever unsaddled in."

"Who was it?" asked Grenard.

"He's worked this section before," said the boy. "Should have known it was him. Modesto Obispo."

CHAPTER
FIVE

Built more than a century before Columbus discovered America, Pecos had been, in the 1300s, one of the largest Indian pueblos in New Mexico, its immense communal dwellings capable of housing over 1,000 families. It was known by its Tewa name of Cicuye when Coronado discovered and conquered it in 1540. During the ensuing centuries, however, war with Apaches wiped out most of its manpower, and smallpox caused it to be abandoned in 1838. Hunkered down now on a rise overlooking the village, Kelly Grenard felt the eerie spell its moonlit ruins held.

The boy Grenard had saved from drowning was in no shape to travel, but he had assured the detective that he was only one of half a dozen Lazy M hands staked out along Ute Creek in an attempt to trap the horse thieves, and that, drawn by the shots, the other Lazy M men would undoubtedly find him. With this assurance, Grenard had left him there and gone back to get Sable, knowing this was a chance he would probably never get again. Exhausted and beaten as he was, he had forced the black mare hard on the trail left by the two men. Evidently scared off by the appearance of the boy and indications of other Lazy M hands in the region,

Modesto and his saddlemate had abandoned the horses at the mouth of the cañon.

In the wet spring earth, however, the trail of their two ridden horses was visible in the first mile or so of their ride away from Ute Creek. They had made the mistake of starting to hide their tracks on a top land, for, although the trail petered out and Grenard would not have been able to follow farther if he had been in a valley, he had access here to a ridge that overlooked a whole range of foothills, and, sitting the crest for a few moments, he soon spotted movement far below that proved to be the two men.

Through afternoon and night, keeping them in sight, he had followed the riders past Glorietta Mesa to Pecos, where, from this rise, he had seen them unsaddle their horses in the ancient village. He waited till they had their kaks off and had hidden the animals in the ruined communal dwelling. Then he stepped back on Sable and turned her down into the trail running up the lower ground, making sure he was far enough away from the village for a good run before he booted her into a gallop.

The black mare's hoofs formed a clattering tattoo against the hard earth that rang back and forth through the hollow. She was wet and blowing by the time he rounded a low, cedar-covered swell and raced in among the ruins. He hauled Sable up to a vicious halt and stepped off, pulling the fretting mare into the shelter of a crumbling wall. Then he crept to the edge of the wall and peered around it, looking anxiously down the back trail.

"Damn that sheriff anyhow," he told the horse in a loud voice. "You'd think he'd have something better to do than scare honest men in the middle of the night. Getting so a man can't even stop a stage any more without there's a badge on it. Whoa there, mare, take it easy . . ."

"You having a little trouble, señor?"

Grenard whirled around as though surprised. The man facing him was taller than Grenard, with a hint of singular breadth to his stooped shoulders, his hips still slim despite the pot-gut shoving at his red sash. The strong, dominating planes of his face had degenerated into slack, grizzled furrows, and his neck was wattled like a turkey gobbler's.

"If the sheriff's down there, Modesto," said someone not visible behind him, "we better not palaver."

"Don't be a *simplón*, Jarales," the man with the *charro* jacket said. "Do you think our *amigo* here would be getting off his horse if the sheriff was still around? Where did you leave him, *señor?*"

"Last I saw him he was having a time through Glorietta Pass," said Grenard, and patted Sable's coat. "Never saw the lawman yet this little mare couldn't outrun."

The other man came farther out from the crumbled wall. He was lean and drawn and jumpy-looking, the whites of his eyes flashing as they shifted back and forth, never still in his narrow, gaunt head. The ivory butt of a big Remington protruded from the waistband of his pants in the middle of his stomach.

"*En la cárcel y en la cama conocemos los amigos nuestros,*" he growled. "In jail and in bed we know our friends."

262

"Don't be loco, Jarales," said Modesto, making an expansive gesture toward Grenard. "Can't you see he is one of the brotherhood? *Aquí, amigo*, if you are sure the sheriff has lost you, take your saddle off and join us. We have a place here, no?"

Grenard saw what they meant when he had unsaddled. Modesto ushered him into one of the outer chambers of the huge communal dwelling. There was a fire flickering in the *estufa* at one end of the room, a pile of dirty blankets in another corner, and a litter of dry bones and old tin cans covering the floor. Jarales sat down on his saddle where he had thrown it to one side of the fireplace, his eyes shifting across Grenard with suspicion. Grenard dropped his own kak, shoved his hat back, looking around. Then he let his glance settle on Modesto.

"The Modest Bishop," he said, and grinned.

Modesto failed to hide the pleasure that gave him. "You know me?"

"Who hasn't heard of you?" said Grenard. "From Mississippi to San Francisco. From the Red River to Mexico City. Billy the Kid, Clay Allison, Johnny Ringo . . ." — Grenard dismissed them with a deprecatory shrug, grimacing — "but Modesto Obispo" — he turned his hand over palm up in a grandiloquent way — "the man who has held the whole West gripped in deadly fear for the past twenty years . . ."

Modesto was grinning openly now. "Go on, go on, don't stop. *Dios*, I like to hear you talk. Tell me some more. What do they say in San Fran —?"

"Modesto!" snapped Jarales.

Modesto jerked perceptibly, and turned in surprise toward Jarales. Then he frowned, sniffling like a child caught in some misdeed, turning his eyes to the ground. "*Aí, caracoles*," he said, rubbing the toe of his broken-down Mexican boot in the dirt, "jus' because he talked that way about me . . ." He motioned uncomfortably with his hand. "All right. Sit down, *amigo*. We got some *mula blanca*."

But Grenard had touched his vanity. Sometimes it surprised him, the way his mind worked. The whole procedure had been automatic. He had seen those gaudy clothes and had started probing without any actual conscious sense of his mental processes. A man got that way, in this business. And now he had it. Modesto was vain.

But before he could use it, there was Jarales. Grenard turned his attention to the other man. Modesto had brought out several clay jugs of white wine. Jarales took one and sniffed it, grimacing.

"I got some better stuff," said Grenard, going to his sougan and getting his war sack out, fishing through boots and shirts till he found the bottle. He held it up so the label was toward Jarales.

"Old Kentucky?"

It had come out of Jarales spasmodically, and Grenard looked at the man, something else working in his mind now. They had given him a physical description of Joseph Iderland. Five foot ten, narrow shoulders, 150 pounds, yellow hair, eyes so blue they appeared black sometimes.

"You read English?" he asked.

Jarales shifted on his seat, face enigmatic. "Some." Grenard offered him the bottle, but Jarales did not hold out his hand. "I don't like it," he said tonelessly.

"Go ahead, it's better than that white wine," said Grenard.

"I don't like it." Without changing the inflection of his voice, Jarales managed to convey something deadly and final.

Shrugging, Grenard sat down, pulling out a pack of cards. "Monte?"

Jarales's head raised a bit. "It's not many *gringos* like that game."

"One *gringo* likes it," said Grenard.

The detective began to shuffle the pack of cards in his hand. Jarales had turned his head so the line of his unshaven jaw was silhouetted for a moment against the firelight. The stubble held a saffron tint. Somewhere outside a hoot owl began to mourn. Grenard cocked his head slightly, and murmured, as if to himself, with a wistful little smile:

Sous les ifs noirs qui les abritent,
Les hiboux se tiennent rangés . . .

"Your Mexican isn't very good," said Jarales.

Grenard looked up in surprise. "Surely you know Baudelaire."

"Did he ride with Billy the Kid?" asked Modesto.

"Hardly." Grenard was watching Jarales. "Somehow, I got the impression you would know."

"What was it?" said Jarales.

> **The owls that roost in the black yew**
> **Along one limb in solemn state,**
> **And with a red eye look you through,**
> **Are Eastern gods. They meditate.**

Grenard said it softly, blowing it out in a caressing breath. Modesto looked from Grenard to Jarales, frowning obtusely, and then let his gaze slip back to the detective.

"That's a *loco verso*," he said. "Did you ever hear '*Mi hijito de la Granada*' . . . ?" He laughed, slapping his thigh. "That is a better verse. Listen . . ."

"Cut?" said Grenard.

"*¿Qué?*" said Modesto, raising up in a startled way to throw his shoulders back. They must have been very broad once. Then he slumped forward again, his grin fading, and took the cards. "Sure, sure."

"Let's play poker," said Jarales.

"What's wrong with monte?" asked Grenard.

"I don't like it."

"Most Mexicans do," said Grenard.

"I don't."

"All right. Stud or draw?"

"It doesn't matter. High card for deal?" said Jarales.

They each drew a card, and Grenard got a king to their trey and five, and began to shuffle. "Why do you call yourself Jarales?"

"It's my name."

"It's a Mexican name," Grenard murmured.

"I'm Mexican," said Jarales.

"Are you?" said Grenard.

Jarales leaned forward. "What do you mean?"

"Listen, *señores*," said Modesto, "what is the matter? Can't we even have a little game of poker without a big fight? Come on, now. I'll open with two *pesos*."

Grenard glanced at his cards. "Raise two."

Jarales was pulling at the jug of *mula blanca* in a steady, purposeful way. Modesto took the first hand with two pair.

"I can see why they said anybody who played poker with you was either a millionaire or a fool," Grenard told him.

"*De veras*," said Modesto, grinning in a pleased way. "In truth, General Porfirio Díaz himself would not sit in on a game when I held a hand. But monte is my real talent. There was only one other man in the world who could beat me at that."

"Who was that?" said Grenard.

"Joe —"

"Modesto," said Jarales.

Modesto looked up once more in that surprise, then lowered his gaze uncomfortably from Jarales's, mumbling: "*Caramba*, all right, *caramba*."

The *mula blanca* was taking its effect on both men differently. Modesto grew happier and more loquacious as his inebriation progressed. Jarales grew silent and sleepy. Soon he was sitting slumped over, glazed eyes staring blankly at the ground, closing slowly till they were completely shut. He began to snore.

"Look at the *caracol*." Modesto giggled. "He's getting old. We was only in the saddle about twenty hours today. He never could match me, anyway. I could ride a week straight and still whip my weight in *tigres*."

"You should not judge poor ordinary human beings by yourself," said Grenard. "After all, you are Modesto Obispo."

"*Sí*," said the man, his chest swelling out. "I guess you are right."

"I have heard so many things about you," said Grenard. "The time you and *El Chivato* stood off Pat Garrett and a hundred-man posse for ten days down by the Llano Estacado. And the ride you and Joe Iderland made from Mexico City to Santa Fé in nine days, killing a hundred horses to do it. I think that was the best of all."

"*Sí*, me and Billy the Kid showed Pat Garrett a few things." He grinned. "*Pues*, you are right. That ride with Joe was the best. Those were the good days."

"Maybe they'll come again," said Grenard, shuffling idly. "Who else would Joe go to but the best friend he had in the world, a man even more famous than himself, the Modest Bishop."

"I guess you're right." Modesto was getting maudlin now, staring into the fire slack-lipped, his eyes filled with tears. "I never have a *compadre* like Joe. I told him we could ride down to Mexico and they'd never get him. I wouldn't let them get him. But he wanted to stay here, near his kid or something, I don't know, maybe it was that woman, he always had a soft spot in his heart for her even when she divorced him."

"Not many people know he was ever married," said Grenard, and then he tried something. "Why did she change her name?"

"Because the ranch was in her maiden name. Moraine. She didn't have the boy's name changed, though. She wanted him to have that inheritance. I told Joe he was crazy. They don't care nothing about him. The woman and that damn' boy. They wouldn't save him if somebody else came after him like those first two."

"You did a good job with them," said Grenard. "I guess nobody else could have gunned that tall one. He was pretty fast with an iron."

Once again he had touched the man's vanity.

"He's the only one I had to take on," said Modesto with a grandiloquent gesture. "Joe said there were two, but he's the only one I seen."

It had all been guesswork up to now, about the marriage, and the woman changing her name, and the tall one, but Grenard was getting more sure of his ground as he went along, seeing he was on the right trail. "Joe had changed his appearance pretty well," he hazarded. "I guess you were about the only one in the world who could have recognized him."

"Even the woman didn't recognize him," said Modesto proudly. "You'd think she would, being his wife, but she didn't. Twenty years will change a man, I guess. But I knew him. Even with all the weight he'd lost and dyeing his hair and growing a mustache that way, I knew it was Joe."

"Sure," said Grenard. "You couldn't miss Joe after all you'd been through together. That survey was the best thing he ever pulled, wasn't it? What really happened there? What's behind all this?"

"I don't think you'll ever find out, *amigo*."

Grenard was surprised to see that Modesto's mouth was closed. Then, slowly, he allowed his gaze to slide around to Jarales. The man held that ivory-handled Remington in such a position that Grenard was looking directly into its bore. The oily *click* of the cocked hammer beat into Grenard's eardrums with stunning shock. He felt his breath stop within him.

"Jarales." It came from Modesto in a whisper.

Jarales bent forward, the focus of his eyes changing. Grenard could hear it now, the sound of trotting horses up the same trail he had used. He took that moment, while Jarales's attention was off him. The cards made a fluttering sound, shooting from Grenard's hand. He saw Jarales's eyes jerk, trying to change their focus back to him, and then the fluttering cards hid them, inundating the man, and Grenard's boot knocked the gun upward as he rolled to one side.

Even with the violence of the action, he had to admire Jarales's presence of mind. Another man's gun would have gone off. Jarales must have hooked his thumb across the hammer. He jumped to his feet, playing cards dropping in a stream off his shoulders, trying to bring the gun back down. But Grenard threw himself at the man's legs, going in under the line of the gun, and his weight threw the man back against the wall so hard it shook, knocking flakes of adobe down on them in a shower.

"¡Vámonos, Jarales!" yelled Modesto, on his feet now, scooping up his saddle. "Forget about him, will you. They're too close."

270

Beating wildly at Grenard with the Remington, Jarales fought free, stumbling with his head down after Modesto. The older man had ripped a blanket aside on the wall to reveal the dark maw of a doorway leading farther into the communal dwelling. Grenard got to his feet, shaking his head, but the two men had already disappeared into the maze of rooms beyond. He was still standing in the doorway, staring after them, when the first horse crashed in the other door. They must have heard the sound of the struggle.

A second rider forced his animal in, ducking the beam of the low door, a Winchester in his hand, and, after him, a third. The brands showed boldly on the flanks of these animals. Lazy M. Then Grenard saw that the last horsebacker was a woman.

Firelight made it clearer than it had been in Cartier's stable. She wore a checkered flannel shirt now, instead of a white moiré gown, and a split-leather riding habit, and the chestnut hair hung in rich, wind-blown abundance down about her shoulders, instead of being swept up over her head. But her size was the same, and the Junoesque lines of her figure. Grenard bowed low, his voice mocking.

"Good evening, Missus Moraine. Or should I say Missus Iderland?"

CHAPTER
SIX

It was a tight little spread, set in a possessive fold of hills. A small creek rising from a spring on the upper slopes meandered down to pass within 100 feet of the house. There were two cedar-post corrals in good repair and the square block of an adobe bunkhouse squatting a few hundred yards away from the main building, which sprawled contentedly in the shade of venerable cottonwoods fat enough to make it obvious why they called the ranch Alamogordo. Monte Tennes was first to dismount in front of the flagstoned porch.

"I still think he was in with them horse thieves," he said sullenly.

"No, Monte," said Esther wearily, stepping off her horse. It had taken them four or five hours to ride from the Pecos ruins, and the weariness showed the age in her face for the first time. Back in San Antonio, the sound of her voice, her movements, her sense of hidden fire, all had left Grenard with the impression of a young woman, twenty-five or so. Now he added ten years to that and it still didn't change what she did to him. She waved her hand toward Six Beans. "Take the horse out, will you? My home, Grenard. I think we all need a little sleep."

272

The living room held the cool intimacy characteristic of these adobe-walled houses. The bedrooms were in the north wing, opening off a hall that led from the living room. Esther led down the hall to the last chamber, unlocking the great, pegged-oak door. The room had a musty odor and she swung open the shutters of the window, revealing a view onto the *placita*, which stood between the two wings of the house, a red-roofed well surrounded by greening willow trees.

"Why did you want to stop me in San Antonio?" he asked her, when they had entered the room.

"I'd rather not discuss it." She had paused by the huge four-poster, covered by the hand-woven spread they called a *colcha*, and she made a faint gesture about the room. "Used to be my husband's room. We've used it for guests since."

He studied her a moment, decided it would do no good to press anything now. "You must have been very young when you married him."

"Fifteen," she said.

He stood there, looking around the chamber. "I'm glad I've seen this, in a way. All the time I've been hunting Joseph Iderland, a conception of his personality has been forming in my mind, bit by bit, revealed to me by people who had been associated with him, the places he had been. It gives me a strange feeling sometimes. Like I was hunting someone I'd known intimately in the past."

She moved to the window, staring out into the patio. "I suppose his personality would make a deep

273

impression on you, even second-hand. He was a strange man. I thought he was lonely, at first. It took me a while to find out he wasn't really lonely. Self-confident would be better. There were so few people he was drawn to. The others he would make utterly no effort toward. I guess I was one of them. Our attraction was nothing more than physical. That's why I left him. I wanted something more than that out of marriage. We parted without any bitterness. You could never feel bitterness with him, no matter what he did. There was something so impersonal about everything he did, something so far removed. As long as I was with him, I never saw any evidence of emotion. But there must have been something. Modesto. You can't deny their friendship. And his son, Carl. If there's anything Joe loved in the world, it was his son. It's been a continual fight through the years for me to keep the boy." Her head raised slightly, as if she realized the release she had allowed herself. She turned toward him, a delicate flush of anger tinting her cheek. "You'd better get some sleep. I'll call you for dinner."

"Esther," he said. "You tell me the boy whose life I saved up in Ute Creek was your son. Is that why you allow me here?"

She shrugged deprecation. "I feel obligated."

"I can't believe that," he said. "Why do you really want me here, Esther?"

The *tapicería de matrimonio* was a wedding tapestry woven in colonial times for the bride of a *hidalgo*. The one Joseph Iderland had obtained for Esther hung on

274

the wall of the dining room where they ate that evening. There was a guest from Santa Fé who Esther introduced as Deryl Fages. He was as tall as Grenard, if not as heavy, with a good figure for the impeccable tailoring of his dark blue pinstripe. He had a rich dark head of hair that he wore with heavy sideburns. His healthy pallor should have fitted in with the impression he gave of prosperous, gracious living, but somehow it was wrong.

"Odd name," said Grenard. "French?"

"I suppose it is." The man had a vibrant, cultivated voice, and a quiet assurance. "I never gave it much thought."

Grenard could not believe that Esther would be capable of such an obvious thing, or so foolish, yet, already, it had begun working in his mind, as he watched Fages. The casual polish of each movement, the careful gentility of the mannerisms. After supper they went into the living room, and Esther excused herself to go and see Carl, who was in bed, still weak from his experience the day before. There was a card table to one side, and Grenard pulled a chair from beneath it, seating himself.

"How about some monte?"

Six Beans and Monte Tennes had eaten with them. Grenard had not gained a very definite impression of either man back there in the darkness of Cartier's barn that night in San Antonio. Six Beans was about average height, originally lean, yet inclined to the small pot-gut that sometimes came to a man nearing middle age who had worked hard all his life and now had begun to slack off. He had a narrow face furrowed by weather and wind; his close-cropped hair was beginning to gray at the temples. There was no overlooking the swift, vicious potency of his movements, however, as he opened the spindled door of a *trastero* in the corner of the room and got out a pack of cards.

Grenard was looking at the man's gun. "Because you keep six beans in your wheel?" he said meditatively.

"That's how I got my name," said Six Beans.

"Most men keep one bean out so their hammer's down on an empty chamber," said Grenard. "You're going to jar it someday on that live shell and blow off your foot."

"And most men have their hogleg empty after five shots. That's when I've still got one left, and it's the one that's just as likely to blow a man's head off as my foot," said Six Beans, seating himself across from Grenard. "Maybe I'll show you sometime."

"What was wrong with San Antonio?" said Grenard.

Fages was looking from one to the other with a vague confusion apparent in his face. Six Beans leaned forward a moment, his eyes meeting Grenard's, then he leaned back, dropping his glance to the cards, and began shuffling them with bony, rope-scarred fingers.

"Looks like you've played a lot of cards," said Grenard.

Six Beans raised his eyes again. He sat there a moment, meeting Grenard's gaze. Then he put the deck down.

"You deal."

"Why not honor the guest," said Grenard, shoving them to Fages.

Fages shrugged, took up the cards. Grenard became aware that both Six Beans and Monte were watching him now, with something more than the hostility he had seen earlier in the evening. Something waiting. It came to him, rather sharply, that there might be more in this than just a monte game.

It was just about then the gray cat came from the hall to rub against Grenard's legs. He looked down at her. What was that from *Fleurs du Mal?* Then it came to him. His murmur was barely audible:

Les amoureux fervents et les savants austéres
Aiment également dans leur mûre saison . . .

Fages was taking the first card of the bottom lay-out from the deck in his left hand. It came from him in an absent way.

Indefatigable lovers and austere savants
love equally during their ripe season . . .

It trailed off, and Fages's eyes lifted from the cards in a strange sort of surprise. His brows raised, and he smiled a faint apology, putting the pack out for Six Beans to cut.

"You like him?" said Grenard.

"It's a nice cat."

"Baudelaire?"

"Oh." Fages removed his cigarette, allowing the smoke to escape his mouth meditatively. "Yes, I suppose so. He's like a rare wine."

"What the hell," said Six Beans. "Turn the cards."

Fages put the other card of the bottom lay-out down. The two cards were jack and three of hearts. Grenard noticed it abstractedly. It was harder, he was thinking, with a man like this. A type like Judge Forman was simple, with his pomposity. Even a man like Jarales, with his suspicion. And Modesto, with his vanity. Now it was different. He had failed to find anything. It was more complex. The quiet assurance, the yet impenetrable sophistication. Nothing apparently to hide, nothing to touch. And yet, being more complex, more interesting. With a new relish, Grenard applied himself.

"He owes a lot to Poe," he said idly.

"Absurd. Poe had no effect whatever on Baudelaire." Fages put the top lay-out down, a queen of hearts, a two of spades. "Bets?"

Grenard placed a dollar on the queen. "What makes you say that?"

"Baudelaire himself," said Fages, turning up the gate card. "He found Poe inferior to himself . . ."

"Naturally. You know these geniuses . . ."

"Don't be foolish." An edge had entered Fages's voice. "Even without Baudelaire's statement, a comparison would be enough. An idiot could see there was no similarity. I don't —"

"What the hell!" shouted Six Beans, striking the table with his palm. "Are we playing monte or having a pink tea party?"

Fages sat stiffly a moment, looking at the man. Then he relaxed slowly against the back of his chair. "Gate card's a three of diamonds," he said almost sullenly. "Who's got fifty cents on that second card in the top lay-out?"

"That's my bet on the three of hearts," said Six Beans. "Now let's go."

Fages paid off, raked in the five dealt cards, discarded them. But Grenard had it. Before Six Beans's shout had cut him off, Fages's voice had been steadily rising. And it was in Grenard's mind now to be used. A temper. Beneath all that easy reserve. A temper. And now Grenard's reactions were setting in. It needed no conscious volition from him any more. He could go on playing the game with most of his concentration, and yet his mind would be touching, probing, exploring. It was an old dodge, in a card game. He had done it enough times before. He found himself watching Fages's hands, and wondered how long he had been doing it. Fages dealt the top lay-out. Then he saw where Grenard's gaze was directed.

"What's the matter?"

"*Hmm?*" Grenard glanced up inquiringly.

"Deal," said Tennes. "I don't want to hear no more about this guy Buadelay. I don't care who's spread he roped on."

Fages drew a breath, put down the bottom lay-out. He waited for them to bet, and was about to draw the gate card, when he stopped. "Don't you like the way I deal?" he said.

"Is he doing something?" asked Six Beans.

"What do you mean?" wondered Grenard.

"Go ahead and deal," said Monte.

Fages hesitated, the flush tinting his pale face perceptibly. He put the gate card down. It matched neither of the lay-outs in denomination, and Fages took in the bets.

Grenard could see it in them very clearly now. He had watched enough men wait for something. Six Beans was carefully keeping his eyes off Grenard's face. Monte licked his lips. Only Fages seemed unaware of it. He discarded the played cards and dealt another lay-out. Then Grenard could see him straighten in his chair. The detective raised his eyes from the man's hands.

"What's the idea?" said Fages.

"Of what?" Grenard asked him.

"Don't you like the way I deal?"

"I didn't say a word."

"You were watching my hands!" said Fages.

"Is he pulling marked cards?" asked Six Beans.

"Will you go ahead and deal," growled Monte.

"Listen, Grenard . . ." — Fages had bent toward the detective, his hands tightening on the deck till the cards bent between his fingers — "just what do you think you're doing?"

"What do you think *you're* doing?" said Grenard.

Fages twitched as if he had been slapped. "I'm telling you I don't like your attitude. I don't know what you're trying to do, but you'd better stop it."

"Let's see the cards," said Six Beans.

Fages whirled to him, shuddering with the terrible effort he was making to control his temper. "You stay out of this. These cards aren't marked and you know it. What are you trying to do?"

"Nobody questioned your dealing," said Grenard.

Fages whirled back to him. "Damn you, Grenard . . ."

"Then why are you afraid to show us the cards?" asked Six Beans.

"I don't see how all this started," said Grenard.

"You know how it started!" said Fages, his voice filled with a terrible guttural restraint.

"Show us the cards," said Six Beans.

"Yes," said Grenard. "Why don't you show them the cards?"

"I'll show *you* the cards!"

Fages's hoarse shout filled the room as he leaped to his feet, knocking the chair backward and flinging the whole pack into Grenard's face. Grenard saw the man's movement after that, and tried to gain his feet before it happened. The heavy oaken table tilted up and over into his lap. He went over sideways beneath it, the chair sliding from beneath him, and struck the floor with the weight of the table crashing down on his legs. Shouting with the pain of that, he made a violent effort to roll from beneath the table, reaching for his Smith & Wesson. Even as he rolled, he caught a glimpse of Fages, standing back in the middle of the room with his face flushed scarlet and both hands free in front of him. And when Grenard had fought from beneath the table with his six-gun out, he wasn't turned toward the man who had tilted it over on him.

"All right," he said to Six Beans. "Go ahead. You said you'd show me. Let's see how much good that extra bean does in your wheel."

CHAPTER
SEVEN

Grenard stood in the patio where he had come from his bedroom, drinking in the damp sweetness of the morning air. At first, the only sound had been a striped chipmunk picking seeds from a pine cone downslope. Now, in the distance, the tap of a trotting horse reached him. He moved around the rear of the north wing of the house and up one wall, and was nearly to the corner when he heard the trotting horse hauled to a stop out front. Faintly he heard the squeak of saddle leather.

"Esther?"

It was a man's voice, low, husky, and then the tap of the woman's shoes across the flagstones of the porch, and her voice. "I thought you'd be along this morning. Did you find anything?"

"I stayed in Santa Fé like you said. Heard —"

"*Sh-h*," hissed Esther. "Grenard's here."

"Grenard," the man said in a hollow voice. "How did he get through?"

"I don't know," she muttered. "Nobody else could have, I guess. He reached Judge Forman. Yellowstone couldn't even stop him. And to top it off, he found Modesto . . ."

"And he's still alive?" The man let his breath out in a hoarse, incredulous way. There was a long pause. Then he said it simply: "He's dangerous, Esther."

"Don't you think I know it?"

"What are you going to do?"

"I don't know," she said. "It's like having a cat by the tail. You can't hang on forever, but if you let go, you'll get clawed." Another pause. She drew a heavy breath. "What did you find out in Santa Fé?"

"I heard how you just missed Modesto up in Pecos. It came through the grapevine. A Jemez Indian crossed Modesto's tracks just afterward and Modesto told him. It's the consensus that, if Modesto don't hit for the border, he'll hole up in Bonanza. You know it'd take more than a little horse stealing to make the law go in there after him."

"Then we're riding."

"Esther, don't be loco. I can think of easier ways of committing suicide. No telling who's holed up in there. Last thing I heard of Apple Jack, he was heading that way . . ."

"There's no time, there's no time, don't you understand? I've got to. Are you going with us?"

The man hesitated so long Grenard thought he was not going to answer. "All right," he said finally. "You know I will."

"Can I go, too," said Grenard, stepping around the corner into view.

Esther stood on the flagstones beneath the extension of the roof that covered the porch. The frilly lace of her nightdress formed a froth beneath the bottom of her

284

padded wool dressing gown, and her rich hair made a dark tousled frame about her face, still flushed from sleep. Grenard did not think he had ever seen her so beautiful, or so stunned.

The man was surprised, too. His beard had taken on the ruddy color of the dust from his long ride and his hair was hidden by a flat-topped hat pulled low over watery blue eyes. His thin lips formed the word with a bitter simplicity.

"Grenard?"

"Yes," said Esther. "This is Hogarth, Grenard. He has connections with certain elements of society in various towns around here that sometimes help in a case like Modesto's. I suppose you heard."

"Hogarth?" said Grenard, pulling out a pair of Caliente Puros from his coat. "Cigar?"

"Got my own," said the man, reaching beneath his canvas Mackinaw for a sack of Bull Durham.

Esther was still looking at Grenard, but she spoke to Hogarth. "Go in and get something to eat. Six Beans is probably already up feeding the horses. He'll take care of your animal."

Rolling his cigarette, Hogarth moved past Esther into the opened front door, his eyes on Grenard all the way, till he had disappeared. Grenard moved over to the woman, placing one cigar back, biting the end off the other.

"Bonanza," he ruminated. "It has a reputation. You must want to reach Modesto pretty bad to go in there."

"He's been stealing my horses for over a year now. I'm getting tired of it."

"Has he?" said Grenard.

"Yes." It escaped her harshly. Then, impulsively, she took the step that brought her up against him, clutching at his arm. "Oh, Grenard, you know why. Where is Joe? Did Modesto tell you? Tell me. You know where Joe is and who he is. I've got to know, Grenard, don't you see, I've got to know . . ."

"And you've got to stop me from taking him back," he said. He watched her face twist with that. "I don't know, Esther. Modesto didn't tell me. And if he had told me, do you think I could trust you, after San Antonio, after last night? Why didn't you have Six Beans use his gun in San Antonio?"

"Don't be a fool," she said. "I told them not to do it that way under any circumstances. I didn't have anything to do with those other two men who were killed. I gave you your chance in San Antonio. I offered you four times the bonus you'd get from Iderland, Incorporated, if you saw to it that you didn't find Joe. Do you think that I wanted to do it that other way? I had to, Kelly. Don't you see?"

"And last night . . . ?"

"You forced it. I heard the whole thing. You brought it all about. Why?"

"That's almost funny," he said. "Your asking me why. You know what they were up to. You left on purpose. Do you think I'm blind? I thought I might as well start it before they did. It would give me some kind of a jump on them. It wasn't Fages who had his gun half out."

"I didn't tell them to, Kelly. You've got to believe me," she said. "That was on Six Beans's own hook. Maybe it was getting back at you for the way you beat him in San Antone. I had no idea, believe me. Do you think I'd have left?"

"It doesn't fit," he said. "I can't believe you'd want me here for any other reason, after San Antonio."

"And you came . . ." — her voice was husky — "believing that?"

"I thought there might be a few clues here," he said. "There were."

"Things have changed since San Antonio, Kelly," she said softly. "Remember, you saved my son's life." She swayed toward him. "He's why I've done all this, Kelly. Joe left a trust fund for Carl. It will give him a start in life, a start I could never give him. I'll fight to give him that start, Kelly. I'd almost kill to give him that start."

"Why should it be affected if Iderland is found?"

"I don't know," she said. "I only know it's mixed up in this somehow . . ."

"I think you do know," he said. "You wouldn't be so vehement about it. I think you know a lot of things. Even who Joseph Iderland is, maybe."

She stepped back, her eyes dark, her lower lip twisted. "It was quite a revelation, hearing you work last night. You have a rare touch."

"A man develops certain techniques."

"So you think Fages is Joe," she murmured.

He was lighting the cigar. "I didn't say that."

"Baudelaire." She smiled wryly. "That's a taste Joe must have developed after he left me." The smile faded, and her head lowered.

"You know, you're a lot like Joe. The way you sit back, so detachedly, playing on other people's weaknesses, not allowing your own emotions to interfere, or maybe not having any emotions that would interfere. Joe would have liked you, I think."

She paused, studying him, and then she moved in against him once more, pushing the hand with the cigar aside so it would not be between them.

"Kelly, you're not a man a person can touch easily. If I could only touch you somehow. I told you things have changed since San Antonio. Not just because of Carl. I could have told them to do that last night. As you say, it's the logical thing. But I didn't. And it wasn't only because of Carl. Maybe I would have with another man, Kelly, but I didn't with you. I swear I didn't."

Her bosom rose against him and her perfume was in his hair and he had never felt such weakness. It took a great effort for him to close his eyes and step back.

"No, Esther, not that way, either."

It was a long time before her answer came. He opened his eyes as she said it.

"Very well. There are other ways."

Bonanza had been staked out in 1800, when sulphide ores were discovered there, but not till 1879 did a real strike boom the region. For a few years, the town flourished, its population reaching over 2,000. But it went the way of all boom towns when the mines petered out, and now all that remained was the dilapidated two-story house which had once been the saloon. This structure, rising, haunted and weird, out of the ruins of the rest of the town, had become a rendezvous for every bad hat above the border, and the uncertainty of just who would be there, and the certainty of what would happen if they *were* there, was such that few lawmen could be found who would venture into Bonanza.

They had come west from Alamogordo through the Sandias, and halted in late afternoon on a hogback looking down into the remains of Bonanza. In the unrelieved shadow filling the dense juniper stands at mid-slope, Grenard sat Sable between Hogarth and Esther.

"It still seems rather strange," murmured Grenard, "Fages staying behind that way."

"Somebody had to stay with Carl," Esther told him irritably. "The boy isn't well enough yet for a ride like this. I think it was big of Deryl."

"Do you?" said Grenard. He offered the other man a cigar.

"I got my own," said Hogarth, reaching for that Bull Durham.

As Grenard bit the tip off his Caliente Puro, Six Beans came through the timber on foot, not speaking till he had reached them, then softly. "Somebody there all right. No horses in sight, but we got close enough to hear movement inside. Monte's watching. He figures we better leave our animals here. Make some noise any closer and we're liable to flush the jacks too soon."

Stepping off her dun, Esther pulled an old Henry .44 from the boot, and tied her reins to a sapling. Then she moved down through the timber after Six Beans. Hogarth got off his horse, watching Grenard, who had dismounted from Sable.

"You go ahead," the detective told him.

"You better let me tail," said the man.

Grenard leaned toward him, an edge to his voice. "You go ahead, Hogarth."

The man drew himself up perceptibly, then, after another moment's hesitation, he turned in a sullen way and swung after Esther. They reached the fringe of timber where Monte Tennes hunkered with his saddle gun, eyes squinted with watching the ghost town. He gave an upward, sidelong glance to Esther.

"Catch a varmint in his trap, you better have a man at the back door as well as the front."

"We'll each go in from a different direction. Hogarth, you might as well start from here. Monte, you and Six Beans circle around to the north. Grenard and I'll take the left." Esther indicated westward with her gun. "Sun's almost on Jemez Peak. When it touches the mountain, we'll all start in on the saloon. Don't shoot unless you absolutely have to. All right?"

"All right."

She let her eyes meet Hogarth's before she turned, then Grenard was following the swish of her heavy leather riding habit through the timber. They walked till they were south of the town, looking down the last gentle slope into the crumbling, fallen rears of the row

290

of structures fronting the single street. Esther turned to him.

"No telling what might happen now, Kelly. Before we go out there, I want you to know that, no matter what does happen after this, or what has happened before, I . . ." — she drew in a quick, hesitant little breath — "that . . . under other circumstances, if you . . . and I . . ." — again that breath, and she swayed toward him, her voice husky — "Kelly, you know what I'm trying to say."

He had kept his expression carefully enigmatic, and her face darkened. Then she reached up to catch his arm impulsively. Her voice was low, with a sort of pleading huskiness in it.

"I'm not trying to get anything out of you now. For once, aren't we in a position where we're just a man and a woman, without all that other between us? I want to know now, Kelly, before it happens out there. You're like Joe in so many ways. But there's one difference. He didn't have any emotions to show. You have. It's there, Kelly. I've seen it."

Maybe it was her nearness. "Fages?"

"Don't be a fool," she told him. "Deryl has some ideas that way, I suppose. So have other men. Even Monte, once. They weren't enough. As cold and unapproachable as he was, it would take an awful lot of man to fill Joe's shoes. Anything less wouldn't do."

"All right," he said, and his arms slipped about her. He would not have believed anything could be so savage and so tender at the same time. They stood there a while before she spoke.

291

"Kelly," she said, and the word came out muted and warped with her lips against his face. "Kelly, Kelly," and the last time it held a small, choked sob. And then the blow struck the back of his head.

His consciousness spun in a vortex of agony, through which he was dimly aware of sliding slowly down Esther, trying in a vague desperation to keep himself erect by clutching her shoulders, her arms, her hips, her knees. She stood there with her arms at her sides. He could not see her face; but he felt the rigidity of her body.

Finally he lay at her feet, dimly aware of Hogarth standing there where he had come up from behind to strike. Then the ground seemed to slip away, and there was unconsciousness.

It was the sound of gunshots that permeated the pain first. He raised himself on one elbow, twitching with the agony it caused. Vision returned in agonizing waves. First he could see the town. The sun was almost gone behind Jemez Peak, and saffron dusk shrouded the gloomy ruins. Gun flashes drew his eyes to the vague, shifting shadows at the far end of the main street.

"Modesto!" That was Monte's voice shouting. "They're down by the well, Esther, watch out. I caught him down here getting water."

"Modesto!" called Esther. "Stop shooting. We don't want you for those horses."

"Think I'm loco?" bellowed the old bandit. "Come on. Me and *El Chivato* shot our way out of Pat Garrett and a hundred men down in Lincoln. Think a crowbait crew like you can do any good? Come on."

There was movement through the buildings on the far side of the street. A gun bellowed from the dim bulk of the adobe well at the other end. Someone in the buildings shouted.

"Hogarth! Hogarth? Did he get you?"

"I'm all right. Don't stop. I'm all right."

Grenard rose groggily, stumbling toward the rear walls of the buildings on this side, ducking into the gloom behind the saloon. He was turning the corner toward the front end when the faint rattle reached his ears from inside. He saw the side stairway and turned into it. A wooden overhang had once covered the stairway all the way up, but now the boards had rotted and caved in and dim light sifted in through gaping openings in the roof, illuminating the rickety, sagging stairs.

He almost went through the dangerous steps more than once. The door at the top hung open on broken hinges. He moved through a room that must have once been the office. There was a faded oil painting on the wall and a dust-covered Chippendale desk. The place smelled of musty, rotting wood. The inner door was unlocked, opening onto a balcony that ran around the sides of the building and overlooked the main floor below.

From here he could see the bar on the far side, the long mirror with dusty shards of glass and broken bottles. Tin cans were scattered across the outer floor and in one corner were two saddles and a black sougan.

Grenard stood utterly quiescent on the balcony, searching the shadows of the lower floor. Finally he made it out, a crouching shape, barely darker than the other gloom, at one of the front windows. Then, from the spot, a gun roared. The shock of it left Grenard trembling in the animal fright a sudden unexpected sound will sometimes cause.

"That didn't come from the well!" somebody outside shouted.

"Did it get you, Hogarth?"

"No," answered the man. "But he will if I move any farther, Esther. He's inside the saloon. They have us in a crossfire that way."

Grenard took off his boots and moved from the balcony toward the stairway. He heard the man down there cock his gun again. It made an oily *click*. A shout came from outside, indistinguishable this time, but it covered Grenard's movement till he had reached the bottom of the stairs. In the last dim light of dusk, he could see who crouched there, looking out through the broken, lower panes of the window with the big, ivory-handled Remington in his hand. Grenard had his Smith & Wesson out, and it bore on the man's back. His voice was dispassionate.

"Drop the gun, Iderland."

CHAPTER
EIGHT

There was no sound in the rotting, musty saloon for a long while after Grenard spoke. There was no sound from outside in the street. The gunfire had ceased momentarily, and the shouting. Then the metallic chatter of a gun striking the floor sent echoes rolling dimly through the great, high-ceilinged chamber. The man did not rise from where he was crouching at the window. Both his hands were visible, gripping the paint-peeled sill. His voice was devoid of emotion.

"Grenard?"

"Yes," said the detective.

"How did you know?"

"It's my job," said Grenard.

"No." The man stood, and turned, his back against the wall. He was the one who had called himself Jarales at Pecos. "It's an academic consideration now, I suppose, but I'd like to know anyway. Deduction?"

Grenard could appreciate that, in Joseph Iderland. "Yes."

"You knew so much about me. The way you were working that night. The monte, the Baudelaire, the Old Kentucky. But you must have used that on a dozen other men. I know two in this vicinity who would have reacted more favorably than I did. Six Beans bears a physical resemblance, plays a damn' good game of monte, even carries a bottle of Old Kentucky in his sougan."

"Nobody would be so quick on the draw as Six Beans without a lifetime of practice," said Grenard. "I saw him pull once, and, if you'd been that good getting a gun out, it would have come to light sooner or later in my search. That ruled him out."

"Fages?"

"Fages did have a lot of earmarks," said Grenard. "The monte, the Baudelaire, the discriminating taste. For a while there I thought I'd found you. Only one thing."

"What?"

"The temper," said Grenard. "That wasn't you."

"And yet, why . . . me . . . ?"

"All the other men I considered revealed one or two of the characteristics I sought, some like Fages a surprising number," said Grenard. "But the night at Pecos, your refusal to reveal even one small characteristic wasn't logical. A Mexican who will drink *mula blanca* will usually drink anything, especially such rare liquor as that bourbon. You wouldn't play monte, even when Modesto wanted to. You revealed enough intelligence to have recognized French, yet you pretended to think I was speaking bad Mexican when I quoted Baudelaire. Most men, in trying to change themselves, would not have been satisfied with the physical alterations. But you overdid it."

The man drew in a slow, careful breath. "You know, Grenard," he said, "I wish, somehow, that we had known each other . . . before."

Grenard did not answer for a moment, realizing what that admission meant, from a man like Joseph Iderland. "I know what you're saying." Then his voice took on a decisive edge. "I've satisfied your academic curiosity, now how about satisfying mine. Start with the name you took. Jarales. Does it have any significance?"

"None particularly."

"Why did you disappear?" asked Grenard.

"To get away from me."

It came from behind Grenard, the suave culture of the tone torn by a husky bitterness. It caused the detective to turn that way with instinctive reaction. It was Deryl Fages, standing on the balcony.

"Curdar," said Iderland.

"I've come to get you, Joe," said the man on the balcony.

"Nobody's going to get me," Iderland told them. The utter lack of any vehemence in his voice belied the violent speed of his action, for he had already gotten hold of his Remington there on the floor by the time Grenard was turned back around.

The first gunshot, however, came from behind Grenard. He felt the whining fan of lead past his face and saw the slug shatter one of the upper windowpanes a foot from Iderland's head. Iderland whirled to get behind the bar, laying the long barrel of his Remington across one forearm to fire at the man on the balcony. The only way Grenard could get out of the bellowing crossfire was to throw himself bodily toward the door at the foot of the stairs. The rotten panels splintered with his weight, and then the whole door was bursting open, the lock torn completely out of the doorframe, and he fell heavily into another musty, gloomy room.

It must have been one of the private short-card rooms; he had a dim impression of one round deal table in its center and half a dozen chairs with the green plush rotting off their seats. Then he was crouching just within the door. Iderland had gained the bar, and the shooting had stopped. Grenard could hear someone breathing. He remembered that pallor on the man who had called himself Deryl Fages now, and knew why it had not seemed quite right somehow. A man would get that pale in prison.

"We have two aliases, then," said Grenard.

"That's right." Iderland's voice came from behind the bar, cold, passionless. "I'd heard of a Deryl Fages recently arrived in Santa Fé who was seen at Esther's house frequently. I had no idea it could be Perry Curdar."

"How do you fit in with this, Curdar?" said Grenard. "You owned that Deaf Smith Strip, I understand."

"Yes," said Curdar from above. "My family acquired that Strip in Eighteen Thirty-Six. But with all the confusion over Texas independence about that time they overlooked filing for patents under the Republic, and later, the state. Iderland must have found that out. He was surveying that three million acres of Public Domain for the Land Office in Eighteen Seventy-Six, and, when the survey came up for approval, we found out our Deaf Smith Strip had been included in the

Public Domain. I filed suit against the state. But the courts ruled that our failure to apply for patents made the Strip forfeit. By law, it became a part of the survey of that three million acres."

"Why did you make that false survey, Iderland?" said Grenard.

"I knew there was oil on the land," said Iderland, "and in my clerical work for the Land Office I'd found the Deaf Smith Strip was held only by that Spanish grant. I approached the Eldorado Syndicate with the proposition of altering my maps to include the Strip if they would give me a share in the company. They agreed and I filed the survey for approval. After Curdar's petition for resurvey was not honored, I tried to get the maps back, but they had disappeared. You know the rest, I guess."

Grenard could hear Curdar shifting around above, and he called up to the man. "Listen, don't be a fool! What good will it do you to kill him now? They'll only send you back to prison."

"I didn't say I was going to kill him," Curdar replied. "The only way I can get my land back in time for it to do me any good is for Iderland to sign it over himself. He knew that was what I wanted the minute he got that first sheet . . . damn you, Joe —"

Curdar broke off as the first shot came, and then his voice was drowned in the deafening crash of one deliberate shot after another, as Iderland fired from the bar.

"Joe?" It was Modesto's voice from outside. "Joe, did they get to you? What is it? You all right, Joe . . . ?"

"Don't try to make it!" shouted Iderland. "I'm all right . . ."

"Joe, I'm coming. Hold them off, Joe, I'm coming!" shouted Modesto from out in the street, and shots began thundering from out there.

"Don't be a fool, Modesto, I'm all right . . ."

"Stop him!" called someone from outside. "He's trying to reach the saloon, Monte. What's happening?"

"I don't know. Somebody else is in there."

"Stop him. Monte. Six Beans. Stop him . . ."

And then the sporadic clatter welled into a deafening fire that rolled through the town and drowned out all other sound. The front porch shuddered and a rotten board gave way beneath someone's weight.

"I'm coming, Joe, I'm coming!"

"Modesto, stay out, you'll get killed . . ."

Modesto reeled in the door, clutching a blood-soaked arm. Curdar rose up on the balcony and he was the first one the old bandit saw. Modesto pulled his gun up, still running forward, and started firing. Grenard saw Curdar's body jerk to the bullet and reel heavily against the balcony rail. There was a crack of rotten wood, and Curdar's feeble cry, and then the whole building shuddered as his body struck the lower floor.

"I'm coming, Joe!"

Still stumbling forward, Modesto saw Grenard in the doorway there, and twisted toward him. Maybe he recognized the detective; maybe he didn't. His gun made a cherry-red blast in the darkness. Grenard's Smith & Wesson bucked in his hand.

"Joe," said Modesto, taking one last fumbling step as he tried to keep erect and run toward Grenard, "where are you?" And then he fell forward onto his face.

"Here I am, Modesto," said Iderland, standing up behind the bar.

"No, Iderland!" shouted Grenard. "I had to. Don't do it. I had to."

Iderland climbed over the bar and started walking toward him, firing as he came. Crouched there in the door, there was nothing else to do. Again Grenard had to take the largest part of the man's body. For a crazy moment the whole place was filled with the roar and flash of guns.

Then the Smith & Wesson's hammer *clicked* emptily on a fired shell, and Grenard crouched there in the dark, realizing Iderland had quit firing, too. The porch outside shuddered and someone was framed in the last dim illumination of dusk.

"Grenard?" said Esther.

He took a weary breath, rising. "Yeah." He stumbled over the dead body of Modesto before he reached Iderland, crouching over the man. "Why the hell did you do that?" he said.

"You shouldn't have shot Modesto," said Iderland.

"Let him kill me?" said Grenard.

Iderland made a wheezing sound. "Yes. I guess you're right. He would have. Perhaps it was better this way."

The moon had risen by the time they buried the three men. Monte had gone up to get the horses, and Six Beans and Hogarth were throwing the last rocks on the graves to keep coyotes off. The woman watched dully for another moment, and then turned away. Grenard followed her a few steps.

"It's strange," she said. "I should feel sorrow. I should feel something."

"Whatever you felt for Iderland was so long ago," he said. "You didn't really know which one he was, then?"

"No," she said. "It's amazing a man could change so in appearance."

"How did you know Carl would lose that trust fund if Iderland were found?" he said.

"Joe wrote me before he disappeared. He didn't tell me why he was doing this, but he said he had turned a million dollars' worth of his personal belongings over to Judge Forman to be liquidated and turned into a trust fund for Carl. Joe told me Carl would lose the money if he were found before Judge Forman got the cash in trust where it couldn't be touched. He saw the beginning of the end when Curdar was released from jail and turned up with those maps. Once the courts got those maps, he knew Iderland, Incorporated would fold. And the only way he could save any of his personal holdings was to put them in trust. He knew Curdar wanted him to sign over that Deaf Smith Strip and hoped that, if he disappeared, Curdar wouldn't turn the maps over to the courts at least till Judge Forman secured the trust fund." She turned her face up toward him. "That's what I was fighting for . . . Carl. We've run on a shoestring so long. Do you blame me? Do you blame a woman for wanting her son to get a decent start in life?"

"I'd admire her for it," he said. "And for fighting for it. Only I'm afraid there won't be any trust fund. Judge Forman turned Iderland's holdings into cash, all right.

But he wanted to feather his own nest with a little profit off that million before he put it in Carl's name. He invested the bulk of it in Ojibway Oil."

"That's a subsidiary of Iderland, Incorporated," she said sharply.

"Yes," said Grenard, "it will fold up along with Iderland, Incorporated when the maps are shown to the courts. I guess Judge Forman didn't know Iderland owned Ojibway Oil when he invested the money. He didn't want Iderland found till he had made his profit. That's why he had Yellowstone try to stop me." He paused, watching her head bow, and finally he put his hand on her shoulder. "Is it so bad? Would you want your son to get a start on money made like that?"

"I guess not." She shook her head dully, then looked up at him. "You'll come back with us?"

"There at the edge of timber, this evening," he said.

"I had to do it," she said. "If Modesto knew where Joe was, I didn't want you to find out and reach him."

"Was it all just so Hogarth could sneak up behind and hit me?"

"It started out to be," she said. "But later . . ."

"You said you never thought anyone could fill Iderland's shoes."

"That was before I met you, Kelly."

He looked into her face for a long moment. "I think," he said, "that maybe Pinkerton is going to need a new detective."